Moments la...
adversary appeared

But it wasn't a member of the Lashkar Jihad or the United Islamic Front. It wasn't even human. Instead, Bolan found himself staring at a roiling, slow-moving cloud the color of pea soup. His mind flashed on the briefing papers he'd read on the way to Samarinda: an entire work crew killed in seconds by mingling pesticide vapors.

Trapped, all Bolan could do was watch as the cloud spilled over the side of the precipice and drifted down toward him. It looked almost alive, like some deadly creature on its way to claim a hapless prey that had fallen into its web.

Already he could smell the noxious fumes and his eyes were starting to burn, as well.

This is it, he thought. At long last, his number had come up.

Don Pendleton's Mack Bolan.

Pressure Point

A GOLD EAGLE BOOK FROM

WORLDWIDE.

TORONTO • NEW YORK • LONDON
AMSTERDAM • PARIS • SYDNEY • HAMBURG
STOCKHOLM • ATHENS • TOKYO • MILAN
MADRID • WARSAW • BUDAPEST • AUCKLAND

First edition January 2004

ISBN 0-373-61494-2

Special thanks and acknowledgment to
Ron Renauld for his contribution to this work.

PRESSURE POINT

Victory at all costs, victory in spite of all terror,
victory however long and hard the road may be;
for without victory there is no survival.
                                        —Winston Churchill

Those who promote terror against their fellow
citizens sink as low as men can get. I will risk
everything and stop at nothing to put these
terrorists out of business. Our survival depends
on it.
                                        —Mack Bolan

CHAPTER ONE

INDONESIA

"Okay, I think I've got the hang of it," Mack Bolan said, speaking through the condensor microphone duct-taped to the inside of his gas mask.

"It gets easier once you've done it awhile," Abdul Salim told him. As they both took off their masks, Salim, a decorated major who'd come up through the ranks of Indonesia's Royal Marine Commandos, added, "The biggest thing to remember is not to hyperventilate."

Bolan nodded. The truth was, although this particular mask was new to him, he'd worn similar protective gear on several occasions over the past few years. It was a sign of the times, a concession to the ever-increasing chance of biochemical attacks in the grim, unending war against global terrorism. Bolan missed the days when he could feel secure going into battle shielded only by the thin layer of Kevlar armor beneath his blacksuit. This day he'd even had to forgo the black-suit in favor of a bulky, mud-colored HAZMAT suit. He'd been issued an armored vest, but it wasn't made of Kevlar and, in comparison, felt as heavy as chain mail.

Major Salim was similarly attired. The two men were seated in the rear of a dust-covered white minibus making its way up a narrow, winding, two-lane mountain road seventeen miles north of Samarinda, capital city of Indonesia's East Kalimantan Province on the island of Borneo. The bus was following its usual itinerary, a scenic route that led to a hilltop textile center long popular with the tourist crowd.

Those aboard the bus that day, however, were not tourists, and their ultimate destination was not the textile center, but rather a nearby storage facility managed—or mismanaged as many contended—by the Indonesian Ministry of Agriculture. The other eleven men in the vehicle were members of KOPASSUS, an elite army commando unit that had seen extensive duty of late battling the rise of Islamic extremism throughout the country's sprawling chain of islands. They, too, carried gas masks and were suited up in full HAZMAT gear. When Bolan first rendezvoused with the force at a private hangar at Samarinda's small regional airport, the men had also been issued 10-shot, .45 ACP Heckler & Koch carbines, one of the few such weapons equipped with a trigger guard large enough to accommodate their thick protective gloves. Rounding out their gear, each soldier also carried a belt pack containing ammo clips, three flash-bang grenades and a first-aid kit loaded with ampules and various syringes for use in the event their suits were compromised during the impending raid.

This was the second time Bolan had joined forces with Abdul Salim. Several years ago they'd worked together putting down a rebel coup across the Java Sea in the province of Sumatra. That insurrection, which claimed the life of Salim's uncle, renowned freedom fighter Ismail Salim, had been clandestinely backed by the Chinese military. Beijing was out of the picture now, but in their place an even greater threat to Indonesia's fragile stability had emerged in the form of the notorious Lashkar Jihad. The so-called Soldiers of the Holy War had come into being as a retaliatory force against Christian militants in the Molucca Islands. Over the past two years they had grown in number and expanded their agenda proportionately, embarking on a violent campaign to seize control of the entire country, whose two hundred million Muslims constituted the world's largest concentration of followers devoted to Islam.

The Lashkar had been formidable enough as a self-contained entity, but in recent months it had bolstered its might even further by joining ranks with the United Islamic Front, the global terrorist network cobbled together from the ranks of al-Qaeda and other kindred organizations decimated by the U.S. and its allies in the aftermath of the September 2001 attacks in New York and Washington, D.C. Whereas Abdul Salim had once thought his country was making headway in its efforts to eradicate terrorism within its borders, the UIF connection now tipped the scales in favor of the enemy.

Over the past two weeks both KOPASSUS and a force made up of KIPAM paratroopers had sustained heavy losses during pitched battles with jihad guerrillas in the provinces of Aceh and Sulawesi. Salim had been wounded by shrapnel in the latter attack—his right thigh still throbbed where he'd been hit—while nearly thirty others had been slain. Almost twice that many had fallen in Aceh. Salim had known most of the victims personally, and their loss weighed heavily. Though he still had his full head of coarse, wavy hair, streaks of gray had infiltrated his mane almost overnight, and his once-youthful features had been increasingly eroded by a deepening of the furrows around his eyes and mouth. The major now looked every bit his forty years, if not older, and though his resolve remained, it had been tempered by weariness. Gone was his proud assertion that the Lashkar Jihad could be eliminated by home forces alone. Much as he was loath to admit it, Salim was secretly relieved that evidence of UIF collusion had brought the U.S. back into the Indonesian fray. Perhaps, with America's help, the terrorists could be rooted out once and for all, giving his country, for the first time in its turbulent history, a chance at peace.

A pensive silence fell over the commandos as the bus groaned its way up the mountain. Bolan, himself troubled after the long flight from Islamabad, turned from Salim and stared out through the tinted windows at the surrounding valley. Miles in the distance, tall, steeplelike derricks rose from the oil fields of Muara Badak. Farther to the south, near the seaport of Balikpapan, dark, noxious clouds spewed from several coastal refineries, further polluting a late-summer sky already shrouded with the smoke of countless slash-and-burn fires set by small farmers and large date palm conglomerates looking to clear swaths of rain forest for the planting of new crops. Most of the surrounding hills had already been cultivated. Sarong-clad laborers could be seen working thin ribbons of terraced farmland, clearly oblivious to the impending danger at the agricultural facility less than two miles uphill.

According to the classified files Bolan had skimmed through on the flight from Pakistan, over the past twenty years Indonesia's Ministry of Agriculture had used its Samarinda mountain site to stockpile more than two hundred tons of obsolete, highly toxic pesticides. The compounds—laced with such carcinogenic agents as DDT, heptachlor and dieldrin—were not of Indonesian origin. They were imported from European manufacturers looking to rid their inventory of items banned by the United Nations' Food and Agriculture Organization. Corrupt IMA officials made a fortune off the scheme, accepting bribes from the Europeans to take the outlawed agents off their hands and then passing along inflated invoices to the Indonesian government for reimbursement. A few of the herbicides had been put to use; the rest had been haphazardly stored outside Samarinda with few, if any, safeguards. FAO investigators hadn't caught wind of the enterprise until corrosion breached several containers and unleashed a toxic cloud that had swiftly killed the compound's entire fourteen-man day shift.

That was two months ago. In the aftermath of the initial investigation, which resulted in five arrests and two suicides within the IMA hierarchy, a Malaysian-based waste disposal firm had been hired to safely repackage the volatile chemicals for transport across the treacherous mountain passes of central Borneo to a high-tech incineration facility in Tomani. The firm had seemed efficient and conscientious enough while removing the first loads from the storage site, but less than a week ago FAO overseers had determined, much to their alarm, that barely a quarter of the loaded pesticides had actually been delivered to the incineration plant. Concern over the whereabouts of the other cargo had triggered a wide-scale investigation, and two days ago UN officials—with help from the CIA and Indonesian Military Intelligence—had confirmed their worst fears, unearthing a paper trail that linked the subcontracted transport firm, Bio-Tain Enterprises, to an affiliate of the United Islamic Front. The implications were as clear as they were odious: the UIF, frustrated by failed attempts to amass an effective nuclear and biochemical arsenal, was apparently ready to go the "dirty-bomb" route, hoping the diverted pesticides could somehow be incorporated into a weapon that could duplicate, no doubt on a far larger scale, the same fatal effect they'd had on the day-shift workers at the Samarinda facility.

Once the UN's findings had crossed the President's desk in Washington, they were quickly prioritized and relayed to the Virginia headquarters of Stony Man Farm. There, the covert ops brain trust—Hal Brognola, director of the Sensitive Operations Group, and Barbara Price, mission controller, had reviewed the data and forwarded it once again, this time via an encrypted e-mail, to Mack Bolan.

For Bolan, the timing couldn't have been more opportune. When he'd first received the directive, he was already in Asia, attempting to track down the UIF's founder and mastermind. Hamed Jahf-Al, a charismatic Egyptian known in some circles as the Nile Viper, had risen to the top of the FBI's list of Most Wanted Terrorists back in June, when he was implicated in the ballroom explosion aboard a Caspian Sea cruise liner that had killed more than four hundred tourists, including sixty Americans. Jahf-Al had thus far eluded a four-country manhunt, and after three days in Islamabad the trail there had gone cold as well. Intel as to his whereabouts was conflicting, but the consensus was that the Nile Viper had fled Pakistan and was headed east. News of the UIF link to the missing pesticides, coupled with the Front's already established collusion with the Lashkar Jihad, had given Bolan hope that in Indonesia he might once again pick up Jahf-Al's scent, or at least that of one of his closest lieutenants.

The raid would be a start. During a quick briefing

after his arrival in Samarinda, Bolan had been told that a Bio-Tain crew had shown up at the IMA facility earlier in the morning to load another shipment of pesticides, purportedly for delivery to Tomani. To the best of Major Salim's knowledge, the transporters were unaware that they had fallen under suspicion. As such, there seemed a good chance that, once apprehended, the crew—or at least their transport vehicle—would provide evidence as to where the pesticides were being routed once they left the facility. The key was to storm the site and overpower the crew as quickly as possible, before it had a chance to realize its cover had been blown. Bolan had tackled similar missions dozens of times in the past, and Salim had assured him that most of the KOPASSUS commandos were equally seasoned. If all went well, it would be over in less than an hour.

Bolan was still staring out the window, preparing himself for the pending confrontation, when he saw two farmers suddenly glance up from their labors, shielding their eyes against a faint glare of sunlight that had somehow managed to penetrate the haze. Bolan tracked their gaze and saw two armed helicopters drifting low across the valley toward them. He wasn't concerned. They were friendlies. He'd seen the choppers—both U.S. Black Hawks armed with .50-caliber M-2 Browning machine guns and submounted 2.75-inch rockets—back at the airport. One was being flown by a KIPAM-trained pilot, the other by Stony Man flying ace Jack Grimaldi, who had also been at the controls of the Learjet that

brought Bolan to Samarinda from Islamabad. The Black
Hawks were flying low for the same reason the bus had
been outfitted with tinted windows: to maximize the el-
ement of surprise as they closed in on their target.

As the gunships drew nearer, Bolan glanced at his
watch. Abdul Salim did the same.

"Right on schedule," the major said, echoing
Bolan's thoughts.

Salim rose from his seat and conferred briefly with
his second in command, Sergeant Umar Latek, then
strode quickly down the aisle, passing along last-
minute instructions to the other commandos as well as
the driver. Latek, meanwhile, donned a headset linked
to a portable Heaton 525 field transceiver and patched
through a quick call to the three-man KOPASSUS surveillance team posted on a hillock overlooking the
agri-compound. Bolan could see the sergeant's features darken as he spoke with the team leader. As Major
Salim passed by on the way back to the rear of the bus,
Latek motioned him aside to pass along the news.

"Apparently the smoke from all these fires has
drifted across the IMA grounds," the major explained
as he rejoined Bolan. "Our surveillance team is having trouble seeing the facility."

Bolan stared back out the window at the dark, low-
hanging soot cloud that loomed ahead of them. "Assuming they're having the same problem at ground
level, it could work to our advantage," he stated. "Disguised or not, we'll be better off the closer we can get
before they see us coming."

"True," Salim conceded. "Maybe there's some truth to that saying about every cloud having its silver lining."

Soon the bus came to a turnoff. A posted sign indicated a left turn for those traveling to the textile center. The driver ignored the sign and continued to drive straight, downshifting to better tackle a steep rise in the grade. Bolan knew from the briefing that the agricultural facility was now less than a quarter mile up the road.

"It's time for the masks," Salim said. He pulled on his protective headgear and affixed the seals securing it to the rest of his HAZMAT suit. Bolan quickly did the same.

After rounding a tight corner, the bus came to a straightaway. The road leveled off slightly and it narrowed, hugging closer to the near-vertical rise of the mountain it had been carved out of. To the right, a steel guardrail, corroded by years of monsoons, separated the road from a precipitous drop into a deep, rock-choked ravine. Bolan peered into the chasm and saw a narrow, glimmering band of water swirling its way around an obstacle course of large, fallen boulders.

"The Mahakam River," Salim told him. "It carries water from the upper mountains all the way to the delta near..."

The major's voice suddenly trailed off. Bolan turned and saw Salim staring straight ahead, slackjawed, past the other soldiers and out the front windshield of the bus. Up ahead, less than a hundred yards away, a second vehicle had rounded yet another turn just below the smokeline and was heading downhill toward them.

"The delivery truck," Bolan murmured through his mask.

"It's supposed to still be at the facility! This is all wrong!" Abdul Salim called up to Sergeant Latek, "Why weren't we alerted?"

"I don't know," Latek responded, his voice edged with concern. "Perhaps with all the smoke..."

"I don't care how much smoke there is up there!" Salim ranted. "They had to be able to see the truck leaving!"

Latek had on his headset and was trying once again to raise the field agents. "I'm not getting any response."

"I don't like this," Salim said.

The major was reaching for his carbine when the driver suddenly slammed on his brakes. Bolan had to grab at the nearest armrests to keep from being flung down the aisle by the abrupt stop. A torrent of curses filled the bus. Bolan couldn't understand them, but he knew damn well what had the men so alarmed.

Up ahead, the Bio-Tain transport truck had veered from its lane and was now straddling the median as it bore down on the bus, picking up speed. With no shoulder between the guardrail and the mountain, the bus had nowhere to go to avert a head-on collision with the truck and its lethal cargo.

"A dirty bomb on wheels," Salim mused grimly.

Eyes on the approaching vehicle, Bolan muttered, "A guided missile is more like it."

CHAPTER TWO

"Everybody out!" Abdul Salim shouted as he and Bolan bolted to their feet. "And get your masks on! Hurry!"

Sergeant Latek yanked off his headphones and grabbed for his mask. The other commandos responded just as quickly, and once their headgear was in place, they rose in their seats and quickly unlatched the window safety catches, then leaned heavily into the hinged framework. As the windows swung downward, the men began clambering from both sides of the vehicle, clutching their assault rifles. The driver, meanwhile, wrestled determinedly with the gearshift, trying to throw the bus into reverse.

"There's no time for that!" Salim called out. "Get out! Now!"

The driver either didn't hear the warning or chose to ignore it. He wasn't about to distract himself putting on a gas mask, either. Still cursing, he continued to grapple with the transmission. He finally managed to put the bus into neutral, but while trying to shift into reverse, his foot slipped off the clutch. The bus shuddered violently as the engine sputtered, then died. An eerie silence filled the bus as it began to roll slowly backward. The driver pumped at the brakes but they, like the steering, were power assisted, and with the engine out of commission, it quickly became clear he would be unable to keep the vehicle under control.

Bolan, meanwhile, shouldered open the rear emergency door. Salim shouted again for the driver to get out, but the man refused. He was still fighting the wheel when a bullet smashed through the windshield and plowed into his shoulder. His pained howl was punctuated by more bursts of gunfire. Outside the bus, one of Salim's men took a bullet to the head and pitched forward alongside the road.

Snipers, Bolan thought. From where he stood he couldn't see where the shots were coming from, but he guessed the Lashkar Jihad had to have positioned gunmen somewhere up on the mountain.

"Ambush!" Abdul Salim cried. Assault rifle in one hand, he moved past Bolan to the rear doorway. Another round of gunfire poured into the bus, pummeling the bench seats three feet from where the two men were standing. "Let's go!"

Bolan cast another glance at the driver, who'd hunched over slightly but was still conscious and struggling with the steering wheel.

"He needs help."

"There's no time!" Salim tugged at Bolan's arm as

more gunshots poured into the bus, riddling the seats. "You'll never make it! We have to go!"

Bolan reluctantly followed Salim out the rear exit. Both men dropped hard onto the pocked asphalt, then quickly tumbled to their right to avoid being run over as the bus continued its backward roll down the steep grade.

"Over the railing!" Salim called, vaulting the horizontal beam. Latek and a handful of the other commandos had already cleared the rail and were clinging to the uprights on the other side, sending loose rock tumbling down into the ravine as they tried to secure a footing on the sheer face of the cliff. It was more than a hundred feet straight down to the river.

Bolan hesitated astride the guardrail, leaning away from the bus as it began to drift past him. Up ahead, he saw the Bio-Tain truck closing the gap between the two vehicles. The commandos who'd exited on the mountain side of the bus had taken up positions along the road's shoulder and were firing at snipers above them as well as at the oncoming truck. Even if they managed to take out its driver, Bolan feared the vehicle would continue on its collision course with the bus.

While his instincts told him to follow Salim over the railing, Bolan couldn't bring himself to abandon the man still inside the bus. As the front end of the vehicle rolled past, he cast aside his rifle and sprang forward, landing on the stairwell that led into the bus. The door was closed. Bolan stabbed his gloved fingers through a gap in the rubberized insulation and tugged hard until the door folded in on itself, giving himself enough room to squeeze through.

The exertion took its toll, however. As Salim had forewarned him, Bolan's labored breathing inside the gas mask left him feeling suddenly light-headed. Sagging against the handrail, he clawed at the mask, yanking it off. His face was layered with sweat, and his dark hair was plastered flat against his head. He doubled over and drew in a deep breath. The move saved his life, as yet another burst of gunfire took out the rest of the windshield, showering him with glass.

Bolan stood back up and peered out at the other truck, which had begun to slow. He suspected the plan to ram the bus had been aborted once the ambushers realized that most of their intended victims had abandoned the vehicle. It was a stroke of good fortune, but there was little time for rejoicing. Turning to the driver beside him, Bolan saw that the man had taken another round, this one to the neck. One look and Bolan knew he was dead.

Unmanned, the bus listed slightly to one side. There was a loud scraping sound as it began to brush against the guardrail. Bolan climbed up out of the stairwell and anchored himself as best he could alongside the fallen driver, reaching past him for the steering wheel. There was little play in the wheel, and the soldier knew he'd need better leverage to ease the bus away from the guardrail. He was concerned that the railing would soon give way under the strain and send the bus hurtling to the bottom of the ravine with him still on board.

Desperate, Bolan quickly pulled the slain driver from the seat and took his place. The steering wheel was slick with blood, but he gripped it as tightly as he could and turned it to the left. The wheel resisted at first, but finally he got enough response to guide the bus away from the railing.

Bolan shot a quick glance over his shoulder. The rear doors were still open, and he could see the roadway behind him. He was running out of straightaway, and there was no way he'd be able to maneuver the bus around the coming bend. It was unlikely the bus would even make it that far. Each time it struck another pothole or crease in the road, its course changed slightly, and no matter how hard he worked the steering wheel, Bolan suspected it was only a matter of time before the bus slammed into the mountain or took out the guardrail. Either way, the bus was a deathtrap.

Bolan lunged from the driver's seat and sidestepped the slain driver, staggering back down into the stairwell. The door was still folded open. He braced himself in the doorway and stared down at the ground rushing past him. There was only a few feet of clearance between the bus and guardrail. It would have to do.

Pushing away from the stairwell, Bolan leaped to the ground. He landed hard and unevenly, turning his right ankle. A stabbing pain shot up his right leg as he teetered off balance, smashing into the guardrail. He tried to right himself, but his momentum worked against him.

The next thing Bolan knew, he was tumbling over the waist-high railing, beyond which lay the vast, deep maw of the ravine.

CHAPTER THREE

In Bolan's predicament, ninety-nine men out of hundred would have crashed over the railing, locked in a deadly freefall before they so much as realized what had happened to them. By then, of course, their fate would have been sealed. Bolan, however, had a warrior's reflexes, honed by experience on a thousand battlefields, and even as he was going over the railing, he was acting on his instinct for survival. He flung out his right arm and the moment his gloved hand came in contact with the upper edge of the rail, he curled his fingers and grabbed hold, breaking his fall. Just as quickly, he swung his other hand to the railing and clawed for purchase. The thickness of the gloves made his grip tenuous, and his feet dangled unsupported below him, but, at least for the moment, Bolan had once again cheated death.

Through the pounding of blood in his ears, the soldier could hear the crackle of gunfire and the squeal of the Bio-Tain truck's brakes. The bus, meanwhile, drifted off the road into the side of the mountain. Bolan couldn't see the vehicle, but it sounded as if the bus had only glanced off the rocks, which meant it was likely still on the roll and out of control. If it veered back across the road and struck the railing, Bolan knew he'd be in trouble.

Focusing his full strength on his hands and arms, the Executioner tightened his grip on the rail and began to pull himself upward. He wanted to reach a point where he could swing at least one leg back up onto the roadway. He strained hard against the pull of gravity, slowly rising up to a point where he could see the bus. As he'd feared, it was headed for the guardrail less than twenty yards to his left. He braced himself as it crashed into the barrier. The weathered uprights snapped under the impact, and a thirty-foot section of the railing gave way. The bus went airborne and began to plunge toward the base of the ravine.

Bolan was safe for the moment, but the railing he clung to had loosened and begun to sag under his weight. Freeing one hand, he reached up and hooked his left arm over the upper edge of the barrier. He tried again to swing his right leg up to the edge of the roadway, but it remained beyond reach. As he held on tightly to the railing, there was a loud crash far below him. The bus had slammed into the rocks rising up from the river, and moments later an explosion ripped through the vehicle and echoed across the valley. Bolan glanced over his shoulder and saw a black column of smoke rise from the fiery heap of twisted metal. The farmers on the other side of the river were pointing at the wreckage and shouting to one another as they began to flee their fields.

Bolan's left arm was starting to go numb. When he tried to shift his position, the railing groaned and there was a dull crack as one of the weakened uprights began to splinter. One way or another, he needed to get off the railing fast. There was no way to get back up to the roadway, so he looked down over his shoulder, surveying the cliff face below him. Just off to his right he saw a few small trees growing out of the side of the precipice. Bolan wasn't sure if any of them were strong enough to support him, but they were his only hope.

When yet another of the guardrail supports snapped under his weight, Bolan let go of the railing and kicked at the cliff face with his boots, directing his fall toward the trees. The first two snapped under his weight, but a third remained intact long enough for him to close his fingers around its trunk. He swung precariously to one side, extending his right foot until it came to rest on another of the trees directly below him. It felt as if the tree would support him, so Bolan took a chance and eased his grip on the overhead limb, freeing one hand. With considerable difficulty, he wriggled his hand free of his HAZMAT glove, then switched arms and did the same with the other. The tree's bark bit sharply into his bare palms, but his grip was now more secure than it had been with the gloves.

Spread-eagled against the face of the cliff, Bolan

glanced to his right. Major Salim, Sergeant Latek and the other commandos had managed to pull themselves back up to the roadway. Salim and one of the others were still crouched near the railing, trading shots with enemy gunmen up in the mountains. Between shots, the major looked Bolan's way, then started toward him.

"Hang on!" he shouted, his cry muffled by his gas mask. Once he reached the spot where Bolan had gone over the side, he lay flat against the edge of the roadway and reached down. Even with his arm fully extended, however, Salim's outstretched fingers remained well beyond Bolan's reach.

"Your belt!" Bolan called up to him. "Try your belt!"

The Indonesian nodded. He rose to his knees and was unfastening his gear belt when yet another explosion sounded, this time from the roadway.

"The truck!" Salim shouted to Bolan through his mask. "The driver must've set off some kind of explosive device!"

Salim's voice was silenced in midsentence. He went limp, and his arm dangled uselessly over the edge of the precipice. Bolan could still hear gunfire and assumed the major had been hit by a sniper.

Seconds passed. No one came to Salim's aid. Bolan was stranded. The trees were holding up under his weight, but he had nowhere to go. He was trapped, and as the patter of gunfire increased up above him, he wondered if the commandos were being overrun by their ambushers. If that was the case, any second now he could expect to see one of the jihad gunners standing over him. Pinned to the side of the precipice, he'd be an easy target.

Shifting more of his weight onto his feet, Bolan freed his right hand and unzipped his HAZMAT suit. He reached inside the suit, drawing his .44 Desert Eagle from its web holster. He thumbed off the safety and pointed the pistol at the roadway, waiting for the enemy to show himself.

Moments later, an adversary appeared, but it wasn't a member of the Lashkar Jihad or the United Islamic Front. It wasn't even human. Instead, Bolan found himself staring at a roiling, slow-moving cloud the color of pea soup. Bolan knew the cloud had likely been unleashed by the explosion of the Bio-Tain truck. His mind flashed on the briefing papers he'd read on the way to Samarinda: an entire work crew killed in seconds by mingling pesticide vapors.

Bolan shoved his .44 back in its holster but didn't bother to zip up his HAZMAT suit. Without the gas mask he'd yanked off while on the bus, the suit wasn't going to do him any good.

Trapped, all Bolan could do was watch as the cloud spilled over the side of the precipice and crept toward him. It looked almost alive, like some deadly creature on its way to claim some woesome prey that had fallen into its web.

CHAPTER FOUR

As the toxic cloud drew nearer, Bolan quickly deliberated his chances of surviving a fall into the river below. Even if he managed to elude the boulders, it seemed unlikely the river was deep enough to keep him from slamming into the bottom. No. Like it or not, his best chance was to stay where he was and hope the poisonous vapors wouldn't be as deadly as those that had killed the IMA workers. It was a faint hope. Already he could smell the cloud's noxious fumes, and his eyes were starting to burn.

This is it, he thought. At long last, his number had come up.

The cloud was almost upon him when two shifting shadows began to sweep across the face of the precipice. When he heard the familiar, throaty drone of four 1600 horsepower turboshaft engines, Bolan felt a sudden stirring of hope.

The Black Hawks.

Bolan glanced up and saw one of the gunships bank

slightly as it drifted close to him, so close that he could see the pilot, an olive-skinned Indonesian. The pilot brought the chopper to within twenty feet of the precipice and then hovered in place, its rotors whirring within a few yards of Bolan's head. The vibration of the rotor wash nearly wrested him from the cliff, and for a moment he wondered if perhaps the Lashkar Jihad had somehow managed to seize the gunship. Then, as he glanced up, he realized that the updraft of the rotor wash was diverting the toxic cloud away from him. The cloud itself was dissipating, as well.

After a few seconds, the Black Hawk pulled away, its mission accomplished. Bolan's eyes still burned, but the cloud had all but vanished.

The chopper drifted up over the roadway, directing its mounted guns at the sniper positions in the mountains. The second gunship came into view and hovered directly above Bolan, the sound of its rotors echoing off the cliff walls. As the soldier watched, a rope ladder began to inch out the side door. Once the ladder was fully extended, a figure emerged and began to slowly lower himself down the rungs. The man was dressed head-to-toe in HAZMAT gear and carried an extra mask similar to the one Bolan had shed.

The strength in Bolan's arms was fading. When he tried putting more weight on the tree below him, the trunk began to snap, forcing him to hold tighter to the limb above. His fingers were going numb. He was running out of time.

"Hang tight, Striker!"

Bolan looked up. The man dangling at the bottom of the rope ladder, arm extended toward him, was his longtime colleague John Kissinger. Though officially on the Stony Man payroll as its resident weaponsmith, Kissinger was no stranger to the battlefield. He'd fought at Bolan's side several times and had been on assignment in Islamabad with Bolan and Grimaldi when they'd received the directive to fly to Indonesia.

"How about a lift?" he shouted to Bolan above the din of the rotors.

"If you insist," Bolan shouted back.

Once Kissinger was within reach, Bolan freed one hand and quickly transferred his grip to the other man's wrist. Kissinger responded in kind. When the tree below finally gave way, Kissinger quickly pulled his comrade toward him. With his other hand, Bolan snatched at the ladder. Once his fingers closed around one of the rungs, he swung his right leg up, groping for a foothold.

"Almost there," Kissinger assured him.

Bolan finally planted his foot on the bottom rung. He let go of Kissinger and grabbed hold of the ladder with both hands. On Kissinger's signal, the chopper began to pull away from the precipice.

"Nice timing," Bolan told him once he'd caught his breath.

"Always glad to lend a hand," Kissinger responded. "But in the future maybe you might want to leave the wall-climbing to Spider-Man."

CHAPTER FIVE

Jack Grimaldi was already pulling the Black Hawk out of the ravine by the time Bolan followed Kissinger into the passenger compartment. He called out a quick greeting without taking his eyes off the controls, then added, "Looks like somebody tipped off the Lashkar about the surprise party, eh?"

"Something like that," Bolan replied, coughing slightly. His eyes were still burning. He coughed again, this time with more force. Kissinger, who'd grabbed an M-16 and positioned himself near the open doorway alongside another armed man in camou fatigues, glanced over his shoulder.

"You okay, Striker?"

Bolan nodded. "Yeah. I just caught a little whiff of that fog."

"We better get you checked out."

"I'll be fine," Bolan insisted. He was blinking harder now, however, and his eyes were reddening. Yet another cough shook through him.

"Fine, my ass." Kissinger turned to the man next to him. "Rocky, grab that med kit and help him out."

Although his nickname conjured up images of some towering brute straight out of the boxing ring, Raki Mochtar was, in fact, six inches shorter than either Bolan or Kissinger and weighed barely 150 pounds in full uniform. This was his first field assignment for Stony Man after two years of service with the Farm's Virginia security detail. He'd had medical training during his stint with the Marines, but it was his family background that had earned him this, his long-sought chance to see action beyond the parameters of the Farm's compound in the Blue Ridge Mountains. The grandson of Jakarta shopkeepers killed during a demonstration against Sukarno in the late 1960s, Mochtar had visited Indonesia numerous times over the past twenty years and was as familiar with the country's various languages and dialects as he was with its geography and culture. When asked to fly out and rendezvous with Bolan and the other covert ops in Samarinda, the thirty-year-old Mochtar jumped at the opportunity. And now, less than two hours later, here he was in the thick of things. He was eager to make the most of it.

"I'll see what's here," he told Bolan, unlatching a large footlocker strapped to the cabin floor, "but if you've been exposed, you really need to go through a full decontamination. There's probably a setup at the storage site, so—"

"Decon's going to have to wait," Bolan interrupted. "We're in the middle of a firefight here, dammit!"

"But I'm telling you," Mochtar persisted, "in a case of exposure, it's vital to make sure you've washed off any traces of contaminants before they have a chance to work their way into—"

"Here," Bolan interjected again, coughing as he reached past the younger soldier for a pair of surgical scissors and an intravenous bag filled with saline solution. "Let's improvise, all right?"

Bolan shouted for Grimaldi to hold the chopper steady, then slit the top of the IV bag. Holding it high over his head, he craned his neck and quickly spilled the entire contents over his face. The saline stung his eyes but brought immediate relief. He coughed again, then cast the bag aside and told Mochtar, "Now grab some kind of antiseptic and pour it over my hands."

Mochtar fumbled through the footlocker and uncapped a bottle of hydrogen peroxide. Not wanting another reprimand, he fought back an urge to tell Bolan he ought to get out of his HAZMAT suit. Instead, he followed orders and drained the bottle as Bolan rubbed his hands in its flow.

Once he was finished, Bolan grabbed a roll of gauze. As he wiped his hands dry, he told Mochtar, "I didn't mean to chew you out like that."

"Not a problem," Mochtar said. He reached into the footlocker once more, then handed Bolan a small oxygen canister rigged to a lower face mask. "This might help with that cough."

Bolan grinned at Mochtar. "You catch on fast."

"I'm trying," the rookie replied. "You were right. I guess at times like this you can't worry about going by the book."

Bolan pressed the mask to his face and opened the canister's feed line. He was filling his lungs with pure oxygen when the cabin resonated with the staccato blasting of Kissinger's M-16. Grimaldi had pulled up over the mountain and Kissinger was firing at snipers perched high above the roadway.

The Executioner moved closer to the open doorway and glanced over Kissinger's shoulder. He saw two snipers wearing the long white robes that were a trademark for the Lashkar Jihad, ducking for cover among the rocks. They were under fire not only from Kissinger, but also from the other Black Hawk. At the base of the mountain, clouds of black smoke snaked up from the bombed-out remains of the Bio-Tain delivery truck's front cab, while ruptured containers in the rear hold continued to release clouds of toxic vapor. A handful of bodies were scattered about the roadway near the truck, some felled by the gas, others during the exchange of gunfire. Sergeant Latek and another KOPASSUS commando were crouched near a remaining section of guardrail, flanking Major Salim. Latek was firing into the mountains while the other attended to their fallen commander. Apparently Salim was still alive.

Bolan impatiently tossed aside the oxygen mask and shouted to Grimaldi, "Put her down over there by the railing."

"Will do," Grimaldi shouted back.

Bolan turned to Mochtar. "We'll be upwind from whatever's seeping out of that truck. You think we can skip the gas masks?"

Mochtar stared down at the roadway, then told Bolan, "At this elevation the wind's always shifting. Besides, to get to Salim we've got to go around the truck."

"Masks then, you're saying."

"Full suits would be even smarter," Mochtar said. "And you should put on a fresh one."

"I had a feeling you were going to say that."

There were several unused HAZMAT suits stored in sealed packets behind the footlocker. Mochtar handed one to Bolan, telling him, "Put the gloves on before you change so you don't recontaminate yourself."

As he changed, Bolan asked Mochtar, "You seen combat before, Rock?"

Mochtar shook his head. "Just training exercises," he confessed. "I'm ready, though."

"Good," Bolan said, "'cause if they nail you, there's no playing dead. It'll be the real deal."

Mochtar finished transferring a few first-aid items into a fanny pack, then strapped the pack around his waist. "I'm ready," he repeated.

"Then let's do it," Bolan said.

CHAPTER SIX

Once he'd set the Black Hawk down on the tarmac, Grimaldi left the turboshafts running and remained at the controls.

"Go get 'em, guys!" he called out to the others.

"I'll sit tight as long as I can."

Bolan suppressed a cough, crouched before the side door of the cabin, then leaped to the roadway, rifle in hand. Mochtar was right behind him. Kissinger dropped to the ground last, carrying a lightweight collapsible stretcher along with his assault rifle.

Almost immediately they were greeted by a hail of gunfire from overhead. The men quickly dropped and rolled to the cover of several large boulders crowding the road's shoulder.

"Nothing like a little rain on the parade to spoil a guy's day," Kissinger groused.

Bolan replied, "Yeah, well, at least there's a way to stop this kind of rain."

He raised his rifle to his shoulder and scanned the

mountainside until he had one of the snipers in his sights, then squeezed the trigger. The carbine bucked hard against his shoulder. Fifty yards up the mountain, a sniper reeled off the escarpment he'd been perched on and tumbled headlong down the steep facing, striking the road ten yards from the delivery truck.

Before seeking out another target, Bolan stole a quick glance at Mochtar. The younger man was firing uphill as well, hands steady on his rifle, no sign of fear in his eyes. Bolan was relieved. During his years in combat, he'd come across many a soldier who'd frozen when confronted with his first taste of combat. Mochtar seemed in control, though. That was one less thing to have to worry about.

"Let's see if we can get close to Salim," Bolan said, glancing down the road. He turned to Kissinger. "Give us some cover, Cowboy. We'll return the favor once we reach the major."

"Works for me," Kissinger said, feeding another ammo clip into his rifle.

Bolan advised Mochtar, "Try to vary your speed and zigzag as best you can. Don't make yourself an easy target."

"Got it."

Kissinger tapped the headset built into his helmet and said, "I don't want to rush you guys, but Jack says the bird's taking a few hits and he doesn't know how long he can keep 'er down."

Bolan looked back at the Black Hawk. He could see puffs of raised dust where gunfire was pounding the asphalt around the chopper, and several times he heard the plink of rounds glancing off the Black Hawk's fuselage. The chopper was built to stand up under light fire, but there was no sense pushing their luck any more than necessary.

"Ready?" Bolan asked Mochtar.

"Ready."

Bolan rose to a crouch; Mochtar did the same. The Executioner held out one hand, index finger extended, flexing his wrist for a three-second countdown. On three, he lunged forward, zigzagging up the road, staying close to the stretch of guardrail that hadn't been taken out by the runaway bus. Mochtar followed suit, staying ten yards back. Behind them, Kissinger fired steadily into the mountains. The other Black Hawk, meanwhile, provided additional cover, sending a fierce stream of .23-caliber rounds from its Brownings at other sniper positions.

As he ran forward, Bolan surveyed the roadway, trying to account for all the men who'd evacuated the bus before its ill-fated plunge into the ravine. Latek was still crouched alongside the major with another of the commandos, and Bolan saw three men trying to make their way up the steep mountainside. Another three soldiers lay dead on the road, felled either by snipers or the poisonous fog from the delivery truck. That left two men unaccounted for. Bolan hoped they'd turn up alive, but he feared they might have fallen to their deaths at the bottom of the ravine.

As they made their way past the Bio-Tain truck,

Bolan sized up the remains. He doubted the vehicle would yield any useful information, at least any time soon. The cab had been all but obliterated, and the cargo hold was clearly contaminated by ruptured tanks. Any evidence that hadn't been destroyed by the explosion would likely be ruined once a CBR crew arrived and doused the vehicle with chemical retardant. If they wanted any answers as to where the herbicides were headed, they were going to have to take one of the snipers alive and wring the truth out of him. So far Bolan had counted at least twelve of them up in the mountains, and only three had been killed that he knew of. Judging from the steady flow of gunfire still raining down on the asphalt, Bolan figured they were going to have their hands full.

When they reached Salim, the commando leader was unconscious. Like Latek and the other soldier huddled next to him, he was still wearing his full HAZMAT suit. Mochtar spoke quickly to the others, then checked over Salim while Bolan took up position near the railing and fired into the mountains, covering Kissinger's approach.

Once he'd finished inspecting Salim, Mochtar raided his fanny pack for a gauze pad.

Bolan asked him, "What's the verdict?"

"He took a bullet in the neck, just above his vest," Mochtar reported, reaching inside the major's HAZMAT suit and pressing the gauze against the wound. "It missed the artery, but he's losing a lot of blood. Weak pulse, too. We need to evacuate him back to Samarinda ASAP."

"What about poisoning?" Bolan asked. "That cloud rolled right over him before it came down on me."

"He'll need to be tested," Mochtar said, "but the entry hole was small, and these suits are bulky enough that a fold might've kept out any contaminants. We'll just have to wait and see."

Once Kissinger caught up with them, Bolan relayed the information, then grabbed Salim under the arms and signaled for Mochtar to take his legs so they could transfer him onto the stretcher once Kissinger unfolded it.

"We'll carry him," he told Mochtar. "Follow alongside so you can keep a hand on that wound."

Latek spoke up in halting English. "We will cover you."

"That would help," Bolan said.

Latek spoke briefly to the other commando, then moved ahead of the group, leaving his colleague to guard the rear.

Bolan grabbed one end of the stretcher, Kissinger took the other and together they raised Salim off the ground.

"Okay, let's move," Bolan said.

They headed out, with Latek and the other commando firing into the mountains. Halfway back to the chopper, another commando caught up with them, providing additional protection. It wasn't enough, however. The group had just made it past the Bio-Tain truck when they fell under cross fire from two different snipers. The commando closest to the railing was hit in the skull and pitched sharply to his right, disappearing over the barrier before anyone could get to him. Another few rounds hammered the stretcher, puncturing the fabric and thudding into Salim's legs. The same strafing line of fire found Mochtar, and he let out a howl as several rounds plowed into his chest. He staggered but remained on his feet, wincing in pain. His armored vest had deflected the bullets, but it still felt as if he'd been struck by a jackhammer.

"Rock?" Bolan called out.

"I'm okay," he replied hoarsely, repositioning his hand over Salim's neck wound. "Keep going!"

They made it the rest of the way to the chopper without encountering further fire. Grimaldi left the controls and crouched before the cabin doorway. With help from the others, he pulled Salim into the cabin. Bolan and Mochtar bounded up afterward. The Executioner yanked off his mask, then switched places with Mochtar, tending to the major's neck while the younger man inspected the gunshot wounds Salim had just taken to the legs.

"He's in bad shape," Mochtar said. "We need to get him to surgery, quick!"

"Anyone besides him we need to evacuate?" Grimaldi asked.

"Not that we know of," Bolan reported.

"Then I'm outta here."

"I'll stay," Kissinger called up from the road. "We'll mop up and then wait for you or hitch a ride with the other Hawk."

"I'm staying, too," Bolan said. "Rock, can you manage?"

"No," the younger man said. "I need you to keep pressure on that neck wound while I work on his legs. If he bleeds out much more, we're going to lose him!"

Though reluctant to leave any battlefield before the last shot was fired, Bolan nodded to Mochtar and stayed at Salim's side. Kissinger closed the cabin door on them, then stepped back, joining Latek and the other remaining commando.

The Black Hawk rose and angled away from the mountain. Grimaldi was making radio contact with the other chopper when he spotted the thin contrail of a projectile jetting out from the mountainside.

"Shit!" Grimaldi cursed. "Those bastards have Stingers!"

Without leaving Salim's side, Bolan leaned toward the cabin window and stared out just as the missile slammed into the other chopper, turning it into a fireball. The shock waves were so strong that the men could feel them reverberate through their own craft.

"Fasten your seat belts, boys and girls," Grimaldi shouted, "'cause there's another on the way and it's got our name on it."

CHAPTER SEVEN

"Chaff jam!" Bolan shouted to Grimaldi.

"Already on it," the pilot shouted back. Groping the console in front of him, Grimaldi thumbed a row of toggle switches, releasing a half-dozen high-yield flares from the underside of the chopper. Igniting within seconds after release, the flares gave off scattered blasts of heat intense enough to rival the thermal signature of the copter's turboshafts.

The ploy worked.

As Grimaldi banked sharply to the right, the heat sensors on the second Stinger missile were unable to distinguish between the intended target and the fiery chaff. Drawn off course, the warhead hurtled past the Black Hawk's framework, detonating beyond the range from which it could do any damage. The chopper rode out another shock wave, this one weaker than the one that had taken out the other gunship. Back in the rear cabin, Bolan and Mochtar rocked in place, doing their best to keep Salim stable on the stretcher.

"I'm sorry, but you're going to have to take over," Bolan told Mochtar, rising to his feet. "If I don't get up front and lend a hand, we're all dead."

Mochtar shifted position, transferring one hand to the major's neck while continuing to apply pressure to the worst of the man's leg wounds. "I'll do the best I can," he told Bolan.

By the time Bolan reached the cockpit, Grimaldi had banked the chopper again and changed course, heading back toward the mountain.

"Our turn!" he snarled. "Find me a target, Striker!"

Bolan grabbed a pair of binoculars and scanned the mountains. The sniper who'd just fired at them had dropped from sight, but Bolan could see four others positioned at intervals along a slight trough in the mountain. Peering higher, he spotted a promontory jutting directly above their positions. Pointing, he told Grimaldi, "There. Aim high with the rockets and see if we can get a little help from the mountains."

"Gotcha." Grimaldi locked in on where Bolan had pointed and readied the Black Hawk's 2.75-inch submounted rockets for firing. "One avalanche coming up."

The gunship shuddered faintly as the first four rockets spewed from their launch tubes and streaked toward the mountains. In quick succession, they struck the rock facing, stitch-blasting a crude line ten yards above the source of the last Stinger.

Weakened from underneath, the promontory collapsed, slamming down hard on another, larger outcropping directly below it. The second shelf gave way as well, splintering into sections and sliding into the trough. As they began to tumble down the side of the mountain, the monstrous stone slabs dislodged still more loose rock, quickly widening the slide's path. As Bolan and Grimaldi watched, three of the snipers were swallowed up by the avalanche. Several others, hoping to avoid a similar fate, scrambled out into the open and found themselves easy targets for Kissinger and the surviving KOPASSUS troops on the ground. The tide of the battle was quickly turning.

"Nice shot," Bolan told Grimaldi.

Grimaldi shrugged. "I just wish we'd pulled it off before we lost the other bird."

Bolan stared at the ravine, where smoke and flames issued from the charred remains of the second Black Hawk. It had landed a little over fifty yards upstream from the fallen bus, which also continued to smolder. There was no way anyone could have survived.

Grimaldi kept his eyes on the enemy and fired a steady stream of .50-caliber rounds from the Black Hawk's front-mounted machine gun, bringing down yet another of the snipers. He then banked the chopper, changing course so that he was flying parallel to the mountain instead of toward it.

"I want to help Cowboy with a few quick flybys," he told Bolan. "Go ahead and check on the major."

Bolan returned to the rear cabin. "How are we doing?" he asked Raki Mochtar.

"Better than expected," Mochtar reported. "I've got

the bleeding in his legs under control. The neck's still a problem, but he's got a chance."

"Good. How's the chest?"

"Smarts a little," Mochtar said with a grimace as he tapped the area where he'd been hit. "I can live with it."

"That's the spirit," Bolan said, grinning.

The Executioner was pulling off his HAZMAT gloves when there was a sudden drumming against the side of the chopper. He cursed and grabbed the nearest carbine, then lurched to the doorway and yanked the door open.

Down below, he saw a sniper firing at the chopper from a rock ledge twenty yards to the right of the avalanche. Bolan quickly returned fire, even as a stream of rounds zipped past his head, thunking into the cabin's interior. The sniper reeled to one side, dropping his weapon. He clawed at the mountainside for support but lost his balance and was soon tumbling down the steep incline.

Down on the ground, meanwhile, Kissinger and the others had taken up positions and stayed put rather than advancing within range of the rock slide. It had been a smart decision. By the time the slide reached the roadway, its swath was nearly a hundred yards wide, and its forceful momentum was strong enough to sweep the delivery truck off the tarmac and carry it sideways to within a few inches of the guardrail. The railing creaked and listed under the slide's weight, but held up and managed to keep the truck from going over the side with its deadly cargo.

The jostling, however, unleashed yet another cloud of poisonous gas. Kissinger, Latek and the others quickly moved out, putting as much distance as possible between themselves and the truck. As they moved, they kept their eyes on the mountainside and fired at the last few remaining snipers.

Soon, for the first time since the ambush had begun, there was no enemy gunfire to contend with.

Up in the Black Hawk, Grimaldi made two more quick passes as Bolan surveyed the mountainside, spotting three bodies but no sign of movement.

"I think that's it," he told Grimaldi. "Let's get the major back to the base."

"Let me just check in with Cowboy," Grimaldi said. He was trying to reach Kissinger on his headset when he detected movement amid the rubble high up the mountainside. "I think we got a stray up at around two o'clock," he told Bolan.

"Swing by and see if we can take him alive," Bolan said.

Grimaldi changed course and drifted the Black Hawk closer to the mountain. Bolan spotted the figure in the debris and raised his rifle. Once he got a better look at his target, however, he slowly lowered the weapon and shook his head with disbelief.

"I don't believe it," he murmured.

"What?"

"It's a woman," Bolan said, grabbing for the binoculars. "A tourist, from the looks of it."

"She must have wandered over from that textile

place when the fireworks started going off," Grimaldi speculated.

"Or maybe not," Bolan said once he got a look at the woman through the binoculars. "She might not be a tourist after all."

"What makes you say that?"

"I thought it was a camera she was carrying, but it's not," Bolan replied. "It's a gun."

CHAPTER EIGHT

Grimaldi was setting the Black Hawk on the road as Bolan finished fastening the seals on his gas mask and leaped down to the tarmac. Kissinger was leading Latek and the other surviving KOPASSUS commandos to the chopper. Two more soldiers had been wounded in the last few exchanges of gunfire. One was well enough to walk but the other was unconscious and had to be carried. They were upwind from the Bio-Tain truck. The cloud leaking from its cargo bay had dissipated, but the ground forces still wore their masks. Latek and another commando stood back from the others, assault rifles trained on the woman slowly making her way down the mountain. She'd tucked her gun back in the web holster strapped under her left arm.

"She keeps yelling that she's an American," Kissinger told Bolan.

"We'll see," Bolan said.

Grimaldi left the chopper idling and came over to help hoist the unconscious soldier into the cabin.

"He got caught up in that last billow of gas from the truck," Kissinger explained. "I'm guessing the seals on his mask didn't hold up."

"I'll get him back to the base so they can look him over," Grimaldi stated.

Bolan looked past Kissinger at the battleground. "I think we should keep a couple men down here and make a sweep back to the compound."

"I was going to suggest the same thing," Kissinger said. "So far we've counted nineteen bushwhackers. None of them are in any shape to talk."

"I was afraid of that," Bolan said. From where he was standing he could see a few bodies scattered along the road and amid the piled debris from the landslide.

Further uphill, the woman continued to make her way down the steep slope. She'd lost her footing several times and was covered with dust, but she wasn't wearing any HAZMAT gear and Bolan could see that she was in her early forties, lean and athletic, with dark, medium-length hair. She wore dark khaki cargo pants and a matching T-shirt under her holstered pistol. Staring down at the commandos covering her every move, she shouted angrily, "Point those popguns someplace else, would you? You're making me nervous!"

Bolan frowned. "I know that voice from somewhere," he said.

"You think so?" Kissinger replied.

When the soldiers ignored her command, the woman shouted again, "I keep telling you, I'm on your side! Doesn't anybody here understand English?"

"I'll be damned," Bolan muttered, finally recognizing the voice.

He turned back to the chopper and called out to Sergeant Latek, "Go ahead and lower your rifles."

Latek glanced at Bolan, then back at the woman. Slowly, he lowered his rifle while advising the other commando to do the same.

"Finally," the woman called out cynically. "Thank you so much."

Kissinger turned to Bolan. "So, who is she?"

"Take a good look," Bolan told him. "It's that bounty hunter we crossed paths with in Africa when we were going up against Khaddafi and the Interahamwe."

"Are you kidding me?" Kissinger said. "Jayne Bahn?"

"That's the one."

"Great," Kissinger muttered, "just what we need. It figures she'd show up. I mean, what's the reward on Jahf-Al up to now? Twenty million?"

"Thirty, I think."

"Hell, and here us poor chumps are tracking him down for free." Kissinger shook his head. "What's wrong with... Holy shit!"

Up on the hillside, a bloodied jihad warrior had suddenly materialized out of the debris and was charging Jayne Bahn, brandishing a long-bladed knife.

Bolan spotted the man, too, and started to call out a warning, but Bahn was already in motion, lurching to one side as the blade swept past, missing her by inches. Loose debris shifted under her feet, throwing her off balance. As she fell, she managed to grab hold of her attacker's wrist. Together, they tumbled down the slope, fighting over the knife.

Bahn finally managed to knock the weapon from the man's hand and, once they reached the level ground of the roadway, she fended off a right cross from her would-be assailant and countered with a fierce pair of karate blows. Both connected, one knocking the wind from the man's lungs, the other striking him behind the ear with enough force to knock him unconscious.

Staggering to her feet, Bahn drew her pistol and trained it on the man's face. When she heard Bolan and Kissinger jogging toward her, she turned to them. At first she didn't recognize them, but once they were close enough for her to see past their masks, she smiled faintly.

"You guys," she said. "Small world, eh?"

Kissinger yanked off his mask and stared hard at the woman. "What the hell are you doing here?"

"Crashing the party," she wisecracked. Nudging the fallen terrorist, she added, "I brought you a little something, but I didn't have time to wrap it."

CHAPTER NINE

"No wonder I put him out of commission so fast," Jayne Bahn said, crouching over the Lashkar Jihad warrior she'd felled. The man, it turned out, had been shot twice prior to being caught up in the landslide, which had broken his right leg in at least two places. "I can't believe he was able to get up and take a swipe at me with that knife of his."

"Adrenaline," Kissinger surmised.

"I say we put the squeeze on him till he coughs up Jahf-Al," Bahn said.

"He's in no shape to talk right now," Bolan said, inspecting the man's wounds. "With the blood he's lost, even if he comes to, he's going to be in shock."

"Well, excuse me for sounding like a hard-ass," Bahn countered, "but we're more likely to get something useful out of him if he's in shock than when he's thinking straight."

"We won't get anything out of him if he dies on us," Bolan stated. "We need to patch him up and get him to a hospital."

"Let me know which one so I can send flowers," Bahn replied sarcastically. "Maybe I'll come by and fluff his pillows, too."

"Listen, sweetheart," Kissinger interrupted. "When the time's right, we'll get him to talk, don't worry. And you can bet your ass we won't do it by pampering him. Got that?"

"Temper, temper," Bahn replied with a shrug. "Fine, have it your way."

Kissinger glowered at the woman, then jogged over to the chopper for a stretcher and Mochtar's med-kit. By the time they returned, Bolan had managed to staunch the flow of blood from the prisoner's wounds. Kissinger daubed the wounds with antiseptic, then quickly dressed them and kept pressure on the bandages as Bolan helped the soldiers load the man onto the stretcher. Grimaldi was waiting to help haul him up into the chopper.

"Go ahead and get these people to the base," Bolan told him. "We'll finish up here."

Grimaldi nodded. "I'll swing back later with rein-forcements and some kind of morgue unit for all the bodies."

"Before you go, hand me a couple two-ways," Bolan said.

Grimaldi reached into a bin near the door and pulled out two high-powered two-way radios. "Good luck," he said, handing them to Bolan.

The soldier nodded, then called past Grimaldi to Raki Mochtar. "You did good work, Rock."

"Thanks," the younger man replied gratefully.

"We'll see you back in Samarinda." Bolan saluted the medic, then stepped back from the chopper.

Grimaldi got back behind the controls and lifted off, then drifted back out over the valley. Bolan turned back to the roadway and sized up the situation.

"The truck's not going anywhere," he said, eyeing the bombed-out vehicle. "I say we leave it for now and spread out." He handed Kissinger one of the radios, telling him, "I want to check out the compound. Why don't you and Latek secure the area, then check around for more survivors."

"Done," Kissinger said, taking the two-way Bolan held out to him. "What about our friend here?"

"I'll take Ms. Bahn with me," Bolan said.

"Not so fast," Bahn said. "No offense, but I didn't sign up for a tour of duty here, okay? I call my own shots."

Bolan sighed. "Fair enough." He grabbed a stray assault rifle lying on the ground and held it out to the woman. "I could use your help, if you don't mind."

"That's more like it," Bahn said, taking the weapon.

Bolan exchanged a quick glance with Kissinger, who rolled his eyes, then gestured to Latek and the other commandos. They began to fan out in separate directions, giving a wide berth to the Bio-Tain truck, which continued to leak faintly visible clouds of toxic gas. Bolan, meanwhile, led Bahn the other way, up the road leading to the agricultural compound.

By now the Black Hawk was beyond earshot and the road was eerily quiet. For the first time since the firefight had begun, Bolan noticed a few signs of wildlife: birds, a few small gray squirrels, and a thin black monkey scrambling back and forth along the guardrail.

"I think you can take off that mask now," Bahn told Bolan. "It's not like we're trapped in some kind of enclosed space."

Bolan took off his mask. There was a faint odor of cordite in the air and he could smell smoke from the fires across the valley, but there was nothing that smelled like the chemical stench of the cloud that had nearly enveloped him a short time ago. Bolan also realized his cough had left him, as had the stinging sensation in his eyes. He'd gotten off lucky, he figured.

They walked silently for a short distance, then Bolan asked, "Are you here on your own or still working for Inter-Trieve?"

"I-T," she replied.

Inter-Trieve was a Washington, D.C.-based bounty agency specializing in high-profile cases involving international fugitives. Bahn had joined them five years ago after stints with the Army Rangers and CIA.

"We're on retainer with the insurance company representing that cruise liner Jahf-Al deep-sixed last spring," she explained. "They figure the reward money'll help offset the claims they're paying out."

"Provided you bring him in," Bolan said.

"I'll bring him in, all right."

"You seem pretty sure of yourself."

"Gotta be in this line of work," Bahn responded calmly.

"I take it you're aware that half the free world's tried tracking down Jahf-Al with no luck."

"Well, maybe they didn't try hard enough," Bahn suggested.

Bolan wasn't about to waste his breath arguing with her. Instead, he asked the woman how she knew about the raid. Bahn shrugged, swatting away a cloud of gnats that had appeared on the roadway.

"I have my sources," she said.

"You think you could you be a little more specific?" Bolan asked.

"Sorry," Bahn said. "A girl needs her secrets."

"I'm just trying to figure out who tipped off these guys that we were coming."

"Don't look at me," Bahn replied icily.

"I'm not accusing you."

"Yeah, right."

Once Bolan and Bahn had hiked around the next bend, the road came to a sudden end and they found themselves at the entrance to the seventy-acre IMA facility. The grounds were enclosed by an eight-foot-high cyclone fence, and the entrance gate was guarded by two uniformed men in their early twenties. The men had their carbines aimed at the new arrivals, and the guns quivered slightly in their hands. They'd obviously heard the earlier assault and seemed fearful of being dragged into the bloodshed. One of them shouted a warning in his native tongue.

"I seem to remember you speak a few languages," Bolan murmured.

"So that's why you wanted me to tag along, you little weasel," Bahn taunted. "And here I thought you were after my body."

Bolan suppressed a smile. "Business before pleasure," he responded evenly.

Bahn called out to the guards in Bahasa Indonesian, then quickly explained what had happened back on the roadway. Once she'd finished, the men conferred briefly, then one of them raised the security bar while the other waved them past.

"That was easy enough," Bahn whispered to Bolan. "Hell, no wonder the Lashkar had such an easy time of it."

"Ask them how many men were on the Bio-Tain truck when it first showed up," Bolan suggested.

The bounty hunter stopped alongside the raised bar and spoke again to the guards. Afterward, she and Bolan continued up the driveway, heading toward the storage facility, a two-story building set back a hundred yards from the gate.

"They say there were only six men on the truck," Bahn reported, "and that includes the driver."

"There were at least four times that many in on the ambush," Bolan recalled.

"I know," Bahn said. "I mentioned that, but they insist they inspected the truck coming and going and there were only six of them."

"Then there must be a camp around here somewhere," Bolan theorized.

"That'd be my guess, too," Bahn said, staring past

the grounds, where hazy ribbons of smoke stretched over a vast sprawl of rain forest.

As they continued up the drive, Bolan abruptly changed the subject. "Are you still on speaking terms with your ex-husband?"

Bahn was taken aback. "Excuse me?"

"Frank Dominico, right? Works CIA out of Africa."

"I know who my ex-husband is, okay?" she retorted. "Why'd you bring him up?"

"You found out about the raid from him," Bolan guessed.

"I already told you, my sources are confidential."

"One phone call and I can find out for myself," Bolan told her.

"All right," Bahn said, sighing. "Yes, I got it from Frank. Last time we talked, I asked him where Jahf-Al might go after he snuck out of Afghanistan, and he turned me on to the whole FAO stink over the agri-compound here. It sounded like a decent lead, so I flew in a couple of days ago and started sniffing around. I got my hands on a map and figured a way to reach the compound without being seen."

"Who'd you get the map from?" Bolan asked.

"Don't push your luck, pal." She sidestepped the question and pointed to her right as she went on, "I made it as far as the fence over there when I heard all hell breaking loose on the road. By the time I'd high-tailed it up over the mountain, the shooting had stopped and you guys had pretty much wrapped things up."

"You didn't really think you were going to find Jahf-Al here, did you?" Bolan asked.

"No," Bahn admitted, "but I was going to plant a homing device on that truck of his and see if it would take me to him. Which is probably what you guys should've tried instead of trying to play John Wayne."

"Hindsight," Bolan said.

There were another two guards posted near the front entrance to the storage facility. As Bahn spoke to them, Bolan looked over the building. It was old and decrepit, the walls overrun with vines and the roof patched in several places with thin sheets of blue plastic. Hardly an ideal environment for storing toxic materials, he thought. There was no way he or Bahn were going to attempt to go inside the building without full HAZMAT gear.

"Okay," Bahn said when she rejoined him. "They said the Bio-Tain crew showed up earlier than scheduled this morning and everything was routine until about an hour ago, when the driver got a call from somebody on his cab radio."

"The tip-off," Bolan guessed.

"Probably," Bahn said. "Anyway, the crew stopped what it was doing and everybody piled back into the truck. The driver said something about an emergency, then drove off."

"That's it?"

"Not quite," Bahn said. "Before they pulled out, apparently one of the workers kept looking up at that hilltop over there. It's a good hundred yards from where I was hiking, so they weren't looking at me."

Bolan glanced up at the hill, half-hidden in shadow. The hill was covered with dense brush and dotted with small trees. Up near the crest was a rock formation that looked vaguely like a raised fist. Bolan told Bahn that KOPASSUS had stationed a surveillance team somewhere in the hills overlooking the compound, adding, "They said they were having trouble seeing the compound because of all the smoke."

Bahn frowned and shook her head. "It was a little hazy up here, yeah, but not that bad. None of the guards mentioned that, either."

Bolan pondered the discrepancy a moment, then got on the two-way radio to Kissinger. Cowboy reported that they'd come up empty-handed in terms of looking for other survivors. Bolan wasn't surprised. He quickly briefed Kissinger on what he had found out, then asked to speak to Umar Latek. Once he had the sergeant on the line, Bolan asked him to think back to the call he'd made to the surveillance team.

"How clear was the reception?" he asked. "Could you tell for sure who you were talking to?"

There was a moment's hesitation, then Latek replied, "There was some static, yes, but I am sure it was the head of the surveillance team."

"Are you positive?" Bolan asked. "One hundred percent certain?"

Again Latek hesitated a moment. "It had to be him," he said finally. "Who else could it have been?"

"I'm thinking the stakeout crew was jumped," Bolan told him. "I think they were killed, and when you called, I think they squelched the frequency just enough to help mask the voice of whoever told you about the smoke making it hard to see the truck. They were covering, because the truck was already on the way, and they wanted to make sure it would take us by surprise."

Yet again it took Latek a moment to respond. When he did, his voice was weary. "If that is the case, I am to blame for the ambush," he told Bolan. "I should have suspected something was wrong."

Bolan tried to assure the sergeant that if his suspicions were correct, Latek's mistake had been an honest one. But Latek was inconsolable. He continued to berate himself until Bolan finally interjected, asking the sergeant to put Kissinger back on. He told Cowboy to stay put until Grimaldi returned or sent back another chopper.

"And keep an eye on Latek," he concluded. "Poor guy sounds like he's ready to commit hara-kiri."

"I'll try talking to him," Kissinger said. "What's your plan?"

"I want to find out what happened to that surveillance team," Bolan said, staring up at the rock formation atop the hillock. "Then we're going to start looking around for the hole our ambushers crawled out of."

CHAPTER TEN

When asked about possible routes to the top of the hill, the IMA guards directed Bolan to a series of switchbacks leading from a rear entrance to the storage facility. The crisscrossed paths twisted their way around tall patches of wild grass, brambly thickets and scattered stands of gnarled trees. As Bolan and Bahn made their way up the incline, they could see, off to their right, the distant mountains of central Borneo. The peaks, some of them nearly ten thousand feet high, were barely visible through the smoky haze, which by now had stretched itself across the entire length of the valley rain forest.

Soon they came upon a firebreak, a thirty-yard-wide band of land hacked clear of brush and vegetation. It ran perpendicular to the switchbacks and stretched in both directions for as far as Bolan could see.

"We take a left here, right?" he said, trying to recall the directions the guards had given them.

Bahn nodded. "Yeah, we follow this for about two

hundred yards, then there's supposed to be another trail that leads up to the peak."

The firebreak was on a slope but the ground was soft, making it easy to walk. There were no signs of boot prints, fresh or otherwise. The break was within plain sight of the storage facility, and there was no way anyone could have used it without being spotted.

"Assuming Jahf-Al's here in Indonesia," Bahn said, changing the subject, "what do you think his agenda is? Other than hiding out, I mean."

Bolan shrugged. "The UIF already has a toehold here. If he can tap into the Muslim unrest, Indonesia's got the makings of a great power base."

"True," Bahn said, "but the Lashkar Jihad's already pretty much cornered the market on the extremist action. I know they've cut some kind of deal with the UIF, but I don't think stepping aside and letting Jahf-Al run things was part of it. He and Pohtoh aren't exactly buddy-buddy from what I understand."

"That's the way I hear it, too," Bolan said.

Moamar Pohtoh was the Muslim firebrand who'd risen to head of the Lashkar Jihad after his predecessor, Halim Alwyi, had been gunned down in a Sulawesi shootout over a year ago. It was Pohtoh who'd widened the group's agenda while at the same time consolidating power by killing off a number of Alwyi's top-ranking subordinates. Pohtoh was no stranger to Jahf-Al, either, and there was supposedly bad blood between the two men dating back to the late 1990s, when they'd trained together at an al-Qaeda terrorist camp in the

Afghanistan mountains of Tora Bora. Pohtoh, who hailed from the slums of Jakarta, was purportedly as suspicious of Jahf-Al's bourgeois Cairo upbringing as he was of the Egyptian's motivation for creating the United Islamic Front. The Indonesian strongman had gone on record as little as six months ago claiming that Jahf-Al was less interested in the cause of Islam than that of amassing power and trying to rival the infamy of Osama bin Laden. Given the antipathy between the two men, many had been surprised when it had come out that the Lashkar Jihad was accepting input from the UIF.

"Must be a strange bedfellows thing," Bolan guessed. "They probably figured they had more to gain by focusing on common ground instead of haggling over their differences."

"Wouldn't be the first time that's happened," Bahn conceded.

By now they'd followed the firebreak nearly a hundred yards. Suddenly Bolan stopped and held out a hand, signaling for Bahn to do the same. She heard it, too: a rustling in the brush to their right. In unison, they both dropped to a crouch and raised their assault rifles, aiming into the foliage. The sound continued, growing louder and moving closer. Finally they could begin to make out the shadowy outline of three figures moving through the brush toward them.

"I've got the one in front," Bahn whispered, nestling her finger against the trigger. "I say we don't give them the first shot."

Bolan shifted his aim toward the rear figures, then stopped and whispered back, "Hold your fire."

"Look, maybe you've got a vest on under that suit of yours, but I don't," Bahn told him. "I'm not going to just wait here like some sitting duck for them to—"

"They're monkeys," Bolan stated.

"Call them what you like, I—"

"Orangutans," Bolan said. "They're orangutans."

"What?" Bahn said, not willing to let down her guard.

But as she took a closer look into the brush, she realized Bolan was right. Three orangutans, all immature males, loped downhill a few more yards, then peered out through the branches. Bahn lowered her rifle and slowly stood, shaking her head.

"Makes sense," she said. "I saw a preserve marked out on the map. Somewhere down there in the rain forest."

The orangutans continued to stare at Bolan and Bahn but made no move to show themselves any further.

"Scram!" Bahn snapped at them. "We're busy here!"

"Let's just leave them alone," Bolan said. He turned his back to the creatures and resumed hiking along the firebreak. Bahn picked up a stone and threw it into the brush to the right of the creatures. When the orangutans refused to budge, she shrugged and quickly caught up with Bolan.

"Smug little bastards," she grumbled.

"They probably knew they could take you out if they wanted to," Bolan taunted.

Bahn scowled at him.

A few minutes later they reached the trail rising up from the firebreak. It was narrow, and they made their way single file, Bolan leading the way. Small trees rose up on either side of them, strangler figs trailing long, woody vines from their lower branches. The large tree Bolan had seen from the ground loomed ahead. They followed the trail toward it and were soon in sight of the fistlike rock formation. For the first time, they also began to see boot prints on the path before them. Whoever had made them had come upon the trail by way of the brush. The tracks led upward.

"Looks like three different sets," Bolan commented.

"Well, unless those orangutans were wearing boots, my money's on the ambushers," Bahn said.

Bolan nodded. "Let's find out."

Assault rifles raised into firing position, they continued up the last few dozen yards of trail and soon found themselves at the base of the rock formation.

"Well, looks like you were right about them being jumped," Bahn told Bolan, staring at the grisly tableau before them.

The three-man KOPASSUS surveillance team lay dead in the grass, facedown, blood caked to their scalps where they'd been shot. Lying on its side a few yards away from the bodies was a transceiver similar to the one Bolan had seen Latek use on the bus.

Bahn crouched over one of the victims and inspected his wounds.

"Small caliber," she said. "I'd guess 9 mm."

"Handguns with sound suppressors," Bolan said.

"Which would explain why I didn't hear anything," Bahn said, speculating as to what had happened. "They popped these guys, then they sent the truck on its way and fed that sergeant that crap about it being too smoky to see anything."

"I want to check something else," Bolan said, stepping over one of the bodies. He inspected the rock formation, then set his rifle aside and climbed up to the top. He looked around briefly, then climbed back down.

"No problem seeing the storage facility," he reported, "but the road's nowhere in sight."

"Meaning what?"

Bolan pointed at the slain commandos. "I think these guys were killed outright," he said. "No interrogations."

"Okay, I follow that much," Bahn said. "Where are you going with this?"

"Just hear me out," Bolan said. "All right. We've got these guys being killed right around the time the truck leaves the facility, right?"

"Right."

"Think about it," Bolan said. "They can't see the road from here, so how did they know we were coming? And even if they *did* see us, we were in that bus. It would've looked like we were just another bunch of tourists headed for the textile center."

"Which brings us back to them being tipped off," Bahn said. "They knew the raid was going down even before they jumped the surveillance team here, which is why they knew enough to get on the radio with that story about the smoke so you'd think the truck was still at the compound."

"Exactly," Bolan said.

"The big question is, who squealed to them?" Bahn asked.

"Hard to say," Bolan replied. "You've got a lot of people in the loop on this. Besides KOPASSUS, you've got the CIA, Indonesia Military Intelligence, the FAO—"

"And you guys," Bahn said.

"What's that supposed to mean?" Bolan countered.

"Easy, big fella," she told him. "I'm just calling 'em as I see 'em. Why should we assume your guys are all clean?"

"I trust them a hell of a lot more than I do you," Bolan said.

"Somehow I don't think that's saying a lot," Bahn said. "Let's try to be objective, okay? Have you guys taken on any new people recently? Anybody who might have some kind of ulterior motive?"

"No, of course not."

But even as the words were coming out, Bolan realized there had, indeed, been a recent addition to the crew.

Raki Mochtar.

But could he be a spy? It didn't seem possible. True,

Mochtar had an Indonesian background, but he'd passed all the necessary security checks before being taken on as a blacksuit, and before being approached for this assignment he'd undergone even more scrutiny. Each time he'd checked out clean. But, then, Bolan also recalled a few other times when Stony Man Farm had suffered security breaches from within; in nearly every instance the culprit had been someone supposedly beyond reproach. Could this be another one of those cases?

"Well?" she prompted.

Bolan didn't answer her. Instead, he grabbed his two-way and started to signal Kissinger. Before he could raise Cowboy, however, he and Bahn heard another rustling in the brush, this time twenty yards to their right.

"Chimps ahoy," Bahn murmured, glancing over her shoulder.

A gunshot suddenly ripped through the foliage, just missing Bahn and ricocheting off the rock formation behind her. Instinctively she dived to the ground and scrambled along with Bolan to the far side of the rock. A second shot rang out, rousing the dirt to their right.

"Okay, maybe it's not the monkeys after all," she said.

CHAPTER ELEVEN

As quickly as it had begun, the shooting stopped. An unnerving silence lingered in its wake. Rifles raised, Bolan and the woman crouched at opposite ends of the rock formation, covering themselves from as many angles as possible. Peering out into the brush, they waited, listening for advancing footsteps, the sound of a weapon being reloaded. Something. Anything.

"Come on!" Bahn whispered hotly. "Show yourselves, dammit!"

She was answered by more silence. Then, finally, several seconds later, there was renewed commotion in the brush. Footsteps and a snapping of twigs. The sounds were receding, however, not drawing closer. Whoever had fired at them was in retreat.

"Sounds like a loner," Bolan murmured.

Bahn nodded. "He runs off after a couple warning shots? What's up with that?"

"Could be he's out of ammo," Bolan said. "Or maybe he's going to try to circle around and have another go at us."

"Let him try," Bahn said, clenching her rifle.

The sounds in the brush continued to fade. Whoever shot at them was headed back toward the far valley, away from the access road and storage facility. Bolan was deliberating their next move when his two-way radio crackled to life. It was Kissinger.

"What's going on there? Over."

Bolan grabbed the radio and quickly explained what had happened, then asked Kissinger, "Where are you? Over."

"Sergeant Latek found a path up the mountain while we were scouting around," Kissinger explained. "We're up on the ridgeline, about a quarter mile from you. I got a glimpse of you up on the rock formation, but the shooting started before I could patch in. Over."

"Whoever it is, they're bound for the rain forest," Bolan told him. "We're going after them. Why don't you head over and give us a little backup? Once you reach the rock formation, it should be easy to pick up our trail. Over."

"We're on our way. Out."

Bolan clicked off, then rose to his feet. "Let's go."

He and Bahn split up and ventured into the brush. Bolan used the barrel of his rifle to clear his way through the bramble, but the thorns still managed to nick him constantly, sometimes piercing the material of his HAZMAT suit. Bahn, navigating the brush twenty yards to his right, was under similar attack, and without the protection of a suit the pricking took a harder toll, prompting a near-constant stream of epithets.

Finally Bolan reached a small clearing where a set of footprints came to a stop and then doubled back on themselves.

"Over here," he called out softly.

When Bahn caught up with him, Bolan was holding a pair of bullet casings he'd found in the dirt. They were still warm and reeking of cordite.

"It's a .22," he said, holding out the shells for Bahn to see. "Revolver, probably."

"Explains why he was so stingy with his shots," Bahn guessed. She plucked a thorn from her forearm and rubbed at the faint smear of blood it had produced. "How about we skip the trailblazing and just stick to the path he made?"

Bolan nodded and led the way. They had followed the footprints another twenty yards, when Bahn suddenly reached past Bolan into the bramble, removing a few strands of black, curly hair glistening with blood.

"Methinks it's the hair of his chinny chin chin," she mused.

"Then we're on the right track," Bolan said. He started to move on, but she put a hand on his shoulder, motioning for him to stop.

"How about if I lead for a change?" Bahn proposed. "Nothing against that nice ass of yours, but I'd kinda like to see where we're going. You'll have an easier time looking over my shoulder than the other way around."

"If you're walking in front, what makes you think I'll be looking at your shoulder?" Bolan replied, doing his best to keep a straight face.

"Ooh, naughty boy." As she stepped past Bolan to take the lead, Bahn smiled up at him. "Try to be a gentleman, would you? At least until we can find a nice hotel room?"

They continued through the underbrush, doing their best to track their fleeing attacker. It was slow going. The grass and bramble grew thicker as they made their way along the slope, and several times they lost sight of the shooter's footprints and had to scout for other signs as to which way he'd fled: snapped branches, bent wildflower stalks, more stray hairs or a scrap of cloth claimed by the thornbushes. At one point they thought they'd spotted someone up in the trees, but it turned out to be another of the orangutans, using strangler vines for support as it moved from limb to limb with deceptive ease.

"Maybe we should try that," Bahn suggested, prying loose yet another thorn from her forearm. "You know, 'Me Jayne, you Tarzan.'"

"I don't think so," Bolan said.

After a few more minutes of navigating through the unforgiving foliage, the two finally emerged into a clearing and found themselves on a broad, flat promontory, not unlike the one Grimaldi had blasted to create the landslide on the other side of the mountain. Before them lay the north valley. Bolan quickly dropped to his stomach and motioned for Bahn to do the same.

"We're like sitting ducks out on this ledge," he whispered.

"I'll take my chances," Bahn said. "Beats the hell

out of having to pick those damn thorns out of my hide all the—"

Bolan squeezed her arm, silencing her, then pointed downhill. Bahn shifted her gaze, just in time to see a young, bearded man frantically making his way down the slope to the valley floor, where the foliage was even denser than up on the hill. One second the man was in clear sight, scrambling through knee-high ferns and wild rhododendrons; the next he'd vanished into the greenery without a trace.

"So much for heading him off at the pass," Bolan said.

"We might as well wait for the others."

As they waited, Bolan looked over the jungle. The valley was easily thirty miles wide and half that distance across, and every square inch of the land seemed veiled by a canopy of trees. The only exception was the foothills on the far side of the valley, where flames could be seen raging through a section of the forest, giving off a thick, dark column of smoke. Beyond the next rise, Bolan could see other, similar columns, all adding to the hazy shroud that stretched over them, blotting the afternoon sun so that it seemed nothing more than a dim bulb. Bolan could smell the smoke. It was so strong his eyes began to burn again. Once more he found himself fighting back a cough.

"It's worse than smog during rush hour in L.A.," Bahn said, stifling a cough of her own.

They continued their vigil atop the promontory for another ten minutes, but there was no further sign of their enemy. Finally they heard a crackling in the brush behind them, followed by a radio call from Kissinger telling them to hold their fire.

"It's just us."

"Stay put," Bolan told him. "We'll come to you."

They retreated from the ledge and backtracked into the brush until they met up with Kissinger, Latek and two of the KOPASSUS commandos. They'd all long since shed their HAZMAT masks, and Bolan looked quickly into each man's eyes for signs of treachery. Each of the commandos returned his gaze unflinchingly, then Latek and one of the others moved past Bolan and headed toward the promontory.

"Flyboy made it back to Samarinda in one piece," Kissinger reported, "but apparently there's a nick in the chopper's fuel line, so it'll be awhile before he can get it airborne again."

"How about another chopper?" Bolan asked.

"He's trying to roust one from the military over in Balikpapan," Kissinger said, "but that'll take time, too."

"How's the major holding up?"

"He's under the knife at the city hospital," Kissinger said. "They say it's going to be a long surgery, and they don't like his chances. That prisoner we took in is in the OR too, but his prognosis isn't much better. The others got by with quick patch-ups. They've probably already been released."

Bolan took Kissinger aside and whispered, "If they haven't been, I think we should have Jack and Rock try to keep an eye on them."

"Why's that?"

Before Bolan could pass along his theory about a spy having tipped off the Lashkar about the raid, Latek returned from the promontory and called out, "I see some smoke."

"That's not exactly 'Stop the presses,'" Bahn told him. "There's smoke everywhere you look."

"Close by," Latek said. "Just down the hill."

Bolan told the others to stay put, then motioned for Kissinger to come with him. When they reached the escarpment, Bolan dropped once again to the ground and inched forward to a point from which he could see back down into the valley. Kissinger did the same.

A hundred yards away, a thin, serpentine finger of white smoke rose through the trees.

"Too small for a slash-and-burn," Kissinger murmured.

"It's in the direction the shooter was headed," Bolan said. "I'm thinking campsite."

"If that's the case, we're in business," Kissinger said.

They crawled back into the brush. Bolan told Bahn and Latek, "If we're going to try to hit them, this is the time, before they head any deeper into the forest."

"I'm with you," Bahn said.

Latek nodded. "What is the plan?"

Bolan thought it over, then laid out a basic strategy. When he was finished, Latek spoke briefly to the other commandos. As they steeled themselves for what lay ahead, one of the men clenched his assault rifle tightly and murmured something in Javanese.

"What'd he say?" Bolan asked Bahn as they prepared to enter the forest.

"Roughly translated," she said, "It's show time."

CHAPTER TWELVE

"Who turned off the lights?" Kissinger whispered.

He'd taken less than a dozen steps into the rain forest, but it was as if he'd crossed time zones to a place where the sun had already set. Engulfed in a bleak twilight, he and the others found themselves surrounded by a preternatural world of looming, shifting shadows.

"Let's take it slow till our eyes adjust," Bolan advised.

"No argument there," Cowboy replied.

The group had split up before entering the forest. Jayne Bahn had paired up with one of the commandos while, somewhere off to Bolan and Kissinger's right, Sergeant Latek and the other commando had already forged ahead and disappeared from sight.

The ground beneath Bolan's and Kissinger's feet was a soft, peatlike layer of decomposed vegetation that padded each step they took. Not that anyone could have heard them above the cacophony. The noise surrounding the men was almost deafening. Up in the treetops, orangutans and smaller monkeys howled to one another, competing with the caterwaul of unseen birds and buzzing of insects, and the unsettling moan of the wind filtering through the upper branches.

And then there was the river, lapping and gurgling its way through the forest. Adding to the sensory overload was a cloying scent of exotic, overripe fruit. The smell was every bit as strong as that of the damp peat and, for the first time since stepping off the plane in Samarinda, Bolan realized he was unable to detect the smell of smoke. So much for sniffing their way to the enemy campfire, he thought to himself.

"Let's stay close to the river," he suggested. "Odds are they pitched camp near it."

Kissinger followed Bolan. Their eyes continued to become accustomed to the darkness, and once they reached the river they were able to make out scores of boot prints along the banks. The tracks led in both directions.

"Seems like we want to keep heading north," Kissinger whispered. "The other way's going to take us back out of the forest."

"You're right," Bolan agreed. "North it is."

As they continued along the river, the men spotted pigs milling near the water's edge. As Bolan and Kissinger drew closer, they quickly scattered, squealing their way into the undergrowth. The commotion spread as a flock of small dark-feathered birds burst out of the brush with a flurry of beating wings. The men froze momentarily, rifles at the ready, wary that their position had been given away.

"I don't know about you," Kissinger muttered, "but this place gives me the creeps."

Bolan nodded. He was looking out at the river.

"Look at the water," he said.

Kissinger took another step closer and peered into the current. The water had a reddish coloring to it.

"It's not blood, if that's what you're thinking," Kissinger said. "I remember reading about tannic acid or something like that in the peat. It gets leeched into the water and turns it—"

"I'm not talking about the color, Cowboy," Bolan interrupted, pointing farther upstream. "I meant that slick over there."

Kissinger shifted his gaze and spotted a wide, luminescent clot suspended on the water. Even in the relative darkness, the shape gleamed, rainbowlike, as it drifted toward them.

"Gotta be some kind of fuel spill," Kissinger surmised. "Outboard motor, most likely. I'll bet you anything these guys use some kind of boat to haul in supplies and any other—"

Kissinger's voice was drowned out by a faint, sudden boom. Seconds later, a vibrant flash illuminated the jungle, momentarily blinding both men with its fiery brilliance.

"Take cover!" Bolan yelled.

Even as he was shouting the warning, Bolan was lunging away from the river and rolling into the nearby foliage. His instincts were once again on target. As he and Kissinger scrambled for cover, the forest around them thundered with the incessant rattle of automatic gunfire. The fusillade was so loud and persistent it quickly drowned out all other sounds save for the muffled thud of bullets plowing into the peat banks where the two men had been standing a moment before.

"You all right?" Kissinger whispered to Bolan.

"Yeah. So far at least."

The flare tumbled through the upper branches of the nearby trees, then dropped straight down to the forest floor, even as another was taking its place, bathing the forest with another blast of harsh light. Bolan blinked his eyes several times, then peered out through the foliage and saw enemy gunmen up in the trees, firing down at the intruders.

Soon there was yet another burst of light, this one down near the river's edge eighty yards from where Bolan and Kissinger had taken cover.

"Flamethrower," Bolan said.

"Oh, man," Kissinger groaned. "Something tells me that fuel spill was no accident."

Moments later, the man with the flamethrower took aim at the water and spewed forth a roaring flame like the breath of a dragon. The river around him turned into a watery inferno as the flames fed on the fuel slick and raced downriver toward Bolan and Kissinger. Some of the flames overshot the banks and ignited the peat. Once again, the stench of smoke assailed Bolan's nostrils.

"And I thought we had it bad out there on the road," Kissinger said. "Looks like we jumped from the frying pan into the fire."

CHAPTER THIRTEEN

Bullets tore through the foliage all around Bolan and Kissinger as they rolled away from the burning peat and crawled to the cover of a fallen tree covered with moss and lichen. The trunk was half rotted but still strong enough to absorb the rounds that pounded into it, giving the men precious seconds with which to scout the treetops and pinpoint the snipers.

"I've got the one on the right," Bolan stated, propping his rifle against the trunk. Once he had his man in his sights, he fired off a 3-round burst. Up in the canopy, the sniper howled and dropped his rifle, falling backward as he clutched at the bullet wound in his shoulder. His foot snagged between the trunk and the limb he'd been perched on, and he found himself dangling upside down by one leg. He flailed his arms, but before he could grab hold of the trunk and wrest himself free, Bolan finished him off.

Kissinger, meanwhile, got off a clean shot of his own, shattering the other sniper's skull and dropping the man to the forest floor.

"Guess I was wrong about the fire," Kissinger said. "The light's helping us a hell of a lot more than it is them."

"We'll take all the help we can get," Bolan replied, shifting his fire to a handful of Lashkar hardmen positioned around the clearing where they'd set up camp. Smoke still rose from the campfire behind them.

There was a third gunman hunched up in the trees behind the campsite, but he, too, went down under a volley of screaming lead from Jayne Bahn's assault rifle. Peering over his shoulder, Bolan spotted the woman forty yards to his right, lying prone at the base of a fruit tree whose elevated roots provided her with a makeshift screen through which to shoot. The commando she'd partnered up with, however, had apparently been struck during the first round of gunfire and lay facedown in a bed of ground vines. Bolan couldn't see Latek or the other commando, but he could hear them firing from positions in the brush far behind Bahn.

Fierce as the initial bursts of light had been, the fires they started failed to take hold, and once the flares had burned out and the fuel slick on the river had been consumed by flames, darkness slowly began to reclaim the forest. If Bolan and the others were going to finish off their adversaries, he knew the time to do it was now, before those at the campsite had a chance to spread out into the jungle.

"Charge and strafe them!" he shouted, switching his assault rifle to full-auto as he bolted over the fallen trunk.

Kissinger followed suit, and together they zigzagged toward the campsite, swinging their rifles from side to side to widen the spray of their gunfire. Return fire whistled past them, but none of the shots came close to hitting their mark.

The terrorist who'd torched the river tried to use his flamethrower against Bolan and Kissinger, but the weapon was low on fuel and gave off only a brief sputter of flame, revealing his position as well as that of two men racing past him toward a thirty-foot hydrofoil moored on the river. Bolan stopped in his tracks long enough to take aim and drop all three men in quick succession.

Jayne Bahn and the two surviving commandos had equal luck, making their shots count while avoiding the panicked firing by the Lashkar troops. By the time they converged on the campsite, only a pair of terrorist gunmen remained. Not about to surrender, the two men leveled their rifles at Bolan and Kissinger, forcing the Stony Man warriors to take them out.

Then it was over.

Kissinger and the KOPASSUS commandos kept their rifles trained on the surrounding jungle as Bolan and Jayne Bahn quickly inspected their adversaries. Seven men in all lay dead within thirty yards of the campfire, and an eighth—one of the men who'd tried to make it to the hydrofoil—stirred only briefly before his wounds claimed him.

"They're all Lashkar Jihad from the looks of it," Bahn said.

"I don't see Pohtoh," Bolan said, turning one of the dead men onto his back. "Not that I'd expect to."

The forest had fallen briefly silent in the wake of the battle, but slowly the sounds of wildlife began to once more permeate the air.

"Perhaps we should scout around to see if there are any others," Latek suggested.

"Go ahead," Bolan told him, "but stick to a quarter-mile radius, then make your way back."

Latek nodded. He and the other KOPASSUS soldier exchanged a few words, then split up and headed off in separate directions. Before they could slip out of sight, Bolan strode over to Bahn and whispered, "Try to keep an eye on them."

"Fat chance," she whispered back. "Hell, I'm not going to be able to see them once they've gone twenty yards."

"That's all I'm concerned about," Bolan said. "I just want to make sure they don't double back and start taking potshots at us."

"A little paranoid, are we?" Bahn said. "Your buddy just vouched for those guys, remember?"

"Just keep your eyes open," Bolan told her.

She snapped a mock salute. "Yes, sir!"

Bolan ignored the sarcasm and rejoined Kissinger. Together they began to look over the camp. There wasn't much to inspect. The terrorists had traveled light. A couple of logs had been set near the firepit and stacked near the hydrofoil were several wooden crates filled with ammunition and some meager provisions:

canteens, bags of rice and a fire-blackened pot. There was more ammo stored in the boat itself, along with several fuel canisters.

"Not a lot of help here," Kissinger grumbled, clearly disappointed at the lack of clues.

Suddenly there was a piercing cry off in the brush. Then, as quickly as it had sounded, the cry ended.

"Sounded like Latek," Bolan said, breaking into a run.

Bahn and Kissinger quickly fell in stride beside him. Leaving the campsite, they passed the KOPAS-SUS trooper killed earlier, then continued to wade through the underbrush toward the source of the cry. Bolan called out Latek's name, but there was no response.

"We better spread out," Bolan told the others.

Bahn broke away and headed to Bolan's right. Kissinger went left.

Bolan stayed put for a moment, then slowly advanced through the ferns. He wasn't sure what to make of Latek's cry. Had something happened to him or was he baiting them into an ambush? Bolan hated being plagued by such paranoia.

He'd taken another two steps when he suddenly stopped. He detected movement to his right and swung around his rifle but held his fire. It was the other KOPASSUS soldier, moving slowly through the brush. After a few steps he called out to Latek. There was no response.

Bolan was about to signal when the commando sud-

denly fell from view. It was as if he'd just fallen
through a trap door in the jungle floor. He let out a startled cry similar to Latek's and it, too, was abruptly silenced. In its wake this time Bolan heard a faint
splashing.

"What the hell?" he muttered.

Kissinger and Bahn had heard the outburst as well,
and they raced toward the sound of the commando's
voice.

"Careful!" Bolan called.

The warning came too late, however. Within seconds after Kissinger strode back into Bolan's line of
sight, he, too, suddenly began to drop from view.

"Shit!" he cried out.

Bolan rushed forward and saw that Kissinger had
stepped into a murky pool of water concealed by a thin
layer of leaves and twigs. A few yards to Cowboy's
right, the KOPASSUS commando's right hand poked
up through the water for a fleeting second, then sank
from view. A little farther beyond that, all that remained of Sergeant Latek was his helmet; it bobbed
on the water's surface like a turtle's shell. It suddenly
became clear to Bolan what Kissinger and the other
men had stumbled into.

CHAPTER FOURTEEN

Bolan moved quickly toward Kissinger until he stepped into the murky water and could feel the ground beginning to give way beneath his feet. Stepping back to dry land, he leaned outward, extending his hand toward Kissinger. Cowboy instinctively grabbed hold, but the water was already up to his chest, and he realized that the more he struggled, the faster he was being pulled under. Rather than risk taking his colleague down with him, he let go of Bolan's hand. Bahn had just arrived and she tugged at Bolan's waist, steadying him as he was about to tumble headlong into the water.

"Stay back, dammit!" Kissinger yelled. "Both of you!"

"No way!" Bolan shouted back at him.

The soldier looked around wildly, desperate to find a way to save Kissinger before he was swallowed by the quicksand. His eyes fell on the vines trailing from a nearby tree. He rushed over and pulled at them, but they were anchored to the upper limbs. Straining with all his might, he continued to yank, cursing. Precious seconds were being lost. Kissinger could already have gone under. He couldn't take time to check, though. He continued to pull at the vines, groaning with exertion.

Then, just as he was about to give up, he heard the rattle of an assault rifle directly behind him. At the same time, one of the overhead vines broke free, severed by the gunfire, and dropped to Bolan's feet.

He grabbed the vine and dragged it back toward the quicksand. On the way, he eyed Bahn gratefully and told her, "I owe you one."

As quickly as they'd risen, however, Bolan's hopes were dashed when he stared into the murky pool and saw Kissinger's fingers slowly sinking below the surface.

"Cowboy!" Bolan shouted. He was about to dive headlong into the pool when Bahn grabbed him.

"Don't be stupid!" she told him, handing him one end of the vine. She'd already begun looping the other end around her waist. "I'm lighter! Give me a few seconds, then start pulling!"

Before Bolan could protest, Bahn finished knotting the vine and turned her back to him. She took two strides forward, then dived into the water, landing close to where Kissinger had just gone under. The vine fed out behind her, and at the last second Bolan grabbed the other end. He crouched, trying to give himself better leverage as he began to pull the vine toward him, but his feet kept slipping out from beneath him. He finally lunged to one side and fed the vine around the base of the nearest tree, then pulled in the opposite direction, using the trunk as a pulley.

His blood pulsed in his ears, making it hard for him to hear anything but his own grunts of exertion. Slowly, short length by short length, he pulled the vine toward him. His arms and legs both began to ache, and it seemed to him that too much time had passed. They were both gone. He was expending all his energy trying to pull bodies from the quicksand's unyielding grip.

Suddenly there was a lapse of resistance, followed moments later by a loud gasp. Glancing over his shoulder, Bolan saw Bahn's head rise above the surface. She spit water from her mouth and greedily sucked in more air.

"Don't stop!" she cried out between gasps.

Spurred on by fresh hope, Bolan tugged harder at the vine while still looking over his shoulder. Soon he saw Kissinger rise to the surface, Bahn holding him around the chest with one arm while she continued to clutch the vine with the other. Kissinger wasn't breathing.

"Cowboy!"

Bolan knotted the vine around the tree trunk, then rushed as close to the water's edge as he dared. He reached past Bahn and grabbed at the collar of Kissinger's HAZMAT suit. Fueled by adrenaline, he pulled hard and dragged Kissinger out of the quicksand. Once he had him on solid ground, Bolan rolled his friend onto his side and pried open his mouth, letting out a stream of brackish water.

Bahn, meanwhile, pulled herself ashore, hand over hand, then knelt on the ground and quickly caught her breath.

"CPR," she told Bolan. "You do the compressions."

Bolan nodded and rolled Kissinger onto his back. Bahn tilted his head back, then quickly pulled her lips away from Kissinger's when he suddenly spit up another lungful of water. Then, coughing raggedly, he opened his eyes and jerked slightly as he fought for his breath.

"Easy," Bahn told him. "Easy, big fella."

She and Bolan helped Kissinger back onto his side. It took a few more retchings before his lungs were cleared, but the color started coming back to his face.

"Man," he sputtered, "that stuff tastes worse than my granny's cod liver oil."

CHAPTER FIFTEEN

"Let's try for the others," Bolan said as he untied the vine from around Bahn's waist.

"There's no point," she told him.

"I figure we can loop the vine over that branch that extends out over the water," Bolan said. "That way we can go straight down instead of at an angle and it'll be easier to—"

"They're gone," Bahn interrupted, raising her voice. "They've been down a long time, and God only knows how deep that sand is beneath the water. We can't get to them."

"We can at least try!" Bolan snapped.

"They're gone!" she repeated, this time more forcefully. "There's a helmet you can fish out if you want, but if we go in there again we're just going to sucked down. It was a miracle we saved one guy. Leave it at that."

Bolan stood at the water's edge. Now even Latek's helmet was beginning to sink from view.

"She's right, Striker," Kissinger called out hoarsely. "If I'd dropped a few inches deeper into that muck, there's no way she could have pulled me out. And they're already buried in it, man."

Bolan listened but refused to move. He continued to stare into the pool, watching the sergeant's helmet disappear below the waterline.

"You feel like shit because you questioned their loyalty, right?" Bahn said, coming over to him. "You want to drown with them just so you can have a chance to apologize? What'll that accomplish?"

Kissinger rose shakily to his feet and hobbled over, favoring a charley horse in his right leg. He put his hand on Bolan's shoulder and told him, "Go ahead and wish them peace or whatever you want, but then we need to move on. We've got a job to finish."

Bolan stared at the brackish pool a moment longer, then turned away, nodding at Kissinger and Bahn. "Okay," he said. "Let's get back to that campsite."

Slowly they began to retrace their steps. Bolan led the way, holding a branch out before him like a divining rod, tapping the ground before them to make sure it was solid. Bahn had Kissinger lean on her so he could take some of the weight off his right leg. Every few steps he stopped and shook the leg, trying to loosen the cramped muscle.

Once they reached the campsite, Bolan and Bahn silently resumed combing the area for clues while Kissinger sat on one of the logs near the campfire and began massaging his leg with both hands, working the cramp out.

After a minute or so, Bolan crouched before the campfire and finally spoke up.

"They weren't here long," he said.

"What makes you say that?" Bahn asked as she came over.

"There aren't any embers," Bolan said, pointing out the base of the fire pit. "From the looks of it, this was their first fire, and it hasn't been going all that long."

They eyed the fire. Though the jihad forces had heaped the pit high with kindling, most of it was too green or too damp to hold a flame. As with the flares and the blaze along the river, the fire had apparently burned hot at first, scorching some of the larger branches, only to dwindle to what was now a weak sputter.

"There aren't any bedrolls, either," Kissinger observed, picking up on Bolan's line of thought. "And if they'd camped here for any length of time, the grass around here would be matted down."

"In other words, they probably showed up sometime during the night or early morning," Bahn guessed. "They came here for the ambush and that's it."

"Looks that way," Kissinger said. "Which makes it pretty certain they had some kind of advance notice."

"What advance notice? The raid wasn't even on the drawing board until yesterday afternoon," Bolan stated.

Kissinger coughed, then shrugged. "Well, they must've gotten word about it from the get-go."

"That's saying their mole's placed pretty high up in the food chain," Bahn said. "If not at the top."

Bolan stared back at the fire pit. "It's not adding up."

"What do you mean?" Kissinger asked.

"Think about it," Bolan said. "Let's assume the only reason they came here was for the ambush. They could only smuggle in a few men on the truck, and this was their way of getting snipers up into the mountains overlooking the road."

"I'll buy that," Kissinger said.

Bolan looked around at the slain terrorists. "The thing is, if they were only here for the ambush, then why'd they leave this many men behind? There's no reason."

"Maybe they weren't left behind," Bahn suggested. "Maybe they were in on the ambush but ran for it when things started to go bad for them."

"Okay, that could be," Bolan said. "But if they were just trying to get away and made it this far, why didn't they just hop in the hydrofoil and try to make a run for it upriver?"

"Good point," Kissinger said. "We haven't tried the engine. Maybe they couldn't get it started."

"If that's the case, they could have fled on foot," Bolan said. "But they didn't. They stayed put and started a fire."

"Well, that part's easy," Bahn said. "They probably had second thoughts about being such chickenshits and decided to make a last stand. You know, send off some smoke signals and draw us into another ambush. Nearly worked, too, in case you didn't notice."

Bolan nodded slightly but he still wasn't convinced. He snapped a branch off one of the logs set near the fire pit and used it to poke through the thick nest of half-burned kindling. A few tongues of flame shot up, but Bolan stamped them out with the stick before they could spread.

"Maybe the fire wasn't just a ploy to get us here," he said, spotting something half-buried amid the burned twigs and branches. "Maybe they were burning evidence."

"I'll be damned." Bahn quickly snatched up another branch and helped Bolan flick the smoldering kindling away from a handful of charred pamphlets and folded papers that had apparently been cast into the fire after it had started. Kissinger limped over and carefully plucked the items from the pit.

"Nice call, Sherlock," he told Bolan.

"Let's have a look," Bolan said.

Much of the paperwork was blackened and a few of the outer pages had been burned away altogether, but enough had been spared that when Bolan helped Kissinger skim the remaining contents, he finally realized what the Lashkar Jihad had in mind for the pesticides they'd been diverting from the agricultural compound.

"The pamphlet's about cloud seeding," he told Bahn. "And the papers are photocopies from a technical journal on chemical dispersion in different types of aerial media."

Bahn frowned. "What, they want to dump the pesticides into clouds? Sounds pretty lame."

Kissinger shrugged. "It'd give new meaning to the term 'acid rain.'"

Bolan read a few underlined passages and notations in the margins of the folded paper. As he did so, he recalled the smoglike haze blanketing the skies over Indonesia. An involuntary chill passed through him.

"They weren't looking to mix it in with clouds," he told Kissinger and Bahn. "They're looking at smoke."

CHAPTER SIXTEEN

SAMARINDA, INDONESIA

"What about crop dusters, Bear? Could they use those?"

Bolan was on the phone at the American consulate in Samarinda, speaking on a secure line with Aaron Kurtzman, Stony Man's wheelchair-bound cybernetic genius back at the Farm in Virginia. It was early morning, more than twelve hours after Bolan and the others had been evacuated from the jungle in a chopper that Jack Grimaldi had requisitioned from the Indonesian military. Bolan had spent half that time enduring decontamination procedures and undergoing medical treatment at Samarinda City Hospital. The rest of the time he'd slept, dead to the world, giving his body a chance to recover from the abuse it had taken the day before. It worked, to an extent. Bolan wasn't quite up for a decathlon, but he had a clean bill of health and it would take more than a few aches and pains to keep him from pursuing the mission.

"Crop dusters wouldn't work," Kurtzman explained.

"The way most of those herbicides are formulated, they'd be too heavy. Spray them and they'd drop right through the smoke."

"What about if they were put together differently?" Bolan glanced down at the singed papers taken from the Lashkar Jihad's jungle campfire. "Most of the jargon in these tech reports goes over my head, but there are a lot of references to methods to break chemicals down into smaller components. Vapor or aerosol, mostly. And there's a whole section filled with schematics for something called a nebulizer."

"I can see what they're up to," Kurtzman replied, "but I still doubt they could pull it off."

"What if they get lucky?" Bolan asked. "What's our worst-case scenario?"

"Again, it would depend on a lot of factors," Kurtzman said, "but with all the fires burning out of control there, they could lace a few smoke clouds headed for some of the bigger population centers and crank up some heavy casualties."

"Casualties or fatalities?"

There was a pause on the line, then Kurtzman suggested, "Look, before we start crying doomsday, maybe I should have a look at what you've got. Is there any way you can scan that stuff and send me a quick file?"

"I'll see what I can do," Bolan said.

"Good. Meantime, I'll run these names through the databases and see what we come up with."

Bolan had already given Kurtzman the names of every high-ranking official he knew had been in on the planning stages for the ill-fated raid on the agricultural compound. He'd come up with ten people, but he knew there were probably more. Major Salim could give him additional names, but the officer had just come out of surgery and was still unconscious. Bolan wasn't about to go to anyone on the list with his suspicions about a mole in the ranks. Until he had reason to believe otherwise, he had to go on the assumption that any one of them could be the one who'd tipped off the Lashkar Jihad about the raid.

"How's the rookie holding up, by the way?" Kurtzman asked, changing the subject.

"He's fine," Bolan told Kurtzman. "Already earned his first battle scar." He quickly explained how Raki Mochtar had taken a bullet to the chest armor while tending to the wounded at the ambush site.

"Hal says to keep him on if you think you can still make use of him," Kurtzman said.

Bolan didn't have to think about it long. After what happened to Latek and the other KOPASSUS commando back in the jungle, Bolan had rid himself of the paranoia Jayne Bahn had stirred up regarding Mochtar and anyone else who'd taken part in the aborted raid. The spy they were looking for, he reasoned, wouldn't have run the risk of being killed in the ambush; he would be more valuable positioned away from the front lines. More likely it was someone on the list he'd just given to Kurtzman, one of the planners who could have made quick contact with the Lashkar Jihad once the raid had been laid out and officially approved. As for

Mochtar, the man proved his mettle as well as his loyalty during the aftermath of the ambush; to respond to his valor by placing him under suspicion would be foolhardy and disrespectful.

"I think keeping him on is a good idea," Bolan told Kurtzman. "What about the other guys, though? I've got a feeling we'll be fighting on five different fronts before this is over."

"I wish we could help, Striker, but we're stretched pretty thin." Kurtzman quickly reported that Stony Man's two other special op groups, Able Team and Phoenix Force, were locked into priority assignments in New York and Greenland, respectively. "But if either of them wrap up while you're still out there," he offered, "we'll do our best to get them on the next available plane."

"Understood." Bolan checked his watch, then told Kurtzman, "Look, Bear, that briefing's about to start and I need to be there for the whole show."

"I'll let you go, then."

"And I'll e-mail you once the briefing's over."

Bolan hung up, then left the office he'd made the call from. A handful of uniformed Marines were stationed throughout the consulate, one of them in the hall outside the briefing room.

The soldier snapped a salute as Bolan walked past him, then called out, "Permission to speak, Corporal!"

Bolan had changed into nondescript camou fatigues with no rank designation, but he'd shown up at the consulate with military papers identifying him as U.S. Army Corporal Don Whittler. It was one of a handful of aliases he used as a way to keep secret his association with Stony Man Farm, an agency itself so secret that scant few even knew of its existence.

"At ease," Bolan told the guard, returning the salute. "I'm in a bit of a hurry, but what can I do for you?"

"Is it true?" the soldier said. "About Pohtoh and Jahf-Al?"

Bolan frowned. "You're going to have to be more specific."

"There's word they were killed up in the mountains yesterday during some raid on an agricultural compound."

Bolan smiled grimly. He was no stranger to the rumor mill and, given the blanket that had been thrown over the details regarding the raid, it came as no surprise that there was some wild speculation going on. In this case, he saw an advantage to the gossip. He knew that both Jahf-Al and the leader of the Lashkar Jihad had egos as large as their appetites for power. If word started circulating that they were dead, it might provoke them into showing themselves, if only to refute the rumors.

"Sorry, soldier," he told the guard, "I can neither confirm nor deny that. Now, if you'll excuse me..."

Bolan continued down the hallway, certain that the guard had taken the bait and would soon be spreading confirmation that the two terrorist leaders had been taken out during the raid. In truth, however, the briefing he was headed for would deal with the more likely reality that both Hamed Jahf-Al and Moamar Pohtoh were very much alive and conspiring to launch some new attack involving the cache of herbicides they had been diverting from the agri-compound.

After taking a flight of stairs up to the top floor, Bolan passed through a security checkpoint outside the computer room. Given an access code for use of one of the computers, he quickly began scanning the documentation he'd retrieved from the campsite. He'd hoped to make photocopies as well, but the machines, located on the other side of the room, were being serviced. He tried printing out a black-and-white copy of each sheet as he ran it through the scanner, but the process was too slow; he'd never finish in time for the meeting. He decided he'd have to make do with the disk copy once he turned over the originals.

Once the scanning was finished, Bolan went down the hall to the consulate briefing room, a large, converted den dominated by a fireplace made of river rock and a laminated oak table large enough to seat twelve people. Half the seats were already taken. Bolan exchanged greetings with the others. General Yuchen Suseno, Major Salim's immediate superior, was a squat, jowly man with a dull expression. To his right was Colonel Medwic Tohm, head of Military Intelligence, a tall man whose shock of white hair contrasted sharply with his deep-hued, ruddy skin. A third uniformed officer, Lieutenant Dari Wais of the Counter-Insurgency Strike Force, sat directly across from them, next to the only woman in the room, Lu Novotai, General Suseno's personal secretary. A stenograph machine rested on the table in front of the woman and her fingers were already working the keys, taking everything down for future reference.

That left two Americans, Lyle Stansfield, the deputy U.S. ambassador to Indonesia, and Herb Scoville, newly appointed head of CIA operations in Southeast Asia. Stansfield was an aristocratic-looking Ivy Leaguer in his early sixties who had most recently served as West Coast director of the President's successful re-election campaign. Forty-year-old Scoville, in contrast, was a disheveled, unshaven Midwesterner dressed in jeans, lizard-skin boots and a lightweight parka sporting several bullet holes complete with splotches of dried blood. A toothpick bobbed up and down between his teeth as he idly drummed his fingers on the tabletop.

"Take a load off, Corporal," Scoville told Bolan, gesturing at the vacant chair beside him. "I understand you went through the wringer out there yesterday."

"We had our hands full," Bolan conceded, taking the proffered seat.

"Better get used to it," Scoville said. "You ask me, we're sitting on a powder keg surrounded by kiddies who like to play with matches. Any day now...boom!"

General Suseno cleared his throat and stared at Scoville and Bolan. "If we could wait until everyone is here to start the meeting..." he suggested, speaking in fluent English.

"Of course," Bolan said.

Bolan stole a glance across the room. Colonel Tohm was staring at him and Scoville with obvious contempt. Bolan remembered Major Salim mentioning that Tohm had reservations about allowing Americans to take part in the battle against the Lashkar Jihad, which he considered to be in-house problem. Bolan could understand the sentiment, but with Jahf-Al and the UIF thrown into the mix, it was a whole different ballgame.

Bolan met Tohm's gaze and held it briefly, then looked away and busied himself jotting a few notes on one of the legal pads that had been set before each man at the table. The group was joined by two other men, Indonesian vice president Kari Hafidz and Nass Buchori, a member of the Indonesian parliament. Once Hafidz and Buchori had taken their seats, General Suseno leaned forward and began his introductory remarks.

As Suseno spoke, Bolan casually glanced around the room. Kurtzman had the names of everyone present, including the stenographer, but rather than having to wait for the results of the computer search into their backgrounds, Bolan hoped the traitor in their midst would tip him- or herself off. Unfortunately, with the exception of Colonel Tohm, everyone in the room seemed totally focused on General Suseno's address. Tohm continued to shoot angry glances at Scoville, but Bolan suspected the colonel was guilty of being territorial rather than treacherous.

Once he'd finished his opening remarks, Suseno said, "And so, let's begin with the incident in the mountains yesterday afternoon."

He turned to Bolan. "I understand, Corporal, that you were exposed to some of the pesticides after the truck explosion."

Bolan nodded. "I went through decontamination and I'm fine."

"And your colleagues?" Suseno asked.

"A few minor injuries, but they all pulled through," Bolan said.

"Which is more than can be said for our KOPAS-SUS troops," Colonel Tohm interjected. "Strange, isn't it, how you were fighting side by side, yet they sustained such high losses."

"I've been in battles where it's been the other way around," Bolan assured the colonel. "It happens."

"I see," Tohm said, though he sounded unconvinced.

"Are you trying to make a point, Colonel?" Suseno asked Tohm.

"Merely an observation." Tohm smiled thinly and nonchalantly ran his fingers through his white hair.

"Your observation is duly noted." Suseno turned to Bolan. "My apologies for the interruption, Corporal. You have the floor."

As the others listened attentively, Bolan briefly related the specifics of the various skirmishes he'd been caught up in the previous day. He laid it out straight, for the most part, divulging everything from the suspicious dispatch received from the surveillance team prior to the ambush to the discovery of the half-burned papers found at the makeshift campsite in the rain forest. Aside from any mention of Stony Man Farm, the only other information he held back, for obvious reasons, was his suspicion that someone in the room had forewarned the Lashkar Jihad about the pending raid, giving them time to set up the ambush. As he spoke, he continued to scrutinize those around him. By the time he'd finished speaking, however, he was no closer to knowing who the culprit was than when he'd begun.

As Bolan had expected, following his remarks Lieutenant Wais of the Counter-Insurgency Strike Force asked to see the campfire papers. Bolan turned them over without hesitation. If there was a spy in their midst, word would get back to the Lashkar Jihad, and while they might not abort whatever plans they might have for the herbicides, they would likely be given pause while they reevaluated their options. That would buy Bolan and the others some much-needed time.

Bolan, it turned out, wasn't the only one concerned about a breach in the ranks. Colonel Tohm was the first to speak after Bolan had finished his briefing, and his suspicions, predictably, were directed at an American, though not one sitting in the room.

"This woman who wandered onto the scene," he said, glancing at the notes he'd jotted on his pad. "This Jayne Bahn. How confident are you in her story about why she was in the area?"

"I've encountered her before," Bolan said. "I believe her. Of course, I had my people touch base with Inter-Trieve to verify her story. It checked out."

"I can vouch for her, too," Herb Scoville added. "She had top-level security clearance when she was with the CIA, and there's nothing in our files on her that would suggest she's not on the up-and-up."

Colonel Tohm smiled wanly. "I'll have a file on her in my office by the time this meeting is concluded. Perhaps we can share notes."

"Sounds lovely," Scoville replied.

Bolan sensed the mutual animosity between the two men and wondered if there was something more to it than Tohm's purported bias against the Americans.

"Where is this woman now?" vice president Hafidz asked Bolan.

Before Bolan could respond, Tohm interjected, "She's having dinner with several of Corporal Whittler's colleagues. At the seafood restaurant in the New Millennium, where they're all staying."

"What, you've got nothing better to do than peep down her dress?" Scoville snapped.

There was a sudden murmuring among the others as Tohm and Scoville faced off across the table.

"Mr. Scoville," Stansfield pleaded, "let's try to keep this civil."

Scoville ignored the deputy ambassador and scowled at Tohm. "Hell, if you did half as good a job tailing Pohtoh and Jahf-Al as you do anything wearing a skirt, we wouldn't be having this meeting!"

Tohm remained unperturbed. Smirking, he told the others, "It would appear our friends with the CIA are still upset that we don't jump through their hoops every time they hold them up for us."

"Kiss my ass," Scoville muttered, triggering another round of gasps and murmurs.

"That's quite enough!" General Suseno slammed

his fist on the table, and a flush of color crept across his pallid face. "We have more pressing concerns than rivalries between intelligence communities!" he shouted emphatically. "I would suggest that we stick to the matter at hand!"

Order was quickly restored, though Scoville and Tohm continued to glare at each other like boxers awaiting the bell for another round in the ring.

Dari Wais took the floor and quickly shifted the focus back to the papers Bolan and the others had found at the Lashkar Jihad's jungle campsite. "I don't have to tell any of you about the fires we're having," he said. "You can't walk out the door anywhere between Aceh and Irian Jaya without seeing smoke. If these people start infusing these clouds with poison, it could spread like the plague."

"But would they really do such a thing?" Hafidz wondered aloud. "The smoke would affect them as much as it would anyone else. And if their fellow Muslims start falling, what kind of support do they think they would have for their cause? The whole thing sounds self-defeating."

"You have a point," said Nass Buchori, the parliamentarian, "but let me ask you something. When the al-Qaeda madmen crashed into the World Trade Center, more Muslims were killed than in any other terrorist act in history. Bin Laden and his followers shrugged it off as, how you say, 'collateral damage.' Who is to say the Lashkar Jihad won't strike somewhere and say the same thing?"

"We have a prisoner in custody from the attack,

don't we?" Stansfield asked. "Can't we get some answers out of him?"

"Perhaps in time," said Colonel Tohm, eager to bolster his credibility in light of the outburst between him and Scoville. "He is still in surgery at the hospital, as is Major Salim."

"They tell me Salim's wounds are more serious than the prisoner's," General Suseno said.

"Yes," Tohm replied calmly, "but both are expected to recover. I am hoping that by morning we will be able to interrogate the prisoner."

"In the meantime, we're left in the dark as to Pohtoh's and Jahf-Al's intentions," Dari Wais said.

The debate resumed; Bolan listened. He was torn between the two viewpoints. He agreed that it would be counterproductive for the Lashkar Jihad to attempt any sort of wide-scale dissemination of poison by way of smoke. On the other hand, some terrorist organizations seemed more obsessed with mounting a high death toll than advancing their cause. Who was to say Jahf-Al or Pohtoh wouldn't greenlight a plaguelike attack that would indiscriminately kill tens—if not hundreds—of thousands of people just to assure themselves a place in the history books?

In the end, it was decided that some kind of preventative action should be taken. There was talk of grounding all aircraft, but exceptions were made to the point where only small planes would be affected. A suggestion that all large outdoor activities scheduled over the next few weeks be canceled was swiftly amended to day-by-day assessments to be made based on conventional readings of a given area's air pollution index.

Everyone seemed to agree that the public might lapse into a wide-scale panic if they were given too much information regarding the possible threat hinted at by the documents Bolan had found. In this respect, it was decided that the country would follow the example of the U.S. government and issue a vague warning of possible future terrorist attacks without dispensing any specifics that could lead to any sort of mass hysteria.

Herb Scoville and Colonel Tohm resumed their verbal sparring during the course of the discussions, much to General Suseno's growing consternation and annoyance. When the vice president tried to interject a reprimand citing Scoville's foul language and poor grooming, Ambassador Stansfield felt obliged to come to the CIA man's defense, which, in turn, forced Suseno and Lieutenant Wais to run further interference in hopes of staving off a schism between the local powers that be and their American counterparts.

Bolan couldn't wait for the meeting to end, and once it was over, he was the first one out the door. His nerves were shot and he had a headache. Given a choice between being trapped in a room full of politicians or terrorists would be an easy decision. At least with terrorists you could cut to chase and settle things quickly.

CHAPTER SEVENTEEN

The U.S. consulate was located at the periphery of the capital's market district, seven blocks from Samarinda City Hospital and from the hotel where Bolan was sharing adjacent suites with Kissinger, Grimaldi and Raki Mochtar. He'd taken a trishaw cab to the briefing but decided to walk back, hoping the air would help clear his head. The haze had grown thicker overnight, however, and after a few steps he found that he couldn't breathe without smelling—even tasting—the smoky residue from the distant fires. In light of the discussion he'd just endured regarding possible threats posed by the Lashkar Jihad, the chalky sky now seemed grim with foreboding. As he passed street vendors, Bolan noticed that several of the hawkers had begun to sell cheaply made surgical masks, really nothing more than handkerchiefs with strings attached. Bolan doubted their effectiveness even under present conditions. If the smoke were to suddenly become tinged with volatile poisons, what chance would any of these tens of thousands of people out on the street have?

Bolan had walked less than a block when a dilapidated Yugo veered to the curb alongside him.

"Hop in," Herb Scoville called out from behind the wheel. "I'll give you a lift."

Bolan hesitated, then climbed in, tucking his six-foot frame into the cramped front seat. The CIA agent pulled into traffic, nearly sideswiping a gray-haired man on a bicycle. The cyclist shouted and waved his fist angrily at Scoville, who, in return, flashed a smile and waved pleasantly at the man.

"Yeah, screw you, too, buddy."

As they stopped for a traffic light at the next block, Bolan asked, "What was that about back there?"

"Old fart wasn't looking where he was going."

"Not that," Bolan said. "At the meeting. That whole thing between you and Tohm."

"Oh, that." Scoville fished through his shirt pocket for a cigarette and quickly lit it before the light changed. "I told you he was a piece of work."

"You didn't answer my question."

Scoville took a drag on his cigarette and wove his way through traffic as he told Bolan. "Basically, a couple of days ago we had a little disagreement on what to do with Jahf-Al, provided we take him in alive. When I said we were going to haul his sorry ass back to the States for trial, he threw a snit about extradition protocols and whatnot."

"There *are* procedures," Bolan said.

"Oh, come on, don't tell me you're taking his side on this." Scoville blew smoke and sped through the next intersection as the light was about to change. "Look, there's no way we're going to risk seeing Jahf-

Al wind up being tried in some Islamic court where his lawyers can wrangle him off the hook on some technicality. Besides, Tohm bugs me. I meant what I said about him tailing Bahn while he lets the Lashkar Jihad come in here and recruit to their heart's content."

"You think they've got him in their pocket?" Bolan asked.

"Wouldn't surprise me," Scoville said, stealing a glance at his rearview mirror. "Just like it doesn't surprise me that he's got some of his goons following us."

"You know that for a fact?" Bolan asked.

"Well, don't turn around and stare," Scoville told him, "but when you get a chance, check your mirror. Three cars back. Green Fiat. Latched onto me the minute I came out of the parking lot."

Bolan stole a look in the side-view mirror and spotted the car. Two men were in the front seat, but he wasn't able to make out their features.

"I think I'll have a little fun with them," Scoville said as he pulled up to the New Millennium hotel. "Go ahead and hop out."

"What are you going to do?" Bolan asked him.

"Go for a little country ride," Scoville said. "This Yugo may not look like much, but I've got it souped under the hood. Hell, one tap on the gas pedal and they'll be scratching their heads wondering where I went."

Bolan got out of the car and peered over his shoulder back at Scoville. "Nice to know you're keeping your mind on the mission."

"Don't bust my balls, okay?" the agent said. "I've got an hour to kill before I'm supposed to meet up with a couple informants. And after being holed up with Colonel Tohm all morning I need to unwind a little, okay? I'm sure you can relate."

"Maybe I can," Bolan said.

"Tell you what," Scoville said. "Buy me dinner, and I'll pass along anything these pigeons cough up to me."

"Deal," Bolan said. "How about the restaurant here?"

"You got it. Eight o'clock okay with you?"

Bolan nodded and closed the door. The passenger-side windows were open, though, and Scoville called out to him, "If you see Jaynie, tell her the Sizzler says hi."

Bolan stared at Scoville. "You're the one who briefed her on the agri-compound when she showed up here," he guessed.

Scoville avoided answering the question and drove off. Bolan veered over to a vendor's cart and pretended to look over a display of sarong cloth, giving him a view of the street. Out of the corner of his eye he watched the Fiat drive slowly past. It continued to stay a few car lengths back of Scoville's Yugo. When both cars stopped for the next traffic light, however, the passenger-side door of the Fiat swung open and one of the men got out. He circled around the front of the car and crossed to the other side of the street, where he paused before a kiosk and glanced halfheartedly at a rack of magazines and newspapers before letting his gaze drift in the direction of the New Millennium.

Bolan realized he was being followed as well.

CHAPTER EIGHTEEN

The New Millennium was the only hotel in Samarinda to rate as many as two stars in any of the better-known travel guides. Built to coincide with Year 2000 festivities at the provincial capital, the Millennium was five stories high, horseshoe-shaped with views of both the city and surrounding mountains. The large main lobby faced the street, but the architects had been determined to play up a sense of isolation, blocking any view of traffic—pedestrian or otherwise—with a seemingly unending row of dense, ivy-laden screens placed a few feet in front of the large floor-to-ceiling windows. Once he was inside, the only way Bolan could see the street was by wandering over to the concierge desk and craning his neck to peer over the brochure stand. Fortunately the lobby was crowded, and he managed the maneuver without drawing undue attention.

Looking through a gap between two of the screens, Bolan saw that the man at the kiosk had bought a paper and moved down the street to an outdoor café, where he ordered coffee, then pulled a cell phone from his shirt pocket. As he spoke, he divided his attention between the paper and the hotel. Bolan figured the man wasn't going anywhere any time soon, a likely indication that all other entrances to the hotel—and perhaps the lobby itself—were already under surveillance.

Moving away from the concierge's station, Bolan strode casually toward the elevators, taking in the other people in the lobby. There was a throng of Japanese tourists milling around the registration desk and off near the entrance to the upscale Begadang Ristorante an elderly couple stood pondering a tall, abstract sculpture that vaguely resembled an Olympic discus thrower. Inside the restaurant, Bolan could see two men—both looked American—sitting on stools at the bar watching a television mounted from the ceiling. All in all, little that struck him as suspicious.

Bolan stopped at a house phone by the elevators and dialed Jayne Bahn's room. He wanted to talk to her about Scoville. He got a recording saying she wasn't available. He didn't bother leaving a message.

A dozen tourists had drifted over to use the elevator, so Bolan took the stairs to the second floor. His room was halfway down the hall, overlooking the courtyard pool area. He was rooming with Grimaldi but the pilot wasn't in, so he rapped on the door to the adjacent suite. Kissinger answered and let him in. Raki Mochtar was off in the corner, seated at a desk, hunched over the laptop Bolan had been lugging around from country to country as he searched for

Hamed Jahf-Al. A sliding glass door in the living room led to a small terrace. The door was half open, and Bolan could hear people splashing around in the pool. The smell of smoke drifted into the room.

"How'd it go?" Kissinger asked.

Bolan shrugged. "About what you'd expect. Where's Jack?"

"Back at the airport," Kissinger told him. "Futzing around with the Black Hawk so it'll be ready in case we need to go up again."

Bolan mentioned Colonel Tohm's remark about having Jayne Bahn under surveillance at the restaurant downstairs.

"Yeah, we saw them," Kissinger said. "They stayed behind after we left, and my guess is they're still floating around here somewhere."

Bolan mentioned the men in the Fiat who'd followed him and Scoville from the briefing. "One of them's posted across the street from the front entrance."

"What I don't get is why they have us under surveillance in the first place," Mochtar called out. "Don't they know we're on their side?"

Bolan quickly told Mochtar and Kissinger about the series of flare-ups between Herb Scoville and Colonel Tohm during the briefing, concluding, "It got to the point where the general looked like a baby-sitter who'd had his fill of the kids yelling at each other."

"This Tohm guy sounds like a paranoid case," Kissinger said. "I don't know if it necessarily makes him our spy, though."

"You could be right." Bolan turned to Mochtar. "Just to be safe, though, can you shoot Bear an e-mail and tell him to dig deeper when he runs his background check on Tohm?"

"Sure," Mochtar replied. "Anything else?"

"Have him do the same with Lieutenant Wais, the guy who heads up their antiterrorist operations," Bolan suggested.

"Will do," Mochtar said. "Bear said something about you sending him a disk of the stuff we found at the campsite."

"Oh, right." Bolan fished out the diskette and handed it to Mochtar, then raided the wet bar for a bottle of mineral water and took it onto the terrace. Kissinger joined him.

The pool area was crowded. Most of the guests were American, although there was a large group of Japanese families taking up the chaise lounges just off the shallow end of the pool. A few grown-ups were in the water, supervising the dozen or so children who were making most of the noise. From where they were standing, Bolan and Kissinger could see the other wing of the hotel as well as the parking lot, which abutted the grounds of the city hospital.

"I called over a few minutes ago," Kissinger said, staring at the hospital. "Salim's been upgraded from critical to serious."

"Glad to hear it," Bolan said. "What about the others?"

"The commandos have already been released,"

Kissinger said. "The prisoner's back in surgery. Something about wanting to take another crack at a bullet lodged near an artery in his leg."

Bolan nodded vaguely, taking in the information. As he sipped his water, he stared out past the city at the smoke funnels rising from the mountains. It looked almost as if a handful of tornadoes had somehow been reduced to traveling in slow motion.

"I've been thinking," he told Kissinger. "I don't think all these fires are just from ground clearance."

"You read my mind," Kissinger said. "Remember that guy with the flamethrower back in the forest?"

"Exactly," Bolan said. "If the Lashkar plan on doing something with smoke, you have to figure they're setting some of these blazes on purpose."

"You mean as a way of targeting where they want to strike?"

"Why not?" Bolan said. "I think we should look into the wind patterns around here, then try to figure out which fires are slash-and-burns and which are arson. We might be able to pick out a pattern of some kind."

"Good idea," Kissinger said. "Did any of this get brought up at the briefing?"

Bolan shook his head. "That would have been too constructive."

Kissinger laughed. "Ah, bureaucracy. You gotta love it."

Bolan changed the subject. "Just out of curiosity, did Bahn happen bring up Herb Scoville's name while you guys were having breakfast?"

"The CIA guy? No. Why?"

Bolan mentioned the last remark Scoville had made before driving away from the hotel.

"Sizzler, eh?" Kissinger said. "Sounds like bedroom talk to me."

"That or he's big on buffets," Bolan said.

"Either way, so what?" Kissinger shrugged. "So they know each other. Big deal. She's ex-CIA herself, and her hubby's still with them, right?"

"Ex-husband," Bolan corrected.

"Whatever. You know what I mean."

"If Scoville was her contact when she showed up here, why didn't she just come out and say it?" Bolan said. "I asked her about it and she got all cat-and-mouse on me. Where is she, anyway? I tried her room and got the machine."

"She said she had a hard time sleeping last night," Kissinger said. "She probably crashed after breakfast and just had them hold her calls."

Bolan finished his mineral water and took the bottle back inside. He called out to Mochtar, "Any word from Bear?"

Mochtar glanced up from the computer and nodded. "He's halfway through that list you gave him." Checking the screen, he reported, "Stansfield, Scoville, Suseno and his stenographer all checked out clean. The guy in parliament weathered a little scandal a couple of years back, but it had to do with kickbacks on some transmigration housing. Doesn't sound like it's connected to what we're looking at. And apparently the vice president was caught up in a prostitution sweep three months ago but managed to keep it out of the papers."

"That's not much help, either," Bolan said. "Listen, I've got one more thing for them look at. See if they can tap into some weather satellites and—"

Suddenly there was a distant shattering of glass, followed by the sound of automatic gunfire. Bolan stopped in midsentence and strode quickly back out to the terrace. Kissinger had moved to the railing and was staring out toward the parking lot.

"The hospital," he told Bolan, pointing.

Bolan stared past the parking lot and saw that two windows had shattered on the third floor of the hospital. The sound of gunfire seemed to be coming from within the hospital itself.

"I might be wrong," Kissinger said, "but I think the third floor's for surgery."

"Damn!" Bolan unfastened the top few buttons of his camou shirt and pulled his .44 Desert Eagle from a concealed shoulder holster. Kissinger had already drawn his gun, a 9 mm Colt Government Model pistol.

"They're after the guy we brought in," he guessed.

Bolan didn't answer. He already had one foot on the terrace railing. He swung one leg over the top, then jumped. Kissinger followed suit. They both landed on the tiled walkway surrounding the pool. There were screams from the guests and children as the two men bounded to their feet and circled around to a side gate leading to a small recreation area, where a mother pushed two young girls on a swing. There were also two men standing near a bench overlooking the parking lot. Their eyes were on the hospital and each man had a hand inside his coat.

"The guys from the restaurant," Kissinger said.

"We don't have time to find out whose side they're on," Bolan told him, veering toward the men.

"Gotcha."

Before the surveillance team could get their guns out, Bolan and Kissinger were on top of them. Kissinger had been a pro linebacker prospect years ago, and he still had the moves. He crashed into one of the men. Caught off guard, the man reeled with the impact and tumbled backward over the picnic table. Bolan, meanwhile, clipped the other man's skull with the butt of his .44, dropping him in his tracks.

Neither of the fallen men lost consciousness, but by the time they'd regained their wits, Bolan and Kissinger were already in the parking lot, headed for the wall separating the hotel grounds from the hospital. Bolan leaped onto the back of a parked Subaru sedan, then used the roof for a springboard, leaping forward and landing atop the wall just long enough to determine where he wanted to land when he dropped to the ground on the other side. Bolan was rising to his feet when Kissinger dropped down next to him, having cleared the wall with the same maneuver. They could still hear gunfire emanating from inside the hospital.

"They should have taken that prisoner to the base hospital instead of here," Bolan said.

"Better facilities here, they said," Kissinger recalled.

"Doesn't matter how good they are if you can't keep them secure," Bolan said as they started for the hospital.

The shootout had apparently drawn away any security personnel posted at the rear entrance. As Bolan and Kissinger charged toward the doors, the only person blocking their way was a terrified nurse fumbling with a cigarette. She shrieked at the sight of their handguns and cowered to one side, letting the two warriors charge past.

Inside, Bolan and Kissinger found themselves in the urgent-care registration area. A handful of patients cowered around the sign-in counter. On the other side, the receptionist had ducked to the floor and was screaming fearfully.

"They might be after Salim, too," Bolan told Kissinger as they charged past the patients and threw open the door to the stairwell.

"He's on the second floor," Kissinger said. "I'll check it out."

Taking the steps two at a time, the men rushed up to the landing. Kissinger split off, heading into the second-floor hallway. Bolan continued up the steps. He was halfway to the next landing when the door burst open and a white-robed gunman rushed into the stairwell, clutching an Uzi submachine gun. Bolan froze on the steps and raised his .44, beating the other man to the trigger. The Desert Eagle thundered loudly, and the robed assailant let out a scream of pain. His robe began to turn red where Bolan's rounds had tapped into his chest. He dropped his gun and teetered off balance before tumbling down the steps. The Executioner side-stepped him and bent over just long enough to grab the man's fallen Uzi.

When he reached the third-floor hallway, it was deserted save for an overturned gurney and the dazed intern who'd apparently been bowled over while pushing it.

"The operating room," Bolan demanded. "Where is it?"

The intern gazed up at him, uncomprehending.

"Surgery! Where is surgery!"

The intern pointed down the hallway behind him.

Bolan rushed past the man, counting off the doors on his right, trying to remember which of the outer windows had been shot out. Halfway down the hall, he came to a double set of swing doors. He pushed inward. One door swung open with no problem, but the other wouldn't budge. Passing through the doorway, Bolan nearly tripped over a nurse lying dead on floor.

She was only the first.

Bleak, smoke-muted sunlight poured into the operating room, which had been turned into a killzone. Two more nurses and three surgeons, all dressed in pale blue scrubs, lay sprawled haphazardly around the operating table. On the table, blood spilled down from the riddled corpse of the Lashkar Jihad gunner who'd been taken into custody after the thwarted ambush in the mountains. He was still hooked up to a monitor, but all the signals had flat lined and the machine was bleating a warning that no one but Bolan was alive to hear.

As Bolan stared at the grisly carnage, more gunfire erupted a floor below him. The soldier's years in the battlefield had trained his ears to be able to distinguish the blasts from various weapons, and it was clear to him that Kissinger's Colt wasn't the only gun being fired. There were at least three others in play, and from the sound of it, Bolan guessed they were Uzis.

Kissinger was clearly outnumbered.

CHAPTER NINETEEN

Instead of heading back the way he'd come, Bolan sprinted to the opposite end of the hallway. He braced himself before opening the door to the stairwell, then yanked it open, Uzi ready to fire. There was no one on the landing, however. He entered the stairwell and took the steps down quietly, not wanting to tip off his approach. The faint reverberation of gunfire rattled the walls around him.

Once he reached the second floor, Bolan paused against the door, slowly turning the knob. He drew in a breath, then yanked the door open and lurched into the hallway. As he'd hoped, he'd come up behind the assailants and they were preoccupied with Kissinger, who they had pinned inside the doorway of the first room at the other end of the hall.

Normally, Bolan was averse to shooting anyone in the back, but under the circumstances he figured the gunmen deserved no more consideration than they had given those who died, unarmed, in the operating room.

He'd already set the Uzi on full-auto, and with grim precision he strafed the unsuspecting terrorists, aiming at their midsections to cut down on the chance a stray bullet might inadvertently make its way to Kissinger.

Two of the gunmen went down quickly, never knowing what hit them. The third managed to twist and fire a volley Bolan's way before succumbing to the last rounds from the Uzi. The Executioner quickly cast the weapon aside and rearmed himself with the Desert Eagle, then strode forward, barrel aimed at the heads of the fallen. None of them were moving, but he stopped before each body, checking for pulses to make sure they were dead.

"Cowboy!" he called out. "You okay?"

Kissinger stepped back into the hall, clutching his left shoulder. "Got me a little nick," he said, tearing open his sleeve around the entry hole for a closer look. "It's nothing. I've had worse mosquito bites."

"Any more besides these?" Bolan asked, indicating the three slain attackers who, like the man he'd killed on the stairwell, were dressed in the white flowing robes of the Lashkar Jihad.

"Not that I know of," Kissinger said. Despite his wound, he had his pistol ready for more action and headed down the corridor, eyeing the room numbers on either side of him. "Salim's in room twelve."

Bolan got there first. Salim had the room to himself. He was still unconscious, lying flat on his bed under a single sheet, three IV drips hooked up to his arm. Judging from the monitor depicting his vital signs, his pulse was strong and regular.

Kissinger caught up with Bolan. He'd taken a gauze pad from one of the other rooms and he held it to his shoulder, blotting the wound.

"How was it upstairs?" he asked.

"Bloodbath," Bolan told him. "Along with our guy, they took out the entire surgical crew."

"Sounds like their style," Kissinger said. "You want to give me a hand with this?" he added, indicating his shoulder.

Bolan tracked down some disinfectant and swabbed the gunshot wound, then applied a fresh pad of gauze to Kissinger's shoulder. He was securing it in place with tape when they heard footsteps down the hall. There were voices, too, one speaking in Bahasa Indonesian, the other in English.

"Security!" the latter cried. "Put down your weapons!"

"U.S. military!" Bolan shouted back, grabbing his Desert Eagle. "Hold your fire!"

Two uniformed security guards appeared in the doorway, each armed with a double action 9 mm Smith & Wesson. The younger of the two glared at Bolan and Kissinger and repeated, "Put down your weapons!"

"You first!" Kissinger demanded, aiming his Colt at the other man's forehead. "We didn't put our necks on the line for *this!*"

The older guard glanced down the hallway at the slain fanatics, then holstered his S&W and leaned close to the man beside him, whispering in his ear. The younger guard nodded reluctantly and slowly lowered his gun.

"I apologize," he said demurely. "We had to take precautions."

"Understood," Kissinger said.

"If you could step into the hall so we don't disturb the patient," the young man said.

Bolan and Kissinger obliged, but as soon as they were in the hall, Bolan took control of the questioning. Gesturing at the slain Lashkar gunner, he asked the guards, "How did they get in here?"

"The service entrance," the young guard replied. "They hid in the back of a supply truck that pulled up to the loading ramp. They took us by surprise."

For the first time, Bolan noticed a bruise under the man's right cheekbone, the kind made by a rifle butt to the face. The older guard had been similarly struck on the right temple.

"How many of them were there?" Kissinger asked.

The guards conferred, then the younger one replied, "I only saw four, but my partner thinks there may have been five. It all happened very fast."

"Well, if it's four, we got them all," Bolan said. "If it's five, you're going to have to lock this place down and run a search."

"We are already in lockdown," the younger guard replied. "Standard procedure."

"Then let's start looking," Bolan suggested.

CHAPTER TWENTY

The hospital was small. There was only one floor above the surgical wing. The men started there and worked their way down as a group. The older guard had passed along instructions to someone over a walkie-talkie, and there was an announcement telling everyone to stay out of the corridors. The message was heeded, and as they went from room to room, Bolan and the others came across not only frightened patients, but also members of the hospital staff who'd ducked out of the hallways, not wanting to share the fate of those who'd fallen in the operating room. None of them had seen another gunman.

As they returned to the second floor and stepped around the men Bolan had gunned down earlier, the younger guard said, "They killed the man who was in surgery so that he couldn't be interrogated, yes?"

"Yes."

"And with the major," the man speculated, "they were looking to retaliate for what happened to them in the mountains."

Bolan stared at the guard. "What happened in the mountains is supposed to be confidential."

"I know," the guard said, taken aback. "We were told as much, but I assumed you already knew, so—"

The guard's voice was drowned out by a sudden rattle of gunfire.

"It's coming from outside," Bolan stated.

They were halfway down the hall. Bolan broke away from the others, rushing through a vacant room to the nearest window. Kissinger and the others followed closely behind. Peering out, they saw a robed figure getting into the driver's side of a supply truck backed up to the service entrance to the hospital.

"He's going to get away!" the younger guard exclaimed.

"I don't think so," Bolan said. He tried the window but it opened only partially; there was a lock mechanism on the lower runner. He took a step back and fired at the mechanism, obliterating it along with a good portion of the windowsill. Throwing the window open, Bolan leaned out and took aim at the truck. He didn't have a good angle on the driver, however, and held his fire. Holstering his Desert Eagle, he quickly climbed onto the windowsill and leaned out.

There was only one way out of the parking lot from the service area, and that was along a narrow access road that ran directly adjacent to the ground floor of the hospital. Bolan crouched, and as the truck was about to pass directly below him, he pushed out from the window and dropped down hard onto the truck's roof. The moment he landed he threw himself flat onto his stomach and grabbed at a rack mounting for support.

Unnerved, the driver swerved from side to side as he raced toward the entrance, nearly colliding with another car that was backing out of a parking space. He wasn't able to shake Bolan from the roof, however. The soldier held on tight to the rack, waiting for the right moment to begin crawling forward. Looking ahead, he saw that there wasn't going to be a right moment. The police had arrived and cordoned off the entrance with two patrol cars. There was no way around the cars, so Bolan braced himself, expecting the gunman below to slam on the brakes any second.

Instead the fleeing gunman floored the accelerator and veered to his right, aiming for the rear quarter panel of one of the squad cars. Bolan realized the Lashkar gunman was going to try to force his way through the barricade. All Bolan could do was hold on to the brackets and await the inevitable.

A split second later, the truck rammed the police car with enough force to spin the car about, creating a gap through which it could clear the driveway and enter the street. The same force thwarted Bolan's grip on the brackets and threw him forward, off the roof and down onto the truck's front hood. Stunned, he slid across the hood and was about to topple into the vehicle's path when he managed to grab hold of the hood ornament and break his fall. He knelt on the front bumper and pressed his body against the front grille, shifting his grip to the hood locks.

The gunman turned sharply and sped recklessly down the street, veering the truck through slower moving traffic. All the while he glared at Bolan, cursing.

When it became clear he couldn't shake his pursuer off the truck, the driver took one hand off the wheel and reached for his gun. Bolan did the same, tearing his .44 from its holster. He nearly lost his grip on the hood in the process but managed to steady himself. He took aim across the hood and when he saw the driver about to fire at him, he pulled the trigger. The windshield shattered and the driver slumped over the steering wheel, dropping his gun.

The truck immediately spun out of control. Bolan looked over his shoulder and saw that he was about to plow into an even larger vehicle parked alongside the curb to his right.

Letting go of the hood locks, Bolan pushed clear of the truck, dropping to the roadway between the two front tires. He tried to fall flat against the asphalt in hopes the truck would pass over him, but things were happening too fast and the underside of the front bumper caught him squarely in the forehead at the same time he hit the ground.

For a moment, Bolan felt as if a flare had gone off inside his head. Everything was bright. Then, just as quickly, his world went black.

CHAPTER TWENTY-ONE

When he came to, Bolan found himself lying on the sidewalk. His skull was throbbing, and he felt a bump the size of an egg rising through his scalp. But he was alive, which was more than he'd hoped for when he'd gone down between the two trucks.

"Striker?"

Bolan turned slightly and saw Kissinger crouched over him, eyeing him with concern. He tried to sit up, but Kissinger gently put a hand to his shoulder and told him to stay put.

"How long was I out?" Bolan asked.

"However long it took me to sprint over here," Kissinger told him. "A minute maybe."

Craning his neck, Bolan saw the delivery truck. Its front end was mangled, half buried in the rear end of the larger truck. The driver had been thrown through the shattered windshield and was bleeding onto the hood. The owner of the other truck, meanwhile, was pacing around the collision point, shouting angrily as he pointed out the damage to anyone who would listen. A crowd had gathered, and Kissinger had to wave them away from Bolan. Off in the distance sirens screamed to life, drawing nearer. Their wailing made Bolan wince.

Soon an ambulance pulled up to the scene, followed by a patrol car. The two security guards from the hospital got out of the back of the second vehicle along with a pair of police officers. The paramedics, meanwhile, rushed over to Bolan with their crash cart and a neck brace. One of them spoke English.

"Don't move."

Bolan waved them away. "I'll be all right," he said, slowly sitting up. He felt dizzy but refused to lie back down.

"You need to be examined," the paramedic insisted. Spotting the welt on Bolan's skull, he added, "You might have a concussion."

"I've already had my checkup for the week," Bolan told him, leaning forward and taking a few deep breaths.

The paramedic turned to Kissinger. "Tell him we need to get him to the hospital."

"Sorry," Kissinger said. "I know the guy. When he says no, he means it. He probably wouldn't turn down some ice, though, if you have some."

The paramedic talked to his partner, who then fished through his med-kit and pulled out a packet of chemical ice. He crumpled the bag in his hands to activate it, then handed the bag to Bolan, who pressed the pack to his head. He could feel it getting colder by the second and just as quickly it brought relief. His dizziness was subsiding as well.

"Go take care of the guy in the truck," he told the medics.

"He's dead," the English-speaking paramedic told Bolan. "There's nothing we can do for him."

"Well, there's nothing you can do for me, either," Bolan said, struggling to his feet. "But thanks for the ice."

The paramedics looked at each other, then hauled their stretcher over to the truck. Kissinger, meanwhile, helped Bolan to his feet.

"Not our lucky week," the soldier stated.

"Maybe not, but we're still in better shape than the bad guys," Kissinger told him.

Bolan grinned faintly. "Let's get out of here."

"I'm going to need to clear it with the cops first." Kissinger helped Bolan hobble over to where the two police officers were talking with the security guards from the hospital. Bolan leaned against the patrol car for support while Kissinger joined in the other conversation. The hospital guards had already filled in the police as to the circumstances leading up to Bolan's gunning down the driver of the smaller truck. Kissinger added a few more details, then the police came over and questioned Bolan briefly, making certain his story jibed with the others'. The police asked where Bolan and Kissinger were staying, said they'd be in touch if they had more questions and told the men they could go.

Kissinger hailed a trishaw and helped Bolan in, then told the driver to take them to the New Millennium. Bolan groaned as the motorized vehicle bounded over potholes in the road, threading its way through traffic. Several times the driver leaned on his horn and the sound went through Bolan's skull like a hot poker.

A few minutes later they were back at the hotel. Bolan stiffly climbed out of the trishaw, leaving Kissinger to haggle with the driver. He glanced up and down the street, looking for any sign that they'd been followed.

"Coast clear?" Kissinger asked, joining Bolan on the sidewalk.

"I think so. They've either dropped the stakeout or else they're being more discreet."

Kissinger casually looked around as he held open the lobby door for Bolan.

"I think we're okay," he said. "Not that it matters. Once we hit the rooms I think some aspirin and a little shut-eye is in order before we make our next move."

"No argument there," Bolan said. As he waited for the elevators, however, he tried again to reach Jayne Bahn on the house phone. When he was routed to her message service, he hung up.

They got on the elevator. On the way up, Bolan checked through his pockets. "Lost my key," he stated.

"No problem," Kissinger said, producing his own card key. "You can go through our place."

A minute later, they stepped into Kissinger's and Mochtar's room and immediately reached for their guns. The room had been ransacked, clothes yanked from overnight bags and cushions displaced from the couch and one of the chairs.

"Rocky?" Kissinger called out. When he didn't get an answer, he moved carefully to the bedroom, pausing outside the doorway before striding in. "He's not here," he told Bolan.

Bolan threw open the connector door and both men charged into the other suite. It, too, had been searched. There was no sign of Grimaldi, either.

"Jack's probably still at the airfield," Kissinger said.

"Yeah, but we know Raki was here," Bolan said as they backtracked to the other room.

"Well, he's gone now." Kissinger's eyes fell on the desk. "And so is the laptop."

CHAPTER TWENTY-TWO

Bolan paced angrily in the small room at the local Military Headquarters office where he and Kissinger had been waiting for nearly an hour to see Colonel Tohm. The headquarters was part of a sprawling government complex taking up forty acres between the airport and the Samarinda military base. They were on the fourth floor, and through the lone window Bolan could see a passenger jet rising up from one of the runways. Within seconds it had vanished in the darkening haze. The sun was down, and neither stars nor the full moon were able to shine through the smoky firmament.

Finally Colonel Tohm entered the room, flanked by a sentry carrying an AK-47 assault rifle.

"I apologize for the delay," he said, half smiling. "I was detained on another matter."

Bolan was in no mood for small talk. Even before their wait, it had taken him and Kissinger nearly three hours to ascertain Raki Mochtar's whereabouts and formulate a plan for insuring his release. He took a step toward the colonel and stared him down.

"Where is he?" he demanded.

Tohm pretended he hadn't heard. "Can I get you anything? Coffee, sandwiches..."

"Where is he?" Bolan repeated.

Tohm again ignored the question.

When Bolan took another step closer, the sentry countered, moving protectively in front of the colonel and shifting his rifle so that the barrel was aimed Bolan's way. Bolan, like Kissinger, had been relieved of his handgun upon entering the facility.

"It's all right," Tohm told the sentry, nudging the rifle with his forefinger until it pointed away from Bolan. "These men are our guests."

Tohm turned and moved behind a desk, taking a seat and removing a hand-rolled cigarette from a silver case in his shirt pocket. He lit the cigarette and blew a lazy cloud of smoke that smelled faintly of cloves. He sat and gestured at the only other two chairs in the room.

"Have a seat, gentlemen."

Neither man took him up on the offer. Kissinger moved past Bolan and leaned across the desk. Like Bolan, he locked his gaze on Tohm and held it.

"Your goons ransacked our rooms and took one of our colleagues into custody, along with a computer containing classified information," Kissinger said. "We aren't interested in an apology because it wouldn't mean anything, but we want our man back, along with the computer. Now."

"You attacked two of our field agents," Tohm countered. "Without provocation."

"We were in a hurry and they happened to be in the way," Kissinger shot back. "There was an attack on the hospital. Of course, you may not have heard about that, since you're so preoccupied with running surveillance on your own allies."

"Sarcasm." Tohm sighed. "You Americans are all alike."

"We're here in Indonesia with full authorization from your government," Bolan interjected. "We pose no security risk, and we've made every effort to cooperate with you as equal partners against a common enemy."

"Your point being...?"

"My point being we want our man back," Bolan said. "No questions asked. We want our computer back, no questions asked. And we want some kind of assurance that you'll back off staring over our shoulders so we can do the job we came here to do."

"A list of demands," Tohm said. "You almost sound like the Lashkar Jihad."

Kissinger turned to Bolan. "Scoville was right," he said. "This guy's got his head up his ass."

"I beg your pardon?" Colonel Tohm sat forward and crushed out his cigarette. For the first time since entering the room there were signs of a weakening in his composure. Kissinger saw the crack and continued to work on it.

"You heard me," Kissinger said. "We're trying to

fight a war here, and all you're concerned about is ruling your little fiefdom."

"Who do you think you're talking to?" Tohm's voice rose a notch. He was quickly losing his composure.

Kissinger continued, "I think I'm talking to a bumbling control freak who doesn't know how to handle the little power he's been given by superiors who'll throw his sorry ass out onto the street if he doesn't wise up and get with the fucking program!"

"Is that so?" Tohm shouted. He pushed away from the desk and rose to his feet, trembling with rage. "No one talks to me like that! Especially some arrogant mongrel American!"

"Sticks and stones," Kissinger responded coolly.

"What does that mean?" Tohm said.

"Sticks and stones can break my bones," Kissinger replied, laying it out like a boy in a schoolyard, "but words can never hurt me."

"Is that so?" Tohm taunted. "Then maybe we should try something else."

"Colonel," Bolan intervened, "we have a lot of work ahead of us. How about if we stop with the games and get down to business. Release our man and give us our computer back."

"Or what?"

"You don't want to find out," Bolan warned the colonel. "Trust me."

Tohm brought himself back under control. "You're right," he said calmly. "Enough with the games." He turned to the enlisted man standing near the door. "Soldier, put them in confinement along with the other one."

The sentry balked, still stunned by Kissinger's denunciation of the colonel. The hesitation was enough to set Tohm off again.

"You heard me!" he roared. "Take them away! And if they offer any resistance, I want them shot on the spot. Is that understood?"

The sentry warily leveled his assault rifle at the Americans and pointed to the door. Neither Bolan nor Kissinger moved.

"You're making a mistake," Bolan told the colonel calmly. "It's not too late to correct it."

"What!" Colonel Tohm cried out. "I'm the one making a mistake? I don't think so!"

"Just release our man and give us the computer back," Bolan repeated. "That's all we're asking."

"You've been placed under arrest!" Tohm retorted. "You've been told to go with the sentry and yet you refuse!"

"You have no grounds to arrest us," Bolan said.

Tohm reached for the pistol holstered under his arm. "In fact," he went on, "you not only refused, you tried to overpower us." The colonel turned his gun on Bolan and Kissinger and thumbed off the safety. "You gave us no choice but to shoot."

Kissinger glanced up at the ceiling and muttered, "You're cutting it a little close here, General."

"General?" Tohm was given pause. "What are you talking about?" He, too, looked up at the ceiling. There was an intercom speaker imbedded in the acoustic tiles a few feet from the overhead light.

"Old American proverb," Kissinger told the colonel. "He who lives by surveillance dies by surveillance."

Seconds later, the door to the room swung open and in strode three men. One was Raki Mochtar, flanked by another armed sentry. The third man was General Suseno. The second sentry aimed his assault rifle at Colonel Tohm.

"What's the meaning of this?" Tohm demanded.

"Put the gun down, Colonel," Suseno advised.

"You were eavesdropping?" Tohm asked, incredulous.

"You left me no choice," the general responded. "I've been on the phone the past hour with Ambassador Stansfield and the vice president. You've gone too far this time."

"Entrapment!" Tohm shouted. "You trapped me!"

"Put the gun down," Suseno repeated.

Tohm lowered the gun slightly but refused to put it down. The quick turnaround of events had stripped him of his rage. He was bewildered now, dumbfounded to find himself on the defensive. "Betrayed by my own people," he muttered. "My own people."

"I'm relieving you of your duties, effective immediately," Suseno told the colonel.

"No," Tohm whispered hoarsely. "This is wrong."

"We are in a state of crisis," the general said, "and yet you care only about your own agenda. You take the law into your own hands out of petty spite and—"

"Lies!" Tohm wailed. "I try to keep the imperialists in check, and for this I am damned?"

"You have become a hindrance," Suseno countered evenly. "Your behavior has disgraced your country and your uniform. Now, I ask you again. Turn over your weapon."

Tohm hesitated, then started to place the gun on the desk. Then, abruptly, he raised the gun again, placing it to the side of his head. "I will not stand for this," he cried out.

Bolan, who was standing only a few feet away, had anticipated Tohm's desperation and, before the colonel could pull the trigger, he dived across the desk, swiping his arm at the hand holding the gun. The gun went off, but instead of taking off the colonel's head, the shot plowed harmlessly into the ceiling.

Tohm began to scream incoherently as Bolan wrestled him to the ground and overpowered him. The two sentries rushed over. One produced a set of handcuffs and, with considerable difficulty, bound Tohm's wrists behind his back. Bolan helped lift the colonel back to his feet, then stepped back as the sentries dragged the man from the room.

"They mean to take us over!" Tohm shouted at the general. "You'll see! You'll see!"

Suseno refused to respond to the outburst. Tohm continued to rant as he was led out, and he could still be heard after the door was closed behind him.

"That was ugly," Kissinger whispered to Bolan.

General Suseno eyed the three Americans. "I am not without my reservations about the power the United States wields," he said, "but concerning the matters at hand, we are on the same side. I owe you an apology for my colleague's behavior. He clearly overstepped his authority. It won't happen again."

"Apology accepted," Bolan said.

Kissinger was less easily mollified. "How could you put a guy like that in charge of your intelligence operations?"

"You have only seen him at his worst," Suseno responded evenly. "He was good at his work."

"Maybe so, but anyone can see he's disturbed."

Suseno smiled faintly. "Perhaps some day when we have more time we can discuss your J. Edgar Hoover."

Kissinger had no choice but to smile back.

"For now, however," the general went on, "I suggest we put this incident behind us and focus our energies on more pressing issues."

CHAPTER TWENTY-THREE

"Home sweet home," Kissinger said as he led Bolan and Raki Mochtar into their hotel room. Grimaldi, who Bolan had spoken to by phone, had already returned from the airfield and straightened the place a little. There was a sign posted on the connector door between the two suites saying he was asleep but wanted to be awakened if the others planned to take any further action.

"I don't know about you guys, but the only action I'm up for right now is sawing some logs," Kissinger said with a yawn. "I think I'm gonna turn in."

"I'm right behind you," Mochtar stated, setting the computer back on the desk. "I just want to touch base with the Farm first."

Bolan fought off a yawn of his own as he checked his watch. "My nap's going to have to wait. I'm supposed to meet Scoville downstairs in twenty minutes. He said he might have something coming in from a couple informants."

"That'd be nice," Kissinger said. "We could use a break or two."

"You think Tohm was able to get into the computer?" Bolan asked Mochtar.

Mochtar looked up from the laptop and shook his head. "Not with the safeguards Bear rigged it with. You can't even access the operating system without a password, and if the computer figures you're making wild guesses, it shuts down automatically and starts encrypting all files off the backup battery."

"What about the disk?"

Mochtar ejected the disk and looked it over. "Hard to say. He probably had a peek, but the only thing on it was the scans from those papers you yanked from the campfire, right?"

Bolan nodded. "And if he wanted to, he could've gotten the originals from Lieutenant Wais."

"Guy's a head case, that's for sure," Kissinger said, cracking open a small, single-serving bottle of Chivas Regal from the wet bar.

"The thing is," Bolan said, "Tohm may be out of the picture now, but we still don't know if he was the mole we're looking for."

"I vote no," Kissinger said. "The way he was blathering at the end there, I got the feeling he would've let it slip. You know, anything to make us feel like he'd at least had the last laugh."

"I don't think it's him, either," Mochtar called out as he skimmed over one of several e-mails that had come in from Stony Man Farm. "If he was double-dealing, it seems like he'd have played his hand a little closer to the vest."

"Under normal circumstances, you're probably right," Bolan said.

"And just because he hates Americans doesn't mean he's pro-jihad," Bolan ventured.

"Hold on," Mochtar said. "I've got the background check Bear ran on him here." He downloaded the file, then pulled it up onto the screen and skimmed the data. "He checked out clean. And Suseno was right. Tohm's got commendations, a lot of them for crackdowns on Muslim extremists."

"What about the others?" Bolan asked.

"Checking," Mochtar said. He read through the rest of the file, then reported, "Zip. The only other one who came up red-flagged was Stansfield, and that was for some stink about fund-raising for the President's re-election campaign."

"Which puts us back to square one," Kissinger said. He downed the last of his whiskey, then told the others, "On that cheery note, I'm off to see the sandman."

After a quick shower, Bolan changed into slacks and a sport shirt, then took the elevator down to the ground floor. It was a little after eight when he got to the restaurant. The place was full, but Herb Scoville wasn't among those seated. Bolan spotted Jayne Bahn, however; she was seated at the bar, sipping a glass of wine as she listened to an Indonesian in a white tuxedo play "Born Free" on a baby grand piano. Bolan gave the

maître d' Scoville's description and said he'd be wait
for him at the bar.

"Hey, there, stranger," Bahn called out as Bolan approached her. "Long time, no see."

"I tried your room a couple times," Bolan said. "I
was beginning to think you'd skipped town."

She shook her head. "Beauty sleep."

"It worked," Bolan said.

"Flatterer." Bahn smiled and tapped the bar stool
next to her. "Have a seat."

Bolan sat across from the woman. She'd been right
about the beauty sleep. She looked well-rested and had
changed into a lightweight pantsuit that had obviously
been tailored specifically to her figure. Her hair was up,
held in place by a handful of strategically placed pins.
Bolan could see that half the men in the bar had their
eyes on her.

"I'm waiting for a table," she told Bolan. "How
about joining me for dinner?"

"Actually, I'm waiting for someone," Bolan said.
"Your friend Sizzler."

Bahn nearly spilled her drink. "That tomcat! I didn't
take him for the kiss-and-tell type."

Bolan shook his head. "He isn't," he said. "He just
told me to say hi. I take it he's the one you touched base
with when you got here."

Bahn managed a laugh. "Actually, we touched all the
bases. But I assume you've already figured that out."

"Why didn't you just tell me up front?" Bolan asked.

"I was afraid you'd think I was a loose woman," she quipped.

"That's not what I meant."

"Don't read too much into it," she told Bolan. "I just don't like bending over backward to accommodate you G-men types. I probably would have told you if you hadn't asked first."

Bolan frowned. "I'm sure there's a thread of logic in there somewhere."

"I'll never tell," Bahn said. She took another sip of wine, then asked Bolan, "So, when are you going to tell me how you got that knot on your head?"

"Long story."

"I'm not going anywhere," she said.

Before Bolan could begin, the maître d' appeared, holding a menu. "Madam?" he said. "Your table is ready."

She turned to Bolan. "Looks like Herbie stood you up. What do you say? You look famished."

Bolan got up from his seat. "All right."

"Dinner for two," Bahn told the maître d'.

Once they were alone, Bolan told her as much as he felt he could about the attack at the hospital and his confrontation with Colonel Tohm over Raki Mochtar's incarceration.

Bahn listened with fascination. When Bolan was finished, she feigned a pout. "Well, that'll teach me to sleep on the job. I missed all the fun."

"Fun isn't what I'd call it," Bolan responded. As he draped a napkin across his lap, he scanned the room, looking for any signs they were being watched. Bahn was the only one drawing any stares, however, and Bolan doubted that it had anything to do with surveillance.

"What did they wind up doing with the colonel?" Bahn asked. "I'm sure they didn't just show him the door."

Bolan shook his head. "They've got him on suicide watch at the military hospital while they wait on a psych exam. I've got a feeling they'll go easy on him. Some kind of honorary discharge."

"Better than just knocking him down a few ranks and keeping him in the loop," Bahn said. "Man sounds like a loose cannon if there ever was one."

For the rest of the meal they hashed over the situation, speculating on where Jahf-Al and Pohtoh might be holed up and when Jahf-Al would start showing his hand more instead of leaving all the dirty work to the Lashkar Jihad. By the time they finished desert, it was past nine-thirty. Scoville had yet to show up. When the waiter came by with the check, Bahn grabbed it.

"This one's on Inter-Trieve," she said.

Bolan didn't argue.

Once she'd paid the tab, she said, "So, what next?"

Bolan said, "I'm not sure. We're waiting on some sat Intel on weather patterns and trying to figure out how many of these fires might have been started by the Lashkar Jihad. Hopefully we can narrow down potential targets and take it from there."

"That's great," Bahn said, "but I was talking about tonight."

"Tonight?"

Bahn looked across the table at Bolan. "I know you're tired, so let me help you out. This is the part where you invite me up to your room for a nightcap."

Bolan smiled. "I'm bunking with three other guys."

"Well, I'm not that kind of girl," she responded. "How about my place?"

"Don't think I'm not tempted," Bolan assured her, "but I have to pass."

"Girlfriend?"

"Fatigue," Bolan said. "I wouldn't want to disappoint you. How about if I walk you to your room?"

Bahn thought it over and shook her head. "Remember, I had a nap. I think I'll stay here and let the wolves hit on me for a while."

"Go easy on them," Bolan suggested.

"I'll try, but they're wasting their time," she said, eyeing Bolan provocatively. "I don't settle for second best."

CHAPTER TWENTY-FOUR

Bolan was lost in the grips of a deep sleep when he heard someone calling out to him.

"Striker!"

He stirred and opened his eyes. Grimaldi had just thrown open the curtains, filling the hotel room with the dull morning light.

"Bad news," the pilot told him, stabbing his legs into a pair of jeans. "They hit the consulate."

Bolan sat upright and threw off the covers.

"When?" he asked, fishing through his overnight bag for a change of clothes.

"Just happened," Grimaldi said. "I don't have all the details, but it was some kind of bomb."

"Suicider?"

"I don't think so," Grimaldi said. "They're saying it went off inside the building."

Bolan glanced at his watch—9:30. "They just opened."

"Afraid so," Grimaldi said. "That's going to jack up the death toll."

"Any word on Stansfield?"

"Not yet, but he stays there."

Kissinger and Raki Mochtar were already dressed in the other room. All four men hurried out and made their way to elevators. There were a handful of people already waiting, including a bellhop with a packed luggage cart.

"Let's take the stairs," Bolan suggested.

None of the men spoke as they bounded down the stairwell, through the lobby and out to the street. It was the tail end of rush hour, and the street was choked with traffic. They piled into a trishaw, but it was making so little progress they got out after less than a block and jogged the rest of the way.

Two blocks from the consulate, they ran into a growing throng of curiosity seekers whose shouts and murmurs nearly drowned out the howl of sirens from patrol cars and the handful of emergency vehicles trying to inch their way through the teeming streets. A pair of military helicopters buzzed overhead, headed toward the consulate. The men were still too far away to get a look at the building.

"Let us through!" Kissinger shouted as he and the others tried to weave their way through the mob. Mochtar repeated the command in both Javanese and Bahasa Indonesian but he, too, was drowned out by the cacophony around them. When the men tried to elbow their way through, some of the bystanders shouted in protest and shoved back, further blocking the way.

"Idiots!" Kissinger shouted. He yanked out his Colt

and motioned for Bolan and Grimaldi to give him a little room. He aimed the gun at the ground and fired an
autoburst into the asphalt roadway. The blasts served
their purpose, getting the crowd around them to back
off. When Bolan and Grimaldi drew their weapons as
well, the mob parted more readily, letting the men
through. Finally they reached the police barricade set
up around the consulate. To their amazement, they saw
that the converted mansion was still intact, showing no
signs of structural damage, inside or out.

"What the hell?" Kissinger said. "I don't get it."

As the men continued to stare at the building, two
men in HAZMAT suits emerged through the front entrance carrying a body. Bolan realized at once that the
situation was far worse than it looked.

"Biochem attack," he muttered.

"Must have been a gas bomb of some kind,"
Mochtar speculated.

The body being hauled out wasn't the first. On the
sidewalk in front of the building, a row of corpses—at
least twenty of them—had been laid out in a grim, neat
row. Paramedics, also wearing full HAZMAT suits,
were busy draping the dead with body bags; they would
worry about getting them into the bags later. Soon another two teams of suited CBR crewmen brought out
yet another pair of fatalities.

The Stony Man warriors approached the police and
flashed their credentials. Mochtar spoke briefly to the
officer in charge. The officer inspected the IDs, then
handed them back and signaled the men through the

barricades, warning them to keep their distance from the building.

"Try to find out what we're dealing with here," Bolan told Mochtar.

He translated the question, then passed along the officer's response. "There's some kind of vapor throughout the building, he says. They're still testing the air inside."

"It's got to be something from the agri-compound," Kissinger stated. "Probably the same mix that killed those workers a couple months back."

"See if anyone got out alive," Bolan asked Mochtar.

Mochtar spoke again to the officer, then reported, "A few people on the ground floor."

"What about Stansfield?" Grimaldi wanted to know.

The officer didn't need a translation to answer. He shook his head and pointed at the row of corpses, then offered Mochtar a quick explanation.

"He says they found him on the second floor, along with Nass Buchori."

"The guy from parliament?" Bolan said.

Mochtar nodded.

The two helicopters, both antiquated Hueys dating back to the Vietnam War, touched down alongside each other in the parking lot next to the consulate. The cabin doors rolled open and a dozen uniformed INI soldiers charged out, brandishing assault rifles. Half of them rushed over to help the police man the barricades. The others fanned out, setting up a defensive perimeter around the consulate, eyeing the rooftops of the surrounding buildings. Bolan doubted the tactic would pay off.

"If there's going to be a second attack, it won't be from snipers," he said, staring out at the thousands of people who had converged on the scene. "Set off another bomb in the street and they can take out a few hundred bystanders, no problem."

"Maybe so," Kissinger said. "But you have to figure with the consulate they were targeting Americans. The mob here's practically all locals."

"I hope you're right," Bolan replied.

They were still fifty yards from the building. Bolan doubted it was safe for them to get any closer without protective gear.

"Let's get suited up," he told the others. "I want to get in there and have a look."

The men circled around to a pair of CBR vans parked next to the fire trucks. Bolan had Mochtar ask the HAZMAT unit for some suits.

"He says they only have two spares," Mochtar reported.

"You and me," Bolan decided. "Cowboy, find a way to get through to the Farm."

"I'll see what I can do," Kissinger said.

Bolan turned to Grimaldi. "Is that Black Hawk ready to go back up?"

Grimaldi nodded. "I'll check with the choppers and see if I can hitch a ride to the air base."

"Perfect," Bolan said. "Hopefully by the time you get back we'll have something to go on."

Grimaldi and Kissinger split up and headed off in separate directions. Once Bolan and Mochtar had pulled on their HAZMAT gear, they headed toward the building. On the way, they passed the bodies laid out on the sidewalk. Bolan didn't see Stansfield or Buchori, but he recognized the Marine who'd asked him about the rumor that Moamar Pohtoh and Hamed Jahf-Al were dead. The soldier lay almost as if he were still at attention, arms straight at his sides, lifeless eyes staring up at the soot-laden morning sky.

Bolan and Mochtar waited while two more bodies were carried out, then strode up the front steps and entered the consulate. Inside it was strangely calm. There were a few papers strewed across the floor and a chair had been overturned, but otherwise the lobby merely looked as if it had been vacated while everybody went out for lunch. It was only when he looked closer at a beam of light passing through one of the open windows that Bolan could detect a faint, misty vapor lingering in the air.

The main corridor was deserted, too, save for a pair of CBR specialists focused on an air duct over the door to a large banquet room. One of the men had pulled over a chair and climbed up on it so that he could sweep the grating with a detection wand. A cord ran from the wand down to a mobile cart outfitted with a keyboard and computer screen. The second man was staring at the screen as he worked the keys.

Mochtar asked the men what they'd found out so far, then told Bolan, "They think it's a mixture of a few different pesticides. The biggest reading is for bipyridyl.

You probably know it as paraquat. Causes suffocation in high levels."

"And it was released through the ductwork?" Bolan asked. The HAZMAT masks weren't outfitted with microphones, so he had to raise his voice.

"Looks that way," Mochtar yelled back. "Apparently it was set off by some low-grade explosive on the top floor and worked its way down."

A sudden chill ran down Bolan's spine. "Where on the top floor?" he asked.

Mochtar queried the workers, then told Bolan, "The computer room."

"Son of a bitch!" Bolan cursed. He broke away from the others and strode quickly toward the stairs.

"What is it?" Mochtar wondered, jogging to keep up with Bolan. "Slow down or you're going to start hyperventilating," he shouted.

Bolan recalled his dizzy spell on the bus two days ago and heeded Mochtar's advice. Still, he pushed himself as fast as he dared, eager to reach the top floor.

The paramedics had been removing bodies from the ground floor up, so the upstairs corridor was still littered with corpses. The hall itself was shrouded with smoke that continued to spill out from the computer room where, the day before, Bolan had scanned the papers retrieved from the Lashkar campfire.

The smoke was even thicker in the room itself. Bolan and Mochtar could barely see from one wall to the other. Two technicians stood atop the photocopiers, carefully removing a charred ventilation duct dripping with foam from a fire extinguisher. The wall area surrounding the duct was blackened as well.

"Looks like they set off some kind of explosive to trigger the gas," Mochtar said.

Bolan didn't respond. His throat tightened with rage and frustration as he watched the workers reach into the ductwork. Moments later, they carefully withdrew the mangled remains of a football-sized plastic cylinder, drenched, like the grillework, with foam retardant.

"Looks like a toner cartridge," Mochtar observed.

"Son of a bitch," Bolan repeated. The tightness in his throat had spread to the pit of his stomach. "Right under my nose."

"What are you talking about?" Mochtar said.

Bolan quickly explained how he'd used the room to scan the papers prior to his briefing with General Suseno and the others. "There was a maintenance crew working on the copiers. They were probably there to set the bomb. Right under my nose," he repeated. "Right under my nose."

CHAPTER TWENTY-FIVE

"Go easy on yourself, buddy," Kissinger said once he'd been told about Bolan and Mochtar's findings inside the consulate. "I mean, how the hell could you have known?"

"I know, I know," Bolan said. "But still..."

The two men were standing with Raki Mochtar in the parking lot next to the consulate. Bolan and Mochtar had already changed out of their HAZMAT suits. Kissinger had just returned to the scene after calling the Farm on a secure line at an American Express office two blocks away. As for Grimaldi, both Hueys were being retained at the site so he hadn't been able to secure a ride back to the air base, leaving him no choice but to brave the crowd again and try to flag a taxi. The others figured it would be awhile before he returned in the Black Hawk.

"I talked to Kurtzman," Cowboy told the others. "Hal's in Washington meeting with the President and Joint Chiefs. After this you can bet the sabers are rattling."

"Not much good that will do," Bolan responded. "This isn't Afghanistan. The government here's not sponsoring the thugs who did this."

"Maybe not," Kissinger said, "but once we get a lock on any Lashkar strongholds where there aren't civilians in the line of fire, there'll be a show of force, you can count on it. Bear said the Pacific fleet is already diverting warships and a couple of aircraft carriers to the South China Sea. I'm guessing the President will authorize some kind of ground deployment, too. Stansfield and the President went back thirty years, so he's going to make sure there's some major payback."

The men stared back at the consulate. Things were still chaotic. Most of the bodies had been removed from the building, and one of the paramedic vans had already headed off to the morgue with its first load of fatalities. The crowd had thinned out slightly, but not to the satisfaction of the authorities. Both Hueys were now back in the air, flying low over the crowd to force them farther back. When a news chopper appeared and began to approach the scene, one of the Hueys rose toward it away. The media had already reached the site by ground. A pair of news vans had muscled through the crowd, and reporters were broadcasting live near the periphery of the police barricade.

"I don't know what it's worth at this point," Kissinger went on, "but Bear also made some headway with the sat Intel."

"What kind of headway?" Bolan asked.

"He's sending all the details by e-mail," Kissinger

said, "but the bottom line is if you take all the fires of unknown origin and calibrate them with the wind patterns, all roads lead to Rome...or, in this case, Jakarta."

"The capital," Bolan said.

"Jakarta's not just the capital," Mochtar reminded Kissinger. "All the country's finances and communications are centered there."

"Along with a few million people," Bolan observed.

"If you're looking for an overthrow," Kissinger said, "what better place to drop the monkey wrench."

"Let's hope it doesn't come to that."

Bolan turned to Mochtar. "You still have family there, don't you?"

Mochtar nodded ruefully. "I was going to visit once we were through. I figured I'd get this big hero's welcome once we'd neutralized Pohtoh and Jahf-Al."

"That still can happen," Bolan assured him.

"Even if it does," Mochtar said, gesturing at the consulate, "after this there can't be any celebration."

While the men waited for Grimaldi to return with the Black Hawk, there was a commotion near the news vans. The crowd surrounding the reporters was expressing outrage. The men wandered over to get the lowdown. Mochtar shook his head with disgust as he listened.

"What's he talking about?" Kissinger asked.

"A fax just came in to one of the news stations," Mochtar said. "Hamed Jahf-Al's taking credit for the attack, and he says this is just the beginning."

CHAPTER TWENTY-SIX

Forty minutes later, one of the two Hueys set down on a back runway at the Kalimantan Royal Air Force Base just outside town. When the Stony Man warriors stepped off the chopper, Grimaldi was there to greet them.

"I'm glad you guys decided not to wait," he told them as they headed across the runway. "It was a bitch getting through that crowd, and finding a taxi wasn't much easier."

"No problem," Bolan told him.

"Of course, even if I'd been able to get here earlier, it wouldn't have mattered," Grimaldi said. He had to raise his voice to be heard over the thundering liftoff of an F-16. Elsewhere on the runway there were two more Fighting Falcons as well as an A-10 Thunderbolt waiting their turn to beef up the country's aerial military presence. "They still can't figure out what's wrong with one of the Black Hawk's turboshafts. I'll give them a few more minutes, then I'm going to roll up my sleeves and check under the hood myself."

"I'm sure they'll appreciate that," Kissinger deadpanned.

"I hear Jahf-Al's finally come out of the woodwork," Grimaldi said. "I'm surprised by the fax, though. It's usually his style to send videotape so everybody can see him puffing out his chest."

"Short notice," Bolan suggested. "He probably wanted to take credit as soon as it happened instead of taping something and having to wait on a courier."

"More likely he knows any videotape's going to be analyzed for some tip-off to where he's hiding," Mochtar said.

"Speaking of tip-offs," Kissinger said. "Aren't we going to be able to figure out where the fax was sent from?"

"I'm sure that's being looked into, but you have to figure they used some kind of safeguard," Bolan said.

Once they'd cleared the runway, the men entered a hangar containing the Learjet Grimaldi used to fly Bolan and Kissinger to Indonesia. The aircraft contained a small trove of weapons and other equipment the men felt might have drawn undue attention from the housekeeping crew at the New Millennium.

One such item was another computer, custom-made by Kurtzman with a built-in printer and wireless modem. It contained several sophisticated programs the other laptop didn't, including the latest generation of Kurtzman's patented Identi-Kit. The computer age's answer to the police sketch artist, the I-K was programmed with more than thirty-seven million variations of facial characteristics, the better to come up with a computer-generated likeness that could be cross-checked against mug shots stored in a number of data-bases. Bolan wanted to use the kit to look for the men who'd planted the bomb at the consulate.

"I only got a fleeting look at one of them, so this is a long shot," he cautioned as Mochtar got the computer up and running.

"Understood," Mochtar said. "Just give me a minute to get my ducks in a row here."

"While you're doing that," Grimaldi said, "I'm going to go check on the chopper again. It's near the PX if anybody wants something."

"Coffee," Bolan and Mochtar said in unison.

"I'll go see if I can steal an urnful," Kissinger said.

Once they were alone, Bolan started giving Mochtar a description of one of the photocopier repairmen he'd encountered at the consulate. There wasn't much to go on. Bolan recalled the man as being short, thin, with wavy, short-cropped hair.

"What color hair?" Mochtar asked as he punched the keyboard.

"Black or dark brown. I'm not sure," Bolan said. "I think his hairline was receding."

"Nationality?"

"Maybe Malaysian or Filipino."

Mochtar entered a few more commands. Bolan peered over his shoulder at the screen. At first there appeared a black-and-white image of a male face rendered so generic as to be useless. As a scroll line tracked down the face, however, the characteristics Bolan had described were applied and the features took on more definition.

"Pull the hairline back a little more and grow it out maybe half an inch," Bolan suggested. When the changes had been made, he stared hard at the image, frustrated.

"This probably narrows it down to what, a few hundred million?"

"It's a start," Mochtar said. "What else can you give me? Eyes? Cheekbones? Facial hair? Anything will help."

"The thing is," Bolan conceded, "I only saw him from the side, and that was just for a few seconds."

"Maybe this will help." Mochtar used the mouse to rotate the head on the screen. "Just tell me when the angle's right."

Bolan watched the head slowly turn. Once it was at a little less than three-quarters' profile, he said, "There."

Mochtar locked the image. "Now, I'm guessing he was looking down, right? At the copiers."

When Bolan nodded, Mochtar cued the image and the head pivoted so that it was facing downward.

"That's good, right there." Bolan stared intently at the image, then closed his eyes, trying to visualize the glimpse he'd had of the repairman. It was a maddening process. He cursed under his breath.

"You're forcing yourself," Mochtar said. "Try to relax and trust your instincts. Most people have a lot better recall than they give themselves credit for, but it just gets buried."

"How'd you get to be such an expert on all this?" Bolan asked.

"My brother's a cop," Mochtar explained. "He works with witnesses all the time. That, plus Bear's been helping me out a little. There's talk of expanding the cybernetics team, and I figured I'd throw my hat in the ring."

"Anything to get off security detail, eh?"

Mochtar smiled. "I'm looking for more of a challenge."

"Well, you've come to the right place," Bolan said. He found it hard to believe he'd thought, however fleetingly, that Mochtar might be a turncoat. The man was clearly beyond reproach.

"Try what I said," Mochtar said. "Close your eyes and let it come to you."

Bolan had his doubts but humored Mochtar. They had set up the computer inside the plane's cabin. Bolan dropped onto one of the bench seats and leaned back, closing his eyes and trying to tune out the drone of the fighter jets. It wasn't easy. The takeoff runway was less than fifty yards away and the entire hangar—along with the Learjet—vibrated faintly each time one of the planes took off. He tried to turn his thoughts off, but he couldn't help putting himself back on the top floor of the consulate the previous morning, and the face that kept haunting him wasn't that of the man fixing the photocopier, but rather that of the Marine he'd spoken to down the hall. And that image, in turn, soon changed to that of the same Marine lying dead on the sidewalk outside the consulate. Bolan struggled and finally blocked the visage from his mind.

He tried again. This time he visualized himself passing through the security checkpoint outside the computer room, then entering, hands on the papers from the campfire, already unfolding them because he knew he was pressed for time and would have to work fast scanning them if he hoped to have time to run them through the copiers as well. But then he saw the copiers being worked on...and one of the repairmen glanced back at him for a moment before turning back to his work.

Bolan was puzzled. Did that really happen or was he just imagining it? He thought back, retracing his steps again in his mind. The same image came back to him. Same man, same fleeting glance. Bolan didn't know why he didn't remember it before, but of course it had to have happened. The men were getting ready to place a bomb. Of course they'd have looked if someone walked in on them.

"Sideburns," he murmured to Mochtar, his eyes still closed. "He had sideburns halfway down his ear. And there was a mark, maybe a mole or birthmark, on his cheekbone."

"Where on the cheekbone?" Mochtar asked. "High up? Near the ear or eye?"

"Right next to the cheekbone," Bolan recalled. "About the size of a pencil eraser. And he had high cheekbones."

"Good, good," Mochtar said, factoring in the new data. "Now we're getting somewhere."

"Small eyes," Bolan said. "Tapered eyebrows, thicker toward the bridge of his nose."

"And the nose?"

"I'm not sure," Bolan confessed. "Nothing out of the ordinary."

"Age?"

"I don't know, late-twenties, early thirties."

"Glasses?"

"No," Bolan said. "No, wait. Yes. Wire-rims. Black frames, round lenses. No, oval. They were oval lenses. Small, below the eyebrows."

"Clean shaven?"

"Yeah. He just had the sideburns."

"Keep going."

Bolan was quiet a moment, then opened his eyes. "That's it."

"That's plenty," Mochtar replied.

Bolan shook his head, incredulous. "I can't believe that all just popped out like that. It's like I was under hypnosis."

"I told you you could do it."

"You sure as hell did." Bolan grinned faintly. "I'm going to have to put in a good word for you next time I see Bear."

"That'd be great," Mochtar said. "Now, let's have a look."

Both men stared at the computer screen. The scrolling was nearly complete, taking into account all the variances Bolan had just recalled. When Mochtar prompted the head to turn back to full-face position, Bolan was amazed.

"Damn spooky," he muttered.

"He look familiar?"

Bolan nodded. The image pricked his memory a little further and he suggested a few more modifications: thinner cheeks, a slightly larger forehead, the eyes set a little farther apart. Once the changes came up, he said, "I don't know who he is, but that's our guy."

"I'll send this to Bear and have him run a cross-reference with the mainframe's terrorist database," Mochtar said. "With any luck, it'll cough up a match."

Bolan was still marveling at Kurtzman's wizardry when Kissinger returned with six cups of coffee. "Hope this'll do."

"Thanks," Bolan said, reaching for one of the cups. "Have a look at what Rocky came up with."

Kissinger looked over the composite. "Nice job, Rock," he said. "You got the printer up and running?"

Mochtar nodded. "Yeah. Why?"

"Why don't you run off a couple copies," Kissinger said. "You can bring them with you."

"Bring them where?"

"Lieutenant Wais wants to see us, ASAP," Kissinger said.

"Counter-Insurgency?" Bolan said.

"He's doing double duty now," Kissinger said, "until they find somebody to replace Colonel Tohm. Speaking of him, it turns out Jahf-Al's not the only one taking credit for the bombing."

"Tohm?"

Kissinger nodded. "I was talking to this guy at the PX, and Tohm's claiming he snuck word out from the rubber room and had his goons plant the bomb during the night. You know, his little way of thanking us for the early retirement."

"I don't buy it," Bolan said.

"Neither do I," Kissinger told him, "especially if we're saying the bomb was already planted before we had our little run-in with him."

"The man's delusional," Mochtar said. "Hell, in his head he might really think it was his doing."

"That's one sick puppy," Kissinger stated. "Hell, I almost feel sorry for him. Almost."

CHAPTER TWENTY-SEVEN

"I'm sorry, but I don't recognize him," Lieutenant Dari Wais said, glancing at the composite. "If I could keep this, however, I'd like to show it to a few other witnesses."

"Other witnesses?" Bolan said. "After what happened, I thought they were all dead."

"There are a few consulate employees who worked yesterday but had today off or hadn't come in yet when the bomb went off," Wais explained. "Plus, we have one of the guards who was stationed out front yesterday when the service call was made. They all say they had a look at the repairmen, so hopefully they will be able to corroborate the description you've given here."

"With any luck, maybe they got a look at the other guy, too," Kissinger said.

Bolan and Kissinger were in the lieutenant's fourth-floor office at the same government facility where they'd confronted Colonel Tohm the night before. A large plate-glass window took up most of the far wall and overlooked a large courtyard where other officers and employees could be seen moving from one quadrant of the complex to another. The office itself was small, and cluttered with paperwork. The lieutenant's workload had been clearly heavy even before he'd assumed his additional duties as interim head of Military Intelligence.

"I take it we're ruling out Colonel Tohm as a suspect," Kissinger said. "Much as he seems to want credit."

Wais nodded. "I didn't put much weight in his claims to begin with, and when I talked to him it was clear he had no knowledge of the particulars behind the bombing. Or, more correctly, I suppose we should call this a gassing. After all, no one was even injured by the blast. It was the poison traveling through the vents that caused all the deaths."

Bolan nodded. "I saw where the bomb went off. It looked like it was more of a triggering mechanism for the chemicals."

"Correct," Wais said. "I have our initial findings from the lab around here somewhere."

The lieutenant's disheveled mounds of paperwork may have appeared disorganized, but he knew where the report was and quickly glanced over it before passing along the details.

"The charge was a low-grade plastique derivative," he told Bolan and Kissinger. "It was placed in the middle of the toner cartridge and flanked on either side by packets of bipyridyl separated from some sort of reactive agent by a thin membrane. I wish I could tell you what this other agent was, but so far the lab results have been inconclusive."

"Some kind of aerosol propellant would be my guess," Kissinger said.

"That's the theory we're working on," Wais replied. "Hopefully we'll have something more specific by morning. In any event, the explosion mixed the two ingredients, if you will, and pushed them out either end of the cartridge with enough force to send vapor clouds through the ductwork. Somehow the toxic byproducts managed to remain suspended inside the clouds as they filtered through the entire consulate."

"So what you're saying is that every time these clouds came out of the ductwork, they worked like those house foggers you use to kill fleas," Bolan said.

"Very similar, yes," Wais said. "Or the way you'd treat a house for termites after you tented it."

"Only the UIF were after bigger game than termites," Kissinger said.

"I'm afraid so," the lieutenant agreed. "We have sixty-one confirmed fatalities so far. Another two victims are in comas and have been placed on life support."

"If we're to take Jahf-Al's fax at face value, he's just warming up. We know for a fact that the UIF has a whole network of scientists and technicians devoted exclusively to creating weapons of mass destruction," Bolan pointed out.

"Yes, we're aware of that as well," Wais said. He spoke matter-of-factly, without rancor, unlike his predecessor, Colonel Tohm. "They also have a whole network of shell companies through which to engage in their jihad."

"The copier repair company," Kissinger guessed.

"I'm afraid so," Wais said. "It's several times removed from Bio-Tain, but I've had men working through the night chasing paper trails, and they feel there is a common parent company for both enterprises."

"There's probably also a connection with that delivery truck they used when they stormed the hospital," Bolan said.

"We're looking into that," Wais conceded. "I know that, in retrospect, it seems we should have pieced this all together sooner, but that is the problem in fighting terrorists. They work so clandestinely that their plottings seem obvious and preventable only once they've been carried out."

"We've been finding that out the hard way ourselves," Bolan said. "That's why they were so eager to take out that prisoner in the operating room. They know how much we'd like to get our hands on some inside information so we can anticipate their next move."

"And, conversely," Wais said, "they are in a similar predicament. Which is the main reason I asked to see you gentlemen. There have been a few other developments I need to discuss with you, with the understanding that anything I say will stay between us."

"I don't have a problem with that," Bolan said. Kissinger nodded in agreement.

"Good." Wais rose from his chair and circled his desk. "Let's go for a walk, shall we?"

The lieutenant led the men from his office and down the hall to the elevators. On the way, he whispered to Bolan, "Forgive the cloak-and-dagger, but we're doing a floor-by-floor sweep for bugs and they haven't yet reached my office."

"Understood," Bolan said.

"Does this have something to do with Tohm?" Kissinger wondered as they stepped into the elevators.

"Perhaps to a degree, but there are also other circumstances...the ones I will discuss with you shortly." As the elevator began its descent to the ground floor, Wais confided, "Before we get into that, however, I need to make a confession regarding Colonel Tohm."

"What kind of confession?" Kissinger asked.

"I'd had my share of concerns about him the past few weeks. Not regarding his loyalty, understand, but his behavior and state of mind."

"You knew he was on the brink?" Bolan said.

"Perhaps I should have drawn that conclusion," Wais admitted. "As it was, I felt it was something more transitory, that he was just letting the stress of events get the better of him."

"It seemed a little more serious than that to me," Bolan said. "And I don't mean last night. He was acting a little manic at the briefing, if you ask me."

Wais sighed. "He may have seemed that way to you, but to those of us who know him, the colonel was just being his normal self. He's always been prone to outbursts, but we'd come to overlook it because it never seemed to affect his performance. I have to tell you, the man's service record is extraordinary."

"General Suseno has already told us as much," Bolan said. "We've confirmed it through our own sources, too."

"All of which takes me back to my original point," Wais told them. "I don't see the colonel as having had anything to do with the consulate bombing. To focus on him would be a mistake, I feel."

"We're on the same page," Bolan assured the lieutenant as they stepped out of the elevator. "So let's move on to this other matter, shall we?"

Wais nodded. "This way, please."

The lieutenant led Bolan and Kissinger across the ground-floor lobby to a side door leading to the same courtyard they'd seen from Wais's office.

"They've swept here twice already since last night," Wais said. "Still, let's wait until we're among the trees."

The trees he was referring to were poplars, two stories high, with wide, sweeping branches. They had been planted around a small fountain whose staggered tiers of hissing geysers would help to mask their conversation. Bolan also suspected the trees would serve as a hedge against the chance that someone might be watching them from one of the upper floors. To some, such precautions may have seemed excessive, but Bolan knew of more than one instance in which critical information had been intercepted by specially trained lip-readers armed with nothing more than a pair of high-powered binoculars.

Once they were beneath the poplars, Lieutenant Wais motioned Bolan and Kissinger close to him, forming a huddle.

"Much as I can't condone the way he acted on it, Colonel Tohm's paranoia was not totally without foundation," Wais divulged. "We have reason to believe that either Jahf-Al or Pohtoh have placed someone within our ranks."

Bolan took the news impassively. He wasn't about to tell the lieutenant that they'd already reached the same conclusion.

"By telling us this, I take it we're not under suspicion?" Kissinger asked.

"That is correct," Wais said. "As I said, Colonel Tohm's focus was misdirected, and I echo General Suseno's apologies in that regard."

"Who do you suspect, then?" Bolan asked.

Wais hesitated a moment, as if weighing how much he wished to reveal, then said, "There is another bit of news that ties into this. Major Salim regained consciousness during the night. The first thing he did was ask to see both me and the general regarding the ambush in the mountains. He fears that one of his own men has been acting as a conduit for the enemy."

"How is the major?" Bolan asked.

"He continues to improve," Wais said, "but let me continue, please."

"Of course."

"Salim points back to a string of missions over the past two months during which KOPASSUS troops have sustained heavy losses. In every instance, he was surprised at the extent to which enemy forces were able to anticipate his strategy and circumvent it. At first he was willing to give Jahf-Al and Pohtoh credit for being fine strategists, but now he is certain there was more to it than that."

"If it's somebody in KOPASSUS, what kind of haystack are we talking about?" Kissinger asked. "How many men are in that unit?"

"At present, about seventy men," Wais said. "And unfortunately, they aren't a single unit. They're spread out across the islands."

"Well, obviously it would have to be someone stationed here, don't you think?" Bolan said.

The lieutenant nodded. "That is my thinking. Which narrows it down to thirty-three men."

"That's still a lot," Bolan said. "What are you going to do, interrogate them one by one?"

Wais shook his head. "That would be too time-consuming. I think it would be more effective to force their hand and hope they'll betray themselves."

"You have something specific in mind?"

"Actually, yes, I've already come up with a plan," Wais replied. "For it to work, however, we will need your help."

CHAPTER TWENTY-EIGHT

"Wais is going to corral all the KOPASSUS troops into the same barracks at the military base so they can be kept under surveillance," Bolan explained to Grimaldi.

They were back at the hotel. Their bags were packed, and they were ready to check out. Raki Mochtar still had the laptop out, though, and was on the line with Stony Man headquarters back in Virginia. Bolan and Grimaldi stood on either side of a table in the living room, where Kissinger had laid out a topographical map of central Borneo. Bolan pointed to the map as he continued.

"Wais is telling them that late tomorrow they're going to attempt a preemptive strike on a suspected Lashkar Jihad stronghold somewhere along the route Bio-Tain was using to transfer the pesticides from Samarinda to the incineration plant in Malaysia."

"Got it," Grimaldi said. "He figures this spy we're looking for will try to leave the barracks so he can sound a warning."

Bolan nodded. "To hedge the bet, he's also setting up a communications center in the barracks itself. They'll be lax with security and see if the guy tries to take advantage."

"So they can trace the call," Grimaldi guessed.

"It's a long shot," Kissinger said, "but if he takes the bait, we'll be able to better pinpoint exactly where the stronghold is."

Grimaldi frowned. "We don't know that already?"

Bolan shook his head. "Wais says they could be in any number of areas." He pointed at the map. "We're talking nothing but mountains and rain forest over a two thousand square mile area. We need this guy to blow the whistle and narrow it down for us."

"Okay, got it," Grimaldi said. "Now, where do we fit in?"

"We'll head for the interior," Bolan explained. "That way, we'll be in better position to strike once we're clear on where the stronghold is."

"What if this guy doesn't go for the bait?" Grimaldi wondered.

"Then we'll be doing recon," Bolan said. "With all the smoke, we're not getting much from the satellites or high-alt planes. We'll be flying lower, below the smoke line."

Grimaldi stared at the map. "Two thousand square miles, huh? Good luck."

"Hey," Kissinger said, "it beats twiddling our thumbs waiting to see where they'll strike next."

"Speaking of which," Grimaldi said. "What are they doing to beef up security around Jakarta?"

"I'm sure they're pulling all the stops," Bolan said. "I passed along all the info Rocky got from Bear, but I didn't press for details. We've got enough to worry about on this front."

"You got that right," Grimaldi said. "I say we check out of this dump and get cracking."

Bolan nodded and turned to Mochtar. "What's the word from home?"

"Bear says he came up empty on the composite," Mochtar told the others. "No match with any terrorists in the database."

"Doesn't surprise me," Bolan said. "It figures they'd used somebody new. Less chance of being found."

"He's got something else, though," Mochtar reported, "and I don't know what to make of it."

"What's that?" Kissinger asked.

"The fax from Jahf-Al," Mochtar said. "It was sent from some postal-box place in Muara Badak. They apparently broke in to use it, so it's kind of a dead end."

"No surprise there, either," Grimaldi said.

"That's not the weird part," Mochtar said. "Bear got his hands on a copy of the fax and figured he'd do his own handwriting analysis to make sure it was authentic."

"That's Bear for you," Kissinger said.

"Get this," Mochtar said. "The message wasn't an original."

"What do you mean?" Bolan asked.

"It was a cut-and-paste job," Mochtar said. "Put together from three different communiqués Jahf-Al's sent out over the past year."

"You're right," Kissinger said. "That *is* weird."

"It explains why there was no specific reference to the consulate," Mochtar said. "Most of it was lifted from a post he made after the cruise liner bombing. Practically boilerplate stuff. You know, your usual 'Down with the West, Allah is great' stuff. What do you guys make of it?"

Kissinger shrugged. "Could mean anything. Maybe it's some kind of cat-and-mouse ploy. You know, trying to mess with our heads. Maybe he's got writer's cramp. Who knows?"

"Or maybe it wasn't Jahf-Al," Bolan suggested. He was on the phone, trying to reach Jayne Bahn. He wanted to let her know they were leaving. Her room line was busy.

"If it's not Jahf-Al, then who?" Mochtar asked.

No one had an answer.

Bolan tried Bahn again, but the line was still busy. "What'd Brognola come back with from Washington?" he asked Mochtar.

"Any kind of plan of attack is still up in the air at this point."

"You let them know what our game plan was?" Bolan asked.

Mochtar nodded. "We've got the green light."

"Well, then, let's get the show on the road," Kissinger said.

"Give me a second?" Mochtar asked. "Bear's putting together some sat Intel on the mountains we're going into. It's from a couple of days ago, before the smoke got in the way. I figure it might come in handy."

"Good idea," Kissinger said. "We can cross-reference with the topo map."

"Look, I'll meet you guys in the lobby," Bolan said, hanging up the phone. "I've got some last-minute business."

Bolan took the elevator up to the top floor. He was on his way to Jayne Bahn's room when her door opened. An elderly woman stepped into the hall. Bolan was puzzled.

"Excuse me, but I was looking for Ms. Bahn," Bolan told the woman. "Is she in?"

The woman looked at Bolan, perplexed. *"Pardon?"*

Bolan repeated the question, this time in French. The woman told him he had to have the wrong room. Bolan checked the room number and shook his head. The woman apologized, saying she didn't know any Ms. Bahn. When Bolan asked the woman if she'd just checked in, she nodded.

"Oui."

It was Bolan's turn to apologize. He excused himself, then took the elevator down to the lobby and checked with the front desk. When he asked about Bahn, the clerk told him, "She checked out late last evening."

"Do you know what time?"

When the clerk hesitated, Bolan flashed his photostat identifying himself as a special federal agent. Technically, it meant nothing, but the clerk was impressed enough to check the computers.

"A little after eleven," he told Bolan.

Bolan thanked the man. He'd left Bahn at the restaurant well before ten. On a hunch, he crossed the room. The maître d' he'd spoken to the previous night had just come on duty. Bolan suspected his badge wouldn't work twice, so he resorted to money, slipping the man a hundred-dollar bill. Instead of a federal agent, he opted to play the possessive lover.

"The woman I had dinner with here last night," Bolan said. "Did she leave here with anyone?"

The maître d' deftly pocketed the bill, then leaned close to Bolan and whispered confidentially, "Yes. As a matter of fact, she left with the man you were waiting for."

Bolan feigned a flash of anger, then thanked the man and returned to the lobby. Kissinger, Mochtar and Grimaldi were just getting off the elevator.

"That was fast," Kissinger ribbed Bolan.

"She checked out last night," Bolan told Cowboy. "With Herb Scoville from the CIA."

CHAPTER TWENTY-NINE

"Scoville was supposed to meet with me after he'd made contact with a couple informants," Bolan told the others as they piled out of the trishaw cab that had taken them to a run-down warehouse just up the road from Samarinda's lone rail depot. The entire block was filled with similar buildings, squat concrete-stone structures with faded paint and sun-bleached signs. A faint breeze had brought smoke down from the hills, and it choked the street like a London fog. A train rolled past behind the buildings but visibility was so low that none of the men could even see it.

"Well, obviously he showed up late and met with Jaynie-girl instead," Kissinger said. "I still don't see why that merits a side trip to the spook house."

"Scoville was hoping for a breakthrough in tracking down Jahf-Al," Bolan said. "If he lucked out, we could use the information."

"I hate to break it to you, Striker," Kissinger said as they made their way down a littered alley to the side entrance to one of the buildings, "but if he had information and ran off with Bahn without telling us, I smell a bounty hunter who doesn't want to slice the reward pie any more than she has to."

"She's not flying solo on this," Bolan reminded Kissinger.

"So what?" Kissinger said. "Even working for Inter-Trieve she still gets a cut. Ten percent probably. That's a three-million-dollar investment she's protecting. Hell, if I were in her shoes, I'd want to keep us out of the loop, too."

The sign over the entrance advertised a metal-plating business. The steel door was locked. It had a peephole, and after Bolan pressed the ringer, he motioned for the others to step back so whoever was inside could get a good look at them. Thirty seconds later they heard the sound of a dead bolt being thrown, then a lean, hardened-looking man in cheap slacks and a polo shirt opened the door.

"Hey, hey, partner," the man said, offering Bolan his hand. "That was quick."

"Hello, Fred," Bolan said.

Fred Byrnes was one of Herb Scoville's subordinates with the CIA. He'd had Scoville's job three years ago when he'd helped Bolan and Major Salim thwart the Chinese in their attempt to gain a toehold in Indonesia. Byrnes didn't care for the responsibilities that went with the job, however, and had asked to step down so he could go back to being a field agent.

Bolan introduced Byrnes to Kissinger and Mochtar,

using their aliases. The men shook hands, then Byrnes led them inside. The reception area was drab and spare, tricked up with just enough business-related para-phernalia to keep up pretenses.

Passing through a door behind the service counter, the men went down a short corridor to the warehouse area. There were a few work benches and an industrial lathe set up on one side of the large room along with a few half-finished projects and a pile of shipping boxes to add to the impression that some plating work was done in the building. Off in the other corner, behind a six-foot-high partition, there was a row of storage lock-ers stocked with munitions and various tools of the spy trade. There was also a computer station, coffee ma-chine, water cooler and, thumbtacked to the partition wall itself, a large map of the island of Borneo. There were color-coded pins sticking out from the map, sup-posedly indicating the location of the plating firm's clientele. In fact, the pins denoted areas where CIA-di-rected intelligence activity was either taking place or being considered.

Byrnes asked if the men wanted anything. When they all shook their heads, he reported, "Scoville still hasn't checked in."

"How long since you've heard from him?" Bolan asked.

"Last night around dinnertime," Byrnes said. "He said he was on to something with these mercenaries we've been keeping tabs on."

"Back up," Bolan said. "What mercenaries?"

"He didn't tell you?" Byrnes frowned. "Shit, I guess I really stepped in it then, didn't I?"

"May as well put the other foot in," Kissinger suggested.

"It's important," Bolan said.

"Okay, let's horse trade," Byrnes said. "I'll show you mine if you show me yours."

Bolan recalled his promise to Lieutenant Wais and kept it vague. "We're here same as we were last time," he said. "Only instead of the Chinese and rebels in Sumatra, we're going up against Jahf-Al and Pohtoh."

Byrnes continued to barter. "Tell me something I don't already know."

Bolan changed tack. "If Scoville's missed his last few check-ins, you guys should be thinking about a search party, only I see from the map there that you're a little overextended. Maybe we can help."

Byrnes glanced over at Kissinger and Mochtar, grinning. "He's good."

"He is at that," Kissinger said.

"Okay, partner," Byrnes told Bolan, "you win. What do you need to know?"

"Let's start with the mercenaries."

"Fair enough. You know, of course, that we occasionally farm out work to these soldier-of-fortune types, usually in cases when we want to keep ourselves once-removed from the action."

"Go on," Bolan said.

"Out in this neck of the woods we throw most gigs to locals," Byrnes explained, "with a few Cambodians and Filipinos thrown in for good measure. A few weeks ago we caught wind that Pohtoh's people were trying to recruit a crew of Americans for some kind of secret operation. Our Intel was that they were after seasoned pros. Guys like you."

"Sorry, our dance card's full," Kissinger said.

"Hang on a second." Bolan now had an idea of what Scoville's plan might have been. "These guys Scoville was dealing with...is it that crew from Seattle that foiled that kidnapping in the Philippines last month?"

Byrnes hesitated a moment, then nodded. "You know about them, huh?"

"Kind of hard not to," Bolan told him, "given all the press they got."

"These are the guys who got on the shit list with those senators back in Washington, right?" Kissinger said.

"The same," Byrnes replied.

Bolan thought back, recalling the incident, in which Takoma real-estate baron William Ruppert had hired a band of retired U.S. soldiers based out of Seattle to deliver a three-million-dollar ransom to al-Arqam terrorists who had kidnapped his daughter during a visit to the Philippines. The men had secured the woman's release, then doubled back and killed her kidnappers before they had a chance to flee the country. They lost one man in the process, but the skill with which they carried out their mission had drawn global praise, as well as criticism from several U.S. senators who felt the use of mercenaries by private citizens was a dangerous precedent and that the Seattle crew's so-called heroics would likely prompt a retaliatory escalation in anti-U.S. activities by al-Arqam. The last Bolan had heard, the head of the mercenary group had countered by calling the senators a pack a whiners who were jealous that freelancers had succeeded in a situation where a sanctioned response would likely have failed. The senators, in turn, had accused the soldiers of fortune of disloyalty, if not outright treason.

"That whole stink with the senators was orchestrated by Scoville," Byrnes explained. "He wanted to make it look like these guys were on the outs with the U.S. so the Lashkar wouldn't be as suspicious of their willingness to work with a known enemy."

"The fact that Pohtoh's at odds with al-Arqam didn't hurt matters, either," Bolan guessed.

"Exactly," Byrnes said. "The old 'the-enemy-of-my-enemy-is-my-friend' angle. They bought into it, too. These Seattle guys haggled for a few days over money, then finally struck the deal yesterday."

"A deal to do what?" Bolan wanted to know. "What kind of operation are we talking about here?"

"That's what Scoville was trying to find out," Byrnes related. "These guys were supposed to get picked up by the Lashkar first thing this morning and taken to Pohtoh. Scoville wanted to meet with them first and nail down some strategy."

"Where?"

Byrnes turned and pointed to the map. "About eighty miles north of here there's an abandoned timber harvesting mill. Right on the river."

Bolan checked the map. They'd be flying within a few dozen miles of the site on the way to the Borneo interior. Obviously they would now be making a detour. There was still one matter that hadn't been touched on yet, and he wanted some answers before they moved on.

"What do you know about Scoville and an Inter-Trieve agent named Jayne Bahn?" Bolan asked Byrnes.

Byrnes laughed. "A real firecracker, that one, eh?"

"Yeah," Kissinger interjected. "She's a regular life of the party."

"All I know is she was by here a couple days ago to see Scoville," Byrnes said. "He made like it was just about hormones, but my guess is there's more to it. Herb's always got an angle."

Bolan asked a few more questions, but Byrnes wasn't able to shed any more light on Bahn's relationship with Scoville or why the Lashkar Jihad had recruited the mercenaries from Seattle.

"How's our friend Major Salim?" Byrnes asked, changing the subject.

"On the mend," Bolan said. "I haven't talked to him, but word is he's going to pull through."

"Glad to hear it," Byrnes said. "Good soldier. We were going to—"

Byrnes was drowned out by a sudden explosion coming from the reception area. The concussive force of the blast shook the warehouse area, dislodging one of the overhead lights and jarring the partition wall. Mochtar and Kissinger had to grab it to keep it from falling over. The storage lockers rocked slightly but remained upright, and as the others instinctively reached for their handguns, Byrnes quickly raided one of the lockers for a Remington 870 Magnum shotgun. As he slapped a 7-round extension tube into place, he told the others, "I think we've got company."

CHAPTER THIRTY

"They took the door out," Bolan guessed, readying his Desert Eagle for action. His ears were ringing from the sound of the explosion.

"We must've been followed," Kissinger said.

"Let's worry about that later," Fred Byrnes suggested. He stepped past the others, finger nestled close to the trigger of his Remington.

Bolan and the others followed. Once they cleared the partition, the warehouse rattled with a second explosion, this one milder than the first. Twenty yards away, an acrid cloud of smoke rose from the floor and began to fill the warehouse.

"Shit," Kissinger murmured. "We're dead."

"No, wait," Raki Mochtar yelled, coughing as he sniffed the air. "It's just tear gas."

"I stand corrected," Kissinger said. "We'll gag and go blind crying before they come in firing. *Then* we're dead."

Bolan stepped back from the mushrooming cloud,

aiming his .44 at the doorway across the chamber. Whoever had fired the tear gas was apparently waiting for the gas do its work before making their next move; no one had yet charged in from the reception area. For the third time in as many days, Bolan began to feel as if his eyes were on fire.

"Is there another way out?" He coughed, trying futilely to wave the gas cloud away from him.

"The loading dock," Kissinger suggested, pointing to a set of large bay doors to their right.

"Too risky," Byrnes said, blinking tears from his eyes. "They've probably got men on the other side. There's a better way. C'mon, give me a hand."

Holding their breath, the men followed Byrnes through the thickening cloud of gas to the work area. Bolan's lungs were aching and he was beginning to feel nauseous, but he fought off the sensation and rubbed his eyes with the back of his hand. He saw Byrnes crouch before the large industrial lathe and crank a lever mounted on the floor.

"There's a trapdoor underneath," he told the others. "We just need to swing this baby out of the way."

The lathe weighed several tons but rested on casters. When the men pushed, the machine rolled to one side, revealing the trap door.

"Quick!" Byrnes said, yanking open the door.

Mochtar went down first, followed by Kissinger. As he waited his turn, Bolan glanced back toward the doorway. The tear gas, however, had created a smoke screen, blocking it from view. By the same token, it was keeping the attackers from seeing what their intended victims were up to.

As Bolan started to lower himself into the opening in the floor, he asked Byrnes, "Can we swing the lathe back in place behind us?"

Byrnes nodded. "Wouldn't be worth much if we couldn't. Go on, I'm right behind you."

There were metal rungs anchored in the vertical shaft leading from the warehouse, and once Bolan had climbed all the way down, he found himself in what seemed to be a utility tunnel dating back to before the CIA had set up shop in the building.

Once Byrnes had repositioned the lathe and closed the trapdoor behind him, he joined the others, who were all hacking and coughing from the effects of the tear gas.

"This connects with most of the other buildings and runs all the way to the depot," he told them.

The commandos followed Byrnes for fifty yards, then he stopped and pointed at another vertical shaft similar to the one they'd taken down from the warehouse.

"It comes up to an alley one building over from where you guys came in," he explained. "Careful, though, 'cause there's no guarantee they won't have somebody up there waiting for us."

"I like the odds better than at the warehouse," Kissinger said. "Let's do it."

Bolan headed up first. The shaft wasn't lit, and he had to grope for the rungs in darkness. When he felt a manhole cover above him, he paused a moment, steeling himself, then unfastened the undermounts and pushed on the plate, slowly raising it as he climbed up another rung.

Peering out, Bolan saw that the smoke-filled alley was deserted save for a woman and two children picking through a garbage bin. When they saw him climbing up out of the manhole, they froze, eyeing his gun with horror. He quickly put a finger to his lips, signaling for them to be quiet, then reached back into the shaft, giving Kissinger a lift up. Mochtar followed and Byrnes brought up the rear.

"So far so good," the CIA agent said, surveying the alley.

Bolan listened. He could hear the distant rumbling of a train and the hum of traffic out on the streets, but there was no sound of gunfire.

Byrnes pointed out a fire escape jutting from the side of the building next to them. "How about if a couple of us take the high road while the others circle around from both sides?"

"I'll go high," Bolan said. He turned to Mochtar. "You come with me?"

Mochtar nodded.

The lowermost section of the fire escape was a retractable ladder folded up against the underside of the second-story landing. Bolan figured it would make too much noise to pull it down, so he had Kissinger give him a lift up to where he could reach the landing framework. He pulled himself up and reached down, lending Mochtar a hand. Kissinger, meanwhile, headed toward the rear of the building, leaving Byrnes to circle around the front.

The fire escape groaned slightly under their weight as Bolan and Mochtar made their way up the steps. The smoke seemed to get thicker the higher they went, and by the time they reached the flat roof their visibility was down to less than ten yards. Bolan was concerned about wandering headlong into a sniper concealed by the smoke.

"Take it slow," he whispered to Mochtar over the hum of a nearby condensor.

The roof was topped with a layer of gravel, making it difficult, if not impossible, to walk across without making any noise. The droning of three other air-conditioning units helped mask their footsteps, but Bolan still cringed each time he heard the stones crackle underfoot.

They'd stolen their way less than thirty feet across the roof when a flurry of gunshots suddenly erupted at the far end on the building. Apparently Kissinger or Byrnes was drawing fire and, as Bolan had feared, some of it was coming from a sniper posted somewhere on the roof. Bolan dropped to a crouch behind one of the condensors and motioned for Mochtar to do the same. Both men peered around the bulky unit. The far edge of the roof was less than twenty yards away, but they couldn't see where the shots were coming from.

Leaning close, Bolan whispered to Mochtar, "Look for muzzle-flash."

Mochtar nodded. Both men took aim, and several seconds later, they got their opportunity. Another round of gunfire sounded from the roof, and they could see the faintest trace of a muzzle-flash coming from the barrel of the gun the man fired.

Bolan drew bead with his .44 and fired. Mochtar's shots echoed right behind those of the Desert Eagle. There was a dull cry in the smoke, followed by the sound of a body plummeting to the alley below. Both men quickly drew back behind the condensor, bracing themselves for return fire. When there wasn't any, they moved clear of the unit and advanced warily toward the sniper's last position. Down in the alley, they could hear the rattle of two submachine guns, punctuated by blasts from Byrne's Remington and 3-round bursts from Kissinger's Colt pistol.

Soon they could see the edge of the roof. Both Bolan and Mochtar dropped to their stomachs and inched forward the rest of the way. They could hear only one SMG, and seconds later the other was silenced as well.

Once Bolan reached the roof's edge, he peered down. The smoke was less dense in the alleyway below. Two enemy gunmen were sprawled on the asphalt near the charred opening where the steel door had once been; the door itself had fallen inward, blasted off its hinges by the initial explosion. Bolan shifted his gaze and looked directly below him. The sniper he and Mochtar had felled lay in a twisted heap atop the piled trash inside a garbage Dumpster.

Bolan was about to call down to Byrnes and Kissinger

when he detected motion behind the Dumpster. A surviving attacker had risen from cover and was about to fire his Uzi at Kissinger. Bolan let out a cry, startling the man, then fired down at him with his Desert Eagle. The man fired aimlessly into the side of the Dumpster, then dropped his weapon and pitched forward to the ground.

"Nice save," Kissinger shouted up to Bolan.

Byrnes called up next, telling Bolan and Mochtar that the fire escape on this side of the building was ten yards to their right. They found it and quickly clambered down to the ground.

Byrnes stepped over one of the bodies and stared at the ruined doorway. "I was ready to move out of the neighborhood, anyway," he said.

Kissinger crouched over the body closest to him, getting a better look at the man's face. "Indonesian, from the looks of it. Whether he's Lashkar or some traitor, who knows?"

"If they're from KOPASSUS or Military Intelligence, it'll be easy enough to identify them," Mochtar said.

Bolan ventured over to the Dumpster to inspect the two men he'd slain. When he got a close look at the sniper, he did a double take, stunned. He waved over Mochtar and pointed to the man's face.

"Does this guy look familiar to you?"

Mochtar nodded, incredulous. "The guy in the composite."

Bolan nodded back. "The guy who set the bomb inside the consulate."

CHAPTER THIRTY-ONE

"His name is Iman Agung," Lieutenant Wais told Bolan, showing him the dossier he'd brought with him from MI headquarters. The two men were standing with Kissinger on the tarmac at the Kalimantan Royal Air Force base. Fred Byrnes had stayed behind at the CIA facility, while Raki Mochtar was helping Jack Grimaldi load a few things into a nearby Sultan EG-23 firefighting helicopter borrowed from the Samarinda Emergency Response Corps. The Black Hawk's turboshaft problems had finally been resolved, but Bolan and the others had decided that a gunship would be too conspicuous for their upcoming mission in the Borneo interior. The Sultan, though unarmed, would not seem out of place given the number of fires still raging along the Central Mountain Range. In it, the Stony Man crew would likely be able to infiltrate closer to any Lashkar Jihad stronghold without finding itself targeted by another round of Stinger missiles like those that had been fired by

Lashkar snipers during the ambush on the mountain roadway two days ago.

Wais continued to brief Bolan and Kissinger on the man responsible for placing the chemical bomb in the consulate. "He was an explosives expert with the Jemaah Islamiah before they folded in with the Lashkar Jihad last year. He had been taken off file because we thought he perished in a bomb raid at a training camp of theirs in Sulawesi. Obviously, we were mistaken."

"Well, he's dead for good this time," Kissinger said.

"We had to have been followed from our meeting," Bolan told Wais. "That would seem to throw suspicion on somebody at MI."

"Perhaps," Wais conceded. "But you have to remember we are just down the road from the military base, and the KOPASSUS commandos are only now reporting to their new barracks. A handful of them are coming in from off-base, so it's still conceivable they had a hand in your being followed."

"What about the other men who were in on the attack?" Kissinger asked. "Have they been identified?"

"Only insofar as they were wearing the robes of the Lashkar Jihad," Wais said. "But given their nationality and the fact that Agung was among them, it seems obvious they were Pohtoh's men. I can tell you for a fact that they weren't KOPASSUS or MI officers in disguise."

Changing topics, Bolan asked the lieutenant, "Do you know anything about the Lashkar trying to recruit American mercenaries?"

Wais stared at Bolan. "No," he said. "That is the first I've heard of such a thing."

Bolan decided there was nothing to be gained by holding back what he knew, so he explained to Wais what Byrnes had told him about the Seattle-based mercenary force Herb Scoville was dealing with.

"I know of these mercenaries," Wais said. "After their mission in the Philippines, they turned up in Jakarta. Colonel Tohm had placed them under surveillance, but they disappeared on him."

"With Scoville's help, no doubt," Kissinger guessed.

Wais frowned with irritation. "This whole development should have been brought up during the briefing," he said. "If not before."

"Scoville probably held back because of Tohm," Bolan suggested.

"You're probably right," Wais said. He drummed his fingers on the dossier file. "This is all very troubling. It is bad enough we have been infiltrated. If your efforts wind up being compromised by security breaches as well, it will make this whole business more difficult for the both of us."

"I don't think that's a big concern," Bolan said. "It seems pretty clear to me that these mercenaries are on our side all the way."

"And if you're mistaken?" Wais countered. "What if they have plans to act as triple agents?"

"I just don't think that's the case," Bolan insisted. "And even if they aren't on the level, these soldiers of fortune run in a whole different circle from our military and intelligence operations. They wouldn't be able to cross over that easily."

Wais wasn't convinced. "If they run in different circles, as you say, then how did they wind up working for the CIA in the first place?"

"Good point," Bolan said. "Unfortunately, the only man who can answer that question is missing."

"I suspect that as you look for the Lashkar Jihad's stronghold in the mountains, you might very well find Mr. Scoville in the process. Not to mention these mercenary acquaintances of his," Wais said. "In fact, if I were a wagering man, I would bet Mr. Scoville has gone incommunicado because he is closing in on the enemy and wants to avoid giving away his position."

"I hope you're right," Bolan said. "Tell me something, Lieutenant. As long as we're talking about odds, what are the chances that Pohtoh and Jahf-Al are hiding out in one of these strongholds we're looking for?"

"It's very possible," Wais said. "After all, the last report we had on Pohtoh, he was in Banjarmasin, on the south coast two hundred miles from here. It would make sense for him to move inland to the rain forests, especially now that he knows we will be stepping up efforts to find him. The same for Jahf-Al, assuming, of course, that he is indeed in the country."

"You have doubts?" Kissinger asked.

"Again, this is confidential," Wais said. "We have been analyzing the fax message sent by Jahf-Al after the consulate incident. There are serious questions about its authenticity."

"Our people back in the States just reached the same conclusion," Bolan said. "They're saying it was patched together from other messages he's sent."

"It's very puzzling," Wais said.

"At the same time, it's a little beside the point, too," Kissinger said. "I mean, we know for sure now that the Lashkar Jihad was involved in the bombing, and since they've gotten in bed with the UIF, that still leaves you with Jahf-Al. One way or another, the finger points at him."

"True," Wais said. "But given the circumstances, one would have thought Pohtoh would have made sure he got his share of the credit. He's not the sort to shy away from the spotlight."

Kissinger was getting impatient. "You know, we could stand around guessing from now till Ramadan and it won't get us anywhere. I say we quit yapping and go hit the mountains and try to find these guys."

"Of course," Wais said, smiling faintly. "As I mentioned, we'll have all the KOPASSUS officers under surveillance within the hour. If our ploy works and our turncoat tips his hand, I'll pass along any details on the stronghold's location to you via radio."

"And vice versa," Bolan said.

"Be sure your pilot takes care," Wais advised. "All this smoke has made the skies treacherous for flying. On the way here I learned we lost a fire-fighting plane in the same general area where you're headed."

"What happened?" Bolan asked.

"We're not certain at this point," Wais said. "From

what I've been told, we lost radio contact without warning and then the plane just dropped off the radar. The smoke is so thick up in the mountains we're afraid they may have flown into a peak without realizing it was there."

"If you can give us the plane's last coordinates, we can do a flyover," Bolan offered.

"A good idea," Wais said. "It would be appreciated."

The lieutenant excused himself, saying he had a meeting with General Suseno and the vice president regarding plans to beef up security in Jakarta in light of Intel pointing to a possible terrorist attack. Bolan and Kissinger strode across the tarmac and joined Mochtar and Grimaldi alongside the fire-fighting chopper. The Sultan was somewhat similar to the AH-64 Apache, but the one Grimaldi would be flying had been retrofitted for its fire-fighting duties, stripped of armament and outfitted with side-mounted release tanks filled with E-33 grade fire retardant. The cabin, likewise, had been reconfigured to carry half-a-dozen firefighters and their equipment.

"If it was up to me, we'd take the Black Hawk," Grimaldi told the others as they piled into the cabin. "I mean, if the visibility's so bad, who's going to see us anyway?"

"They'll be sentries posted, Jack, you know that," Bolan stated. "All it'd take would be for us to pass through one clearing at the wrong time and our cover could be blown."

"Yeah, yeah," the pilot grumbled, firing up the engines and giving the controls a final check. "But if they start taking potshots at us and we don't have any way to shoot back, just remember I told you so."

"Duly noted," Bolan said. "We're ready when you are."

Grimaldi lifted the chopper into the hazy sky. They'd gone up less than a hundred yards when the ground below became obscured by smoke. The men could smell the smoke, even with the chopper's doors closed and sealed.

"Play it safe," Bolan told Grimaldi, passing along Wais's warning about the even greater visibility problems they were likely to face as they moved farther inland.

"Hey," Grimaldi joked, "aren't you the one who's always saying I could fly with my eyes closed if I had to?"

"Don't remind me," Bolan said.

"Okay, boys and girls," Grimaldi stated, setting the Sultan on a northward course, "ready or not, here we come."

CHAPTER THIRTY-TWO

Central Mountain Range,
Kalimantan Province, Indonesia

As daunting as the flying conditions were, Grimaldi soon determined that there was no uniformity to the smoky pall enshrouding the Borneo interior. Given wind currents and the proximity of the nearest blazes, there would be stretches where he could pick out a flight path that avoided the denser concentrations of smoke. It made for slower going, as he was constantly shifting course to seek out better visibility, but despite his boasting, Grimaldi wasn't foolish enough to think he could fly blindly on a straight course without courting the same fate that had apparently met the SERC's larger C-130 Hercules fire-fighting plane.

Bolan rode up front in the Sultan next to Grimaldi, helping him scout the way and passing along their coordinates by radio to the Emergency Response Corps controller orchestrating the movements of air traffic between Samarinda and the Central Mountains. The controller had already passed along the coordinates for the missing Hercules, and, as best he could, Grimaldi tried to home in on them. As it turned out, the plane had gone down less than thirty miles from the timber mill where CIA agent Herb Scoville had arranged to rendezvous with his mercenary informants. The proximity was fortuitous, because it would allow Grimaldi to pass over both areas without unduly straining the Sultan's fuel tanks. As it was, Grimaldi knew he'd be cutting it close fuel-wise given the meandering course forced upon him by the fire clouds.

In the rear cabin, meanwhile, Mochtar and Kissinger were busy cramming gear into the backpacks the men would don once their insertion point had been determined. Along with the usual items—first-aid kits, flares, walkie-talkies, canteens, spare ammo clips, topo maps and protein bars—the packs included infrared goggles for searching caves and a more lightweight version of the HAZMAT suits worn during the aborted raid on the agricultural compound.

"Tight fit," Kissinger grumbled as he stuffed the last few items into one of the packs. "Lugging all this crap I'm going to feel like Santa Claus on the first leg of Christmas Eve."

"It does seem like a lot," Mochtar agreed.

"Let's not kid ourselves, though," Kissinger was quick to add. "Odds are it'll all come in handy before we're out of this."

The men had been in the air nearly an hour when they finally found themselves close to one of the larger

fires. It was a harrowing sight. A mile-wide swath of
flames, some reaching as high as sixty feet into the air,
was burning its way up a mountain pass filled with old-
growth forest. The wind was pushing the fire up the
pass, and in its wake it had left more than eight thousand acres of rain forest blackened and denuded. All
foliage had been reduced to ash, and once proud trees
were now nothing more than charred shafts. From a
distance they looked like a discarded heap of burned
matches.

"Gives you an idea why the big firms go this route
to clear land," Bolan said. "It'd take them months to
cut down that much timber with work crews."

"You don't have to pay a fire, either," Grimaldi
replied as he banked the Sultan slightly to veer clear
of the thick, dark fire clouds rising up from the blaze.

"Some trade-off," Bolan said, eyeing the devastation.

Grimaldi veered wide of the fire and cleared the ridge,
then continued north across an emerald valley that had
been thus far spared from the fires. The surrounding
mountains served as a buffer from the smoke, and the
air over the valley was the clearest they'd seen since ar-
riving in Samarinda. Bolan checked the instrument panel
and passed along their coordinates, then took advantage
of the increased visibility and unfolded a topo map on
top of his map. For once, he could actually compare the
land below with the map and printouts of the sat-Intel
images Raki Mochtar had downloaded back at the hotel.

"We're getting close," he told Grimaldi. "You want
to cut right and head toward that peak over there. In
about a mile or so we'll come on a old logging road
that runs parallel to the river."

"I think I see it already," Grimaldi said.

"The road dead-ends at the lumber camp. We'll fly over for a quick look, then cut across the valley and see if there's any trace of the Hercules."

"Got it."

As they drifted eastward, Bolan spotted the road as well as the glittering waters of the Saralesi River. The river was far wider than the road in most places and the current seemed strong, an obvious consideration for those who'd set up the camp. As they drew closer, he could see a four-hundred-acre tract of forest that had been cleared before the mill had shut down. The land was still green, and a new generation of trees was already growing up through the undergrowth.

"Looks like they went by the rule book here and tried some reforestation," Grimaldi said. "No wonder they went out of business."

The camp itself was made up of only a few structures. A large mill was set near the river's edge, its feed chutes rusted by monsoons, and on the other side of a makeshift dirt parking lot stood a row of clapboard barracks.

"Nice place for a terrorist training camp," Grimaldi suggested as he brought the Sultan lower.

"Yeah," Bolan said, reaching for binoculars, "except you've got an access road leading right to your front door."

Grimaldi nodded. "Yeah, I guess that would be a problem."

"I could maybe see some mercenaries driving up here for a couple days, though," Bolan said. "Nice way to bone up on their woodcraft."

Kissinger and Mochtar had also brought out their field glasses and were surveying the campsite from both sides of the rear cabin.

"Looks pretty deserted," Kissinger said. "I see some tire tracks in the parking lot, but other than that..."

"Hold on." Mochtar called up to the front of the chopper. "Can you swing back toward the mill? I think I saw something over near that chute that feeds into the river."

"Will do."

Grimaldi passed over the barracks, then looped back, chasing the Sultan's faint shadow back toward the mill.

Bolan fixed his binoculars on the feed chutes, then followed their angular drop to the river's edge.

"I see it, too," he murmured. "Looks like a car."

Once Grimaldi saw the vehicle, he brought the chopper down another fifty yards and hovered in place above the chutes. The car lay on its side, halfway in the river. The framework was crumpled, as if the vehicle had rolled down the embankment before coming to a rest. Bolan looked over the vehicle, then slowly lowered his binoculars. This wasn't going to be a quick fly-over, after all. They were going to have to touch down and get out for a closer look.

He told Grimaldi and the others, "It's Scoville's Yugo."

CHAPTER THIRTY-THREE

Grimaldi set the Sultan down in the center of the timber mill's parking lot and cut the engines. He tried to radio the SERC controller back in Samarinda but was unable to make contact.

"Mountains must be blocking the signal," he guessed.

"You can try again once we're back up," Bolan said, rising from his seat.

Kissinger opened the cabin door and leaped to the ground, followed by Mochtar and Bolan. Grimaldi brought up the rear. All four men had armed themselves with M-16s; they weren't sure what to expect and weren't about to take any chances.

"This place is crawling with tread marks," Kissinger noted, eyeing the dirt lot. "Most of them look fresh."

"Same with footprints," Bolan said.

The tracks led in all directions, so the men split up. Kissinger went to check out the barracks while Mochtar and Grimaldi took the mill. Bolan, meanwhile, followed a set of tracks leading to the embankment where the Yugo had gone over. The slope was steep but the soil was loamy, cushioning Bolan's steps as he carefully made his way down. The vehicle had left deep gouges in the earth en route to the river, but the only prints leading back up from the wreckage were those made by animals: pigs from the look of it, Bolan thought.

It wasn't a good sign.

As he drew nearer to the vehicle, Bolan felt a gnawing dread at what he might find. The Yugo had clearly gone into a roll once it had gone over the side and the roof had collapsed, shattering the windows. The driver's side of the car was almost completely submerged as well, and the river rushed noisily through the passenger compartment. Bolan wasn't sure, but it seemed to him as if the Yugo had moved a few feet since he'd first spotted it from the air. The current was clearly doing all it could to wrest car from the embankment and claim it for its own.

Bolan scrambled down the last few yards to the water's edge and peered into the wreckage.

Empty. And even though the roof had flattened, there were gaps in the side windows large enough to crawl through. Bolan felt a twinge of relief. It looked as if whoever'd been inside the car had managed to escape. There was still hope.

Bolan circled the car and followed the embankment downriver another fifty yards, looking for signs that someone swam before being able to get out of the water. Again, however, none of the tracks he came across were human. Finally he reached a point where the embankment abruptly ended and was replaced by a rocky cliff that rose up sharply from the water's edge. Rather than risk the precipice, Bolan turned back, retracing his way upstream to the Yugo.

Getting back up the embankment was far more difficult than coming down, but Bolan finally made it back to level ground. Kissinger had finished searching the barracks and called out, "Not much there but some food wrappers and cigarette butts. Could have been left by anyone." When he caught up with Bolan, he added, "Behind the barracks there's a dirt road with some fresh tread marks leading into the jungle. What'd you come up with?"

Bolan quickly described what he seen down by the river.

"Let's check on the others," Kissinger suggested. "Then we can fly down the river a bit and see if anybody turns up."

The abandoned mill was a tall building with corrugated steel siding. Bolan and Kissinger followed a warped wooden ramp up to the closest entrance. Inside was a large, musty-smelling work area, two stories high and faintly illuminated by sunlight coming in through the broken windows. Most of the equipment had been removed, but there were a few benches and empty tool sheds as well as the rusting remains of a large ripsaw that had been used to trim roots and branches off logs before they were sent down chutes into the river.

"Yo, Jack! Rocky!" Kissinger called out.

"Over here," Grimaldi shouted back.

Bolan saw the pilot standing alongside Raki Mochtar at the end of the wide conveyor belt used to carry logs from the ripsaw to the chutes. They were both looking grimly at the area where the chute ran level before angling down toward the river.

As they headed over, Kissinger murmured, "Something tells me this isn't going to be pretty."

He was right.

Once they reached the chute, Bolan spotted a man's body tethered to the chute. One look at the man's lizard-skin boots, and he knew it was Herb Scoville. If not for the boots, identification would have been difficult, because the man's head was missing. Judging from a still-glistening streak of blood trailing down the chute, it was clear that the head had rolled all the way down into the river.

"Looks like he was tortured first," Grimaldi said, pointing to bruises and lacerations along Scoville's arms.

"What a way to die," Kissinger said with disgust.

Bolan stared at the body, filled with revulsion and anger.

"The question is, who did it? Mercs or Lashkar?" Grimaldi said.

Mochtar still looked a little queasy from the discovery, but he pulled himself together enough to take a closer look at what little remained of Scoville's neck.

"Beheadings aren't that uncommon in the islands,"

he told the others. "They use a *carok,* something like a cross between a machete and a hunting knife."

"Lashkar, then," Bolan said.

"Unless it was the mercs trying to throw us off their scent," Kissinger interjected.

"Any sign of Bahn?" Bolan asked Mochtar and Grimaldi.

Grimaldi shook his head. "We haven't searched the whole place yet, though."

"Let's do something about the body, then look around," Bolan suggested.

Mochtar had a folding knife, which he used it to cut through the ropes that had secured Scoville to the chute. Then the men dragged him back inside the mill. They turned one of the tool lockers on its side and placed the body inside, then closed the door and placed a bench over it to keep it secure from predators. There wasn't much more they could do, at least for the moment.

The task completed, the men silently spread out and quickly searched the rest of the mill. Coming up empty-handed, they went back outside and combed the grounds. Again, there was no trace of the female bounty hunter.

"I don't think she was in the car," Bolan stated. "I think they just drove it to the edge, then got out and let it roll down the embankment."

"Provided she came out here with Scoville, that leaves the road into the jungle," Kissinger said. "They must've taken her hostage."

Bolan fell silent. Given Scoville's grisly fate, Bolan didn't want to think about what the Lashkar might have done with a female prisoner.

"Well, we've got a decision to make," Kissinger said. "If we go looking for her, it's going to take us away from our mission, and it's not like we've got a lot of leeway time-wise."

"On the other hand," Grimaldi countered, "if the Lashkar have her, it seems like she's going to wind up at the same stronghold we're looking for. If anything, following that road lets us have it both ways."

Bolan decided on a compromise. "Let's take the bird back up," he said. "We'll fly low and follow the road as best we can. As long as it stays on course toward where the Hercules went down, we'll stick with it."

"And if it strays off course?" Kissinger asked.

For Bolan, like it or not, the decision was a no-brainer. "If the road strays off course," he said, "we stick with the mission."

CHAPTER THIRTY-FOUR

Following the road from the air was no easy task. One moment they would have it in view and the next it would disappear, concealed beneath the dense jungle canopy. Usually Grimaldi would be able to evaluate the terrain and make a guess as to where it was headed, but there were places where he proved off the mark and they would have to backtrack and circle around with Bolan, Kissinger and Mochtar all peering through the foliage with binoculars before they were able to pick up the trail. It was a slow, tedious process, and even though they continued on a general course in the direction of the downed Hercules and purported jihad strongholds, there came a point when the Sultan's dwindling fuel became the determining factor.

Grimaldi broke the news. "Sorry, Striker, but this puppy's going through fuel faster than I figured. We gotta cut back on all this bobbing and weaving."

Bolan had seen it coming. Without hesitation, he

said, "Let's call it off, then. Take us up higher and see if we can get back in radio range."

Grimaldi nodded and pulled the chopper up another two hundred feet, then veered course toward the mountains to the north. Checking the instrument panel, he told the others, "Another few miles and we'll be within range of where the Hercules went down. Keep your eyes open."

"A lot of good that'll do," Kissinger called out from the rear cabin. "This haze is getting worse the higher up we go. We aren't going to be able to see squat."

"Do the best you can," Bolan said. "If we can't establish radio contact with Samarinda, we're wasting our time."

Grimaldi took the Sultan up another thousand feet. Visibility quickly dwindled to the point where they could no longer see the ground. Bolan kept trying the radio, but all he could get was static.

"This sucks," Grimaldi vented. "Hell, you'd think in this day and age you could reach out and touch somebody from anywhere on the planet."

"We're in no-man's land," Kissinger called out from the rear cabin. "The last relay tower was probably just north of the agri-compound."

"We aren't supposed to need relay towers," Grimaldi countered. "That's what we have satellites for."

"Maybe it has something to do with the smoke," Mochtar ventured.

"Whatever it is, it sucks," Grimaldi said.

Bolan tried to make contact with Samarinda a few more times without success, then slapped the radio with frustration and cursed under his breath. Grimaldi, meanwhile, was having problems of his own with the Sultan's controls.

"Great," he grumbled. "It just keeps getting better."

"What's the problem?" Bolan asked.

"Two problems," Grimaldi said. "One, we're down to under half a tank. Even if we turn back, it's gonna be iffy whether we can make to Samarinda."

"What about the reserve tank?" Bolan asked.

"That's the second problem," Grimaldi said. "I just tried opening the line. Nada."

"The reserve tank's empty?"

"It wasn't when I checked it back at the base," Grimaldi said. "There's either a leak or some kink in the delivery line."

"Sounds like we need to make a pit stop," Kissinger called out.

Grimaldi traded a glance with Bolan. "Your call, big guy."

Bolan thought it over, then glanced over the topo maps and sat photos before making his decision.

"Let's do this," he said. "We'll make a couple of quick passes over the Hercules's last coordinates, then head over the mountains and touch down in this gorge area here where it's mostly flatland. If we've still got the extra fuel and get it to the main tanks, we'll double back to Samarinda and come up with another game plan."

"What if we're stuck running on fumes?" Grimaldi wondered.

Eyeing the map, Bolan said, "One of the possible strongholds Wais listed is a day's hike from the gorge. If we can't make it back to Samarinda, we might as well forge ahead and see what we come up with. Maybe we'll get lucky."

Kissinger laughed. "Yeah, we're really on a roll on that front."

Grimaldi took the chopper back down. The smoky haze began to thin out. The men also began to see bits of ash floating in the air like large flakes of snow. Soon they were able to make out the ground below them again. Scattered about the mountainside they saw a handful of small fires.

"Looks like they could have been started by the plane," Grimaldi said.

Bolan grabbed his binoculars and looked for signs of wreckage near where the fires had started. There weren't any. "I think it's from all this falling ash," Bolan said. "Some of the flakes floating around down there look big enough to carry a little heat."

"What's that up on the right over there?" Grimaldi said.

Bolan trained his field glasses in the direction Grimaldi was pointing. He saw a small clearing on the ridgeline where boulders had been stacked in a half-circle, then partially covered by a screen of leafy branches.

"Looks like a sentry post," he told Grimaldi.

"Anybody on watch?" Grimaldi asked.

"Not that I can see." Bolan panned with the field glasses, taking in the surrounding terrain. "The brush is pretty heavy, though, so there still might be someone down there."

"Maybe we were wrong about the Hercules," Mochtar said. "Maybe they took it out with a Stinger."

"Let's hope not," Grimaldi said. "Otherwise they're going to be looking at us for dessert."

Bolan eyed one of the small fires snaking its way along the ridgeline. It gave him an idea.

"How about if we kill two birds with one stone," he told Grimaldi. "See if you can douse that fire as we're passing over. It'll make us look legitimate if anyone's watching, and if we dump some retardant it'll lighten our load a little."

"I'll give it a shot," Grimaldi said, "but it's not like I've got a lot of experience at this. If my aim's off, it'll blow our cover."

"I have confidence in you," Bolan told him.

CHAPTER THIRTY-FIVE

It took two passes and all the chopper's retardant, but Grimaldi managed to snuff out the blaze. The feat had apparently gone unnoticed from the ground, however, as the sentry post remained untended and there were no other signs of the enemy. The others also kept an eye on the surrounding peaks for any trace of the missing Hercules C-130, but the plane remained unaccounted for.

"It still might have gone down here," Bolan said as Grimaldi crossed over the mountain, entering a valley even more sprawling and overrun by vegetation than the one they'd just crossed. "With all the clefts around here, we might have missed it."

"I don't know about that," Kissinger said. "That C-130's a big hunk of metal. If it went down around here, I think we'd know it."

"What if they were just having radio problems like us?" Raki Mochtar suggested. "I mean, for all we know, they could still be in the air and on their way back to Samarinda."

Bolan didn't think so. "Lieutenant Wais said something about the plane dropping off the radar. It has to be down here somewhere."

"Whatever the case," Grimaldi said, "the Hercules is the least of our worries right now. I'm more concerned about making sure we don't wind up stranded along with it."

The gorge Bolan had pointed out on the topo map was a deep vertical recess between the two larger peaks separating the two valleys. A three-tiered waterfall cascaded down the center of the crevasse, emptying into a small lake that, in turn, fed a series of tributaries that disappeared into the surrounding rain forest. Near the lake's edge was a half acre of grassland flat enough for Grimaldi to set the Sultan down. Once he'd shut off the chopper's engines, he tried the radio one last time but was still unable to raise a signal.

"It's going to be a few minutes at least," he told the others. "Might as well get out and stretch your legs."

The men piled out of the copter. While Grimaldi investigated the fuel situation, Bolan laid out the maps and satellite photos on a large boulder and motioned for the others to huddle around.

"Let's get our bearings." Bolan pointed to the topo map as he spoke. "The road Bio-Tain was using for its deliveries is over here, about fifty miles east of us. As you can see, everything else is pretty much rain forest."

"What about this?" Kissinger pointed to an undulating line branching off the main road far to the north.

"It's an old service road," Mochtar said. "It leads to

a limestone quarry my uncle used to work at. When it tapped out, they shut it down and tried to convert it into a transmigration settlement. Dayimatan, I think they called it."

"Tried to?" Bolan said.

"It didn't work out." Raki Mochtar went on to explain how Dayimatan had been one of countless remote areas where the government had forcibly relocated nearly nine million people from the more congested parts of the country, particularly Java, between 1969 and 1994. The quarry site had turned out to be a poor choice. "There was a lot of graft on the construction end, and the local tribes rose up in revolt once the transmigrants started moving in. There was a big massacre about ten years ago, and once they evacuated the survivors, there was talk of setting up a campground for day hikers, but the tribes wouldn't have that, either, so the government just pulled out."

"So it's another road to nowhere," Kissinger said.

Mochtar nodded. "Just like the access road to the timber mill."

"What about the tribes?" Bolan asked. "Where do they stand with the Lashkar Jihad? Are they sympathetic?"

"Not that I know of," Mochtar said. "They're mostly Muslim, but they don't have any use for politics. If the Lashkar are holed up around here, they probably just struck some sort of deal to stay out of each other's business."

"Live and let live," Kissinger interjected.

"Something like that," Mochtar said.

They were interrupted by a cursing near the Sultan. Grimaldi slammed a fist against the side of the chopper, then strode over to join the others.

"Well, campers," he announced, "it's a good thing we packed provisions."

"Bad news?" Bolan said.

"Afraid so," Grimaldi said. "Turns out the reserve tank was cocked open the whole time."

"Meaning?"

"Meaning it kept topping off the main tank until was drained out," Grimaldi explained. "That explains why the hell the needle started going down so fast when we were crisscrossing back near the timber mill."

"But we still have nearly half a tank, right?" Bolan said. "Without the retardant weighing us down, we should be able to make it back, don't you think?"

Grimaldi shook his head. "You gotta figure we used up the reserve fuel getting this far, right? That means we used up way over half a tank. Maybe even three-quarters. And the way our luck's been going, if we try to make it back we'll probably needle on empty just as we're flying over one of the fires. I'll pass on that."

Bolan checked the map. "How about if we cut over to the main road? We can follow it back until we're in radio range, then call Samarinda with our position. If the fuel gives out, we can just set down on the road and wait."

"That could work," Grimaldi said.

"Let's give it a try."

The others started back toward the chopper as Bolan

gathered up the maps. He was about to join them when he stopped suddenly.

"Hang on a second," he called out. "I think I heard something."

The others stopped outside the Sultan and listened. The sounds coming from the forest were every bit as pervasive as they'd been back in Samarinda, but soon they heard, above the natural cacophony, the faint drone of an engine. Raki Mochtar instinctively looked upward, searching through the haze for signs of a plane.

"No, I think it's coming from down on the ground," Bolan said. He stared off into the trees, trying to place the sound. It grew louder for a few seconds, then began to recede.

"Sounds a little too high-pitched for a car," Mochtar guessed. "Motorcycle maybe?"

"That or an outboard motor," Kissinger said. "Could be another one of those hydrofoils."

"Try this on for size," he speculated. "Say there was a sentry up at that post when we started coming this way. He scrambles down this side of the mountain and hops in a boat so he can spread the word."

Bolan took the map back out and glanced at it. "If that's the case, maybe Wais was right about that base camp ten miles north of here."

"And if they took your friend Bahn alive," Kissinger told Bolan, "something tells me that's where she's going to wind up."

Bolan stared into the jungle that lay before them. "There's one way to find out."

CHAPTER THIRTY-SIX

Even though the Sultan bore the SERC insignia and was clearly not a military aircraft, the men were concerned it would be too risky to fly it toward the rumored stronghold. With no fires on this side of the mountain the chopper would arouse too many suspicions. They'd braced themselves for a long hike through the forest, but the tributaries feeding out from the lake afforded an alternative and ultimately they decided that the best approach would be by water.

The men had packed an inflatable raft among their provisions. They laid the craft out on the shore and activated its built-in compressor, then returned to the Sultan for their backpacks and weapons, along with a set of oars.

"Hopefully we won't run into anyone until we're close to the camp," Bolan said, "but just in case we do, I think we should go with our suppressors."

None of the men's weapons had been originally designed for suppressors, but Kissinger had years ago used his weaponry skills to fashion lightweight housings adaptable to nearly every gun barrel in the Stony Man arsenal. Each man had a sound suppressor in his backpack, and they quickly rigged them into place.

The raft was nearly ready. While Bolan surveyed the tributaries, trying to determine which one they should take, Kissinger looked back at the waterfall they'd passed over earlier.

"Looks like the lake feeds into the mountain, too," he observed, pointing out a narrow stream gurgling just to the right of the waterfall. It seemed to pass through a small, cavelike opening in the base of the mountain.

"The mountains here are mostly all limestone," Mochtar explained. "They're hollowed out on the inside and riddled with caves."

"We ran into something like that a while back in Africa," Bolan recalled. "Turned out the Interahamwe had set up an entire camp inside one of the bigger caves and had used tunnels as a shortcut from one side of the mountain to the other."

"It wouldn't surprise me if the Lashkar have the same setup," Mochtar said. "If they're camped on this side of the mountain, it might be the way they got to the timber mill."

"If that's the case," Grimaldi said, "it's probably the way they came back, too. Maybe we ought to go that way first. Who knows, maybe we'd wind up cutting them off."

"He's got a point," Kissinger said. "I mean, we're

right here. Why traipse through that damn forest if we don't have to?"

Bolan thought it over. Scoville's body had been cold, but rigor mortis had barely set in, making it likely he hadn't been killed all that long before they'd arrived. And assuming the Lashkar Jihad was traveling by ground, there was a chance Grimaldi had overrun the terrorists in the Sultan. He turned to Mochtar.

"How much of a honeycomb are we talking about with these caves?" he asked.

Mochtar shrugged. "I can't say for sure. When my uncle used to work the quarry, he said on his days off he'd go exploring the caves and they were like a labyrinth. But that's across the valley. These mountains could be different, but not by much, I would think."

"In other words," Kissinger guessed, "there's no guarantee anybody coming back from the timber mill will wind up coming out of this particular hole in the wall."

"It's possible," Mochtar said, "but if we hiked along the base of the mountain we'd probably find a few dozen other entrances just like this one."

"That rules out staying put and hoping we can just ambush them," Grimaldi said. "But I can't see going in after them, either. One wrong turn and we'd wind up chasing dead ends."

"Look, the raft is ready," Bolan said. "I say we stick with the original game plan."

Bolan leaned forward and began to row, heading toward one of the wider tributaries that seemed to wend its way northward into the forest. The others kept an eye out on their surroundings, looking for any signs of the enemy or the missing fire plane.

Kissinger's gaze drifted back toward the cave opening he'd spotted earlier. "I'm thinking maybe we ought to reconsider going into the mountain."

"Why's that?" Bolan asked.

"Have a look yourself," Kissinger said, pointing back across the lake.

Bolan looked over his shoulder. Something had just floated out from inside the cave. They were still close enough that he didn't need binoculars to make out what it was.

CHAPTER THIRTY-SEVEN

As Bolan guided the raft closer, he saw that the corpse, lying facedown in the water, was bloated and distended. All Bolan could tell for sure was that it was a man, olive-skinned and naked, with a stab wound below the shoulder blades a few inches to the right of his spine. It was difficult to tell whether he'd been stabbed in the back or if the blade had entered through his chest and come out the other side.

"Let's turn him over." Bolan handed one of the oars to Kissinger. Once they were alongside the body, they used the oars to flip the man onto his back.

"Oh, man," Kissinger muttered.

Black leeches festooned the front of the man's body as well as his face. Much as the man's features were obscured by the bloodsuckers, Raki Mochtar was still able to make an educated guess as to the victim's nationality.

"I don't think he's Lashkar," he said. "I'd say Middle Eastern. Saudi, maybe Egyptian."

"UIF?" Grimaldi wondered.

"That'd be my guess," Kissinger said. He used his oar to move the man's hair. He was looking for a prominent birthmark along the hairline. He didn't see it. "It's not Jahf-Al," he determined.

"I didn't think it would be," Bolan said. "That'd be too convenient."

"What do you think, Rocky?" Kissinger asked, pointing his oar at the dead man's chest wound. "Did he get nailed by one of those *caroks* you were talking about?"

Mochtar leaned out over the boat for a closer look. "Hard to tell. Maybe. Could be from a stalactite, too, though."

"Stalactite?"

Mochtar nodded. "The caves are filled with them because of the moisture seeping through the limestone. Some of them are as large as gas pumps, but others are like daggers."

Bolan turned to Kissinger. "You're right. I think we better go have a look."

Kissinger handed back the oar. As Bolan rowed toward the opening, the others reached for their guns. The upper arch of the cavity rose only a few feet above the waterline, so they had to crouch low in the raft as Bolan guided it through the gap.

When they emerged on the other side, the men found themselves in a large cavern roughly the size of the CIA warehouse back in Samarinda. There was just enough light seeping in from outside for them to make out a few details. As Mochtar had explained, the upper reaches of the vault were dotted with long, tapering stalactites of various sizes and widths. Stalagmites, their bulkier counterparts, similarly rose from the ground on either side of the waterway.

There was a sudden rustling overhead. Glancing up, the men saw a formation of bats flit between the limestone spikes, then swoop past them toward the opening to the lake. Grimaldi recoiled and eyed the creatures with wary contempt. He fought back an urge to curse at them, and the others remained silent as well. Bolan worked the oars quietly, taking care not to splash them against the surface of the water. Soon they became aware of a few other sounds: water dripping from above, another stream gurgling somewhere off in one of the other passageways and—all along the ground next to them— the scuttling of large insects. Still, compared to the noise of the wildlife outside, the cavern was ominously silent.

They advanced another twenty yards into the chamber. Grimaldi, who was riding up front, pointed and whispered, "There's another one."

The others looked and saw a body floating toward them. Bolan coaxed the raft to one side, letting the corpse drift by, then blocking it with one of the oars so they could have a closer look. The dead man looked much like the other, though the light was too faint to detect any wounds. He hadn't been in the water as long, either, and only a few leeches had attached themselves to his bluing flesh.

"Looks like somebody's doing our work for us," Grimaldi stated.

"The mercs maybe," Kissinger said.

Bolan pulled the oar away. The body floated on,

bound for the mouth of the cave. Bolan resumed rowing, but soon an unmistakable fetid smell began to fill the air.

"There are more bodies somewhere," Bolan whispered.

"Yeah, but where?" Grimaldi whispered back.

Mochtar sniffed the air, grimacing at the odor. "It seems stronger off to the left."

Bolan dipped his oars back in the water and steered left. There was a sudden dull popping sound beneath the waterline, startling the men. Up in front, Grimaldi could feel the raft beginning to deflate.

"Must've hit one of those damn stalagmites," he guessed.

Bolan poked his oar straight down into the water. It quickly touched bottom. "It's only a few feet deep," he told the others. "Everybody out, but be careful. There's more of them just below the surface."

Quietly, the men climbed out and waded ashore, dragging the raft behind them. The insects scattered wildly in all directions, some taking wing. All the while the raft continued to shrink, giving off a snakelike hiss. Kissinger inspected the hole.

"One nasty gash," he said, "but it should be easy enough to patch."

"We'll worry about it later," Bolan said.

They left the raft and ventured toward a series of passageways to their left. The ground was slick beneath their feet, and they moved slowly to avoid falling onto the sharp stalagmites that rose from the ground at irregular intervals on either side of them.

The stench grew stronger until there was no question which of the shafts to investigate. Grimaldi paused before the opening and looked back at Bolan.

"It's pitch-black in there," he said. "What do we use, flares or goggles?"

Not sure what might be waiting for them in the tunnel, Bolan wasn't about to make the same mistake as the jihad forces back in the Samarinda rain forest.

"Goggles," he said. "No sense advertising ourselves any more than we have to."

The men paused long enough to raid their backpacks and don the infrared goggles. With little ambient light to amplify, however, the spectacles were even less effective than they would have been outside in the dead of night. The men had to give themselves a few minutes for their eyes to adjust. As they waited, Mochtar fished through his pack for his HAZMAT mask and suggested the others do the same.

"I know it's a tight fit over the goggles," he said, "but it'll cut down on the smell."

"Good thinking, Rock," Grimaldi told him.

Once they were ready to proceed, Bolan grabbed his Desert Eagle and led the way down the passage. The ground pitched upward slightly for a few yards before leveling off, forcing them to move with even more caution. Soon clouds of insects began to swarm around them, ignoring all attempts to wave them away. Several times Bolan paused and held the men back, allowing snakes to slither across the dirt path ahead of them.

"The masks were a nice idea," Kissinger muttered, "but it still stinks like hell."

"Here's the reason why," Bolan said, bringing the

column to a halt near the mouth of a yet another passageway. He moved to one side, giving the others a chance to peer into the opening, which led to a grotto with a low ceiling free of stalactites.

"Man, I don't believe it," Kissinger said.

Piled high on the ground in the center of the grotto were more corpses, at least twenty of them. In the dark it was difficult for the men to make out any details, even with their goggles, but none of them was in a rush to enter the enclosure. They all hung back in the tunnel, waiting on Bolan's next move.

"I'm going to risk a flare," Bolan said finally. He reached behind him and pulled one from a side pocket in his backpack.

"Hold off until we take off these peepers," Grimaldi told him.

"Go ahead," Bolan told the others, "but hold your breath and get the masks back on as quick as you can."

Bolan fired up the flare and held it at arm's length, squinting against the sudden brightness. He waited a few moments, then strode into the grotto, torch held high to better illuminate the entire enclosure. The glare made everything even more hideous.

The bodies lay in a heap, all in the same state of decomposition. It looked as if most of the men had been stabbed, but there were gunshot wounds as well. A few of the corpses were missing their heads.

"Whoever did these guys wasted Scoville, too," Grimaldi guessed, stepping past Bolan for a closer look. "Same swipe with that *carok* knife."

"Not necessarily," Mochtar said. "Remember, I said

beheading is common in these parts, and it's nearly always done the same way. This could have been done by someone who never laid eyes on Scoville."

Kissinger stepped around the bodies, checking the back of the grotto. "There's a drop-off back here," he said. He kicked a few stones over the side and heard them splash into water. "Must lead back down to the stream."

"Those other guys must've rolled off the heap and dropped into the water."

Leeches hadn't gotten to the bodies yet, but the corpses were crawling with insects. Bolan moved in for a closer look and waved the bugs away, inspecting those few faces exposed to the torchlight. "They're UIF, all right," he said.

"You recognize them?" Mochtar asked.

"That one," Bolan said, pointing to one of the older victims, a hawk-nosed man in his late forties with silvery hair and a matching beard. He was one of those killed by gunfire, with a mottled hole the size of a quarter just below his right temple. "Akhmed Karno. Head of Jahf-Al's personal security force."

"Which is probably who the rest of these guys are, then," Grimaldi said.

Bolan nodded.

"You know what this means, don't you?" Kissinger said.

Bolan wedged the flare in a crevasse and unslung his backpack. "Get some gloves on," he told the others. "We need to sort through these bodies and see if we've got our man."

CHAPTER THIRTY-EIGHT

"He's not here," Kissinger said once they'd completed their grisly task. "Unless he's one of the ones missing a head."

"Or he could've dropped into the stream," Grimaldi said, stepping back from the bodies. The flare was nearly out, and the small cave was growing dark.

"We can check the lake," Bolan said, "but I don't think we're going to find him."

"You think the Lashkar took him prisoner?" Raki Mochtar asked.

"Yeah," Bolan said. "Why, I'm not sure."

"Power struggle," Kissinger guessed. "We know Jahf-Al and Pohtoh had a rivalry going back to their time in Afghanistan. Could be push came to shove, and Pohtoh came out on top."

"Whatever the case, it doesn't change the mission," Bolan said, reaching for his goggles. "Let's get back to the raft."

Bolan still tried to get a handle on the meaning of

their discovery. "I can understand Pohtoh butting heads with Jahf-Al, but to pull something like this...he won't be able to get away with it. Once word gets out, the rest of the UIF will retaliate, and they'll come down harder on him than we would. It's like he cut off his nose to spite his face."

"Crime of passion," Grimaldi guessed. "Things get heated enough, you don't think about the consequences."

"This whole thing sheds another light on that fax that came in after the consulate was hit," Bolan said. "If Jahf-Al's been taken out, no wonder they had to paste together that message of his."

"The question is, if the Lashkar Jihad set the bomb, why pin it on Jahf-Al?" Kissinger asked. "From what I know of Pohtoh, he'd jump at the chance to take all the credit."

"Maybe it's damage control," Bolan speculated. "Maybe Pohtoh's trying to cover up what happened here, at least until he can figure out his next move."

"One thing's for sure," Grimaldi said. "Whether it's at that camp up the river or another stronghold, Pohtoh is somewhere in this valley, and if he's holding Jahf-Al prisoner, that gives us a chance to trim that Ten Most Wanted list down to eight."

Mochtar had been silent, and when Bolan glanced over his shoulder, he saw the medic standing a few yards back from the others, looking the other way.

"Rocky?"

Mochtar turned, finger to his lips. He was pointing back the way they'd just come. The other men fell silent and backtracked to Mochtar's side. Soon they heard it, too.

"Another engine," Bolan whispered. His hand went instinctively to his holster, fingers closing around the butt of his .44.

"It's coming from somewhere past the grotto," Mochtar said.

"A car," Grimaldi guessed. "Maybe a truck."

The drone continued, echoing through the passageway, getting louder. The men drew their guns and followed the sound. As they passed the grotto, Bolan ducked in long enough to quietly stomp out the dying flare.

The tunnel went on for another fifty yards before reaching a junction where it split off in three different directions. The men hesitated, trying to determine which one the sound was coming from. Mochtar finally pointed to his right, then led the men down the smallest of the three shafts.

The offshoot quickly narrowed and stalactites began to appear, forcing the men to first crouch, then crawl on all fours through a thick layer of slime. The passageway curved several times, angling upward and continually shrinking to a point where the stalactites disappeared.

Eventually the tunnel narrowed to an opening barely large enough to squeeze through, one man at a time. Mochtar, leading the way now, found it increasingly difficult to make headway, forcing all four men to inch their way along. Up ahead the droning continued and seemed to be growing louder. As he waited for the others to move ahead of him, Bolan ran one hand along the surrounding rock. It felt scalloped, as if the opening had been chiseled out by hand.

Soon all four men found themselves enclosed on all sides within the cramped shaft, and Bolan began to worry that they'd wandered into a trap. Caught in such close quarters, it would be impossible for them to defend themselves from attack. He considered calling a retreat but decided against it. They were making enough noise as it was. Calling out to the others, even in a whisper, would only draw more attention to themselves.

The shaft continued to angle upward, and after another twenty yards it began to widen again. Bolan was now able to see past the others, and he saw what appeared to be a swatch of light. He saw Mochtar slowly rise to a crouch, then move out of view, followed by Kissinger and Grimaldi. There could be no mistaking it now. Whatever lay beyond the bend the men had taken had a light source of some kind.

Bolan slid his infrared goggles onto his forehead and crawled the last few yards to where the others had disappeared. He saw them crouched together a few feet away on a rock ledge overlooking another large cavern, twice the size of the one they'd first encountered when entering the mountain. And the sound of the car engine was no longer muffled; it echoed loudly off the walls of the cave. More than a hundred feet above them there was a wide opening. Light filtered down through the opening, revealing a long rope ladder that extended all the way to the cavern floor, some twenty feet below them. Bolan wondered if the opening led to the sentry post they'd seen from the air earlier.

At ground level a well-worn dirt roadway ran down the middle of the cavern and reached back into a large tunnel that seemed to lead toward the center of the mountain. The men couldn't see the approaching vehicle, but it sounded as if it would appear on the roadway any second.

Kissinger suddenly tapped Bolan's shoulder and pointed in the other direction. The soldier turned his head looked down at the cavern floor. Forty yards away, set in haphazard rows amid a cluster of thick stalagmites, were more than two dozen large, heavy plastic containers stenciled with biohazard warnings.

CHAPTER THIRTY-NINE

Bolan had no time to reflect on their discovery.

He was still staring at the much-sought containers when an angry cry suddenly echoed throughout the cavern. Startled, Bolan whirled to his right and saw two bearded men in white robes staring up at him and the others.

One of the robed men raised an assault rifle and took aim.

"Down!" Bolan warned the others, even as he was dropping flat against the rock shelf.

A burst of gunfire thundered loudly in the cavern, drowning out the sound of the approaching vehicle. Bullets chipped away at the limestone around Bolan and his companions. Grimaldi winced as one of the shards glanced off his leg.

The second Lashkar gunner shouted at his associate and shoved him hard against the rock facing. The reprimand came too late, however. The gunshots' reverberations echoed so forcefully throughout the cavern that stalactites of all sizes began to snap free and plummet.

Bolan and the others cringed as the stalactites fell past them. They were saved from being impaled or crushed several times when another ledge, several yards directly above them, deflected the falling shafts. The ledge they were huddled on quaked beneath them from the relentless hammering of stone against stone.

One of the plunging columns thudded into the dirt within a few yards of the pesticides. When it toppled onto its side, it clipped two of the containers, knocking them over. It was impossible to know if the seals had broken, because clouds of pulverized limestone had begun to rise from the ground.

"Masks!" Mochtar called out to the others.

"Screw the masks!" Bolan shouted. He wasn't about to call for a retreat, either. There was no way he was going have them crawl back into the cramped passageway that had brought them to the cavern. Instead, he brought his Desert Eagle into play, peering through the dust and squeezing off several rounds, thankful for the suppressor, which negated the odds he would bring down still more of the stalactites. The gunman who'd fired at them went down while the other retreated farther into the mouth of the passageway where he'd already fled to avoid the deadly downpour. Kissinger had a better angle on the second man and quickly dispatched him with a muffled round from his Colt.

Other Lashkar soldiers soon appeared, some emerging from other openings both on the ground and along

the rounded cavern walls across from where the Stony
Man warriors were huddled. Up above men began to
scramble down the rope ladder. Several spotted Bolan
and the others and instinctively fired at them, once
more loosening spires from overhead. Sharp bits of
falling rock had already hacked away the rope, and as
the men scaled their way downward, their cumulative
weight brought down nearly half the ladder and three
men along with it. Grimaldi and Mochtar finished off
the rest with bursts from their weapons while Bolan
and Kissinger continued to fire at those who'd appeared at the lower levels.

In the midst of all the chaos, Bolan finally spotted
the vehicle they'd heard earlier. It was a camou-painted
Hummer. It had come to a stop forty yards away at the
mouth of the tunnel leading from the center of the
mountain. A fallen stalactite had blocked its path. Two
men got out of the front seat and rushed forward with
assault rifles to investigate the disruption inside the
cavern.

Bolan was lining up one of them in the sights of his
.44 when another Lashkar gunner suddenly rose into
view directly in front of him, brandishing a long-bladed
knife. Though he was taken by surprise, Bolan managed to shoot, but not before the terrorist had a chance
to lash out with the weapon. Bolan felt a sharp, jabbing
pain as the blade struck his head. His night goggles,
still propped on his forehead, flew off, having taken the
worst of the blow. His head was still tender from the
incident with the truck on the streets of Samarinda, and

a white flash of pain shot through his head. This time, however, he managed to remain conscious.

Shaking off his pain, Bolan crept forward and peered over the edge. He saw a series of chiseled incisions cutting into the rock wall leading up to the ledge.

"I'm going down," he told the others, wriggling out of his backpack. "Cover me."

Grimaldi nodded, then quickly shifted his attention to the upper reaches. Two more gunmen stood in silhouette before the opening to the outer mountain. The Stony Man pilot fired and one of the men pitched forward, free-falling to his death on the cavern floor. The other ducked to one side and fired back, pelting the rock behind Grimaldi and the others. Kissinger and Mochtar both triggered their guns at the same time, and the second man high dived through the opening, landing a few yards next to his comrade.

Once over the ledge, Bolan carefully lowered himself down the chiseled rungs, gun in hand. He'd made it halfway down when gunshots kissed off the rocks just to his right. He pressed himself against the facing, supporting his weight with his feet and left hand, freeing his right to fire his Desert Eagle at a gunman crouched in the rubble behind a pair of half-severed stalagmites. He had to empty the .44 but finally the other man sagged to one side and slumped into the debris.

Once he reached the ground, Bolan was able to see the stretch of cavern wall that had been shielded from view when he'd been up on the ledge. Set into a wide recess was a wood-framed work station filled with work benches, laboratory equipment and a long rack of full-body HAZMAT suits. Bolan suspected this was where the bomb that had spread toxic death throughout the consulate had been manufactured.

The din inside the cavern began to fade, as did the clouds of dust. Bolan grabbed one of the fallen Lashkar hardmen's Uzis and cautiously began to circle the cavern. Kissinger and the others made their way down from the ledge and joined him. There was no sign of survivors amid the rubble, but they kept a wary eye on all the various passageways.

"Looks like the lieutenant's calculations were a little off," Kissinger whispered as he took in the laboratory and stockpiled herbicides. "If this isn't a stronghold, I don't know what is."

Bolan eyed the slain attackers lying around them. "Check the bodies for Jahf-Al and Pohtoh," he told the others. "I want to have a look at the Hummer."

The Executioner stepped carefully around the fallen stalactites, making his way toward the vehicle. As he passed through the dim shaft of daylight, he glanced up, making sure no one else had appeared at the opening. Once he reached the Hummer, he trained his Uzi on the windows and carefully circled the vehicle. The windows were tinted, so he couldn't tell if anyone was still inside. The driver's-side door was open, however, and as he walked by he could see that the front cabin was vacant. He circled to the back and slowly closed his fingers around the rear door handle, then quickly yanked it open, finger on the Uzi's trigger.

There was movement inside the Hummer, but Bolan held his fire.

Crouched before him, ankles bound and wrists tied behind her back, was Jayne Bahn. Her mouth had been duct-taped.

She wasn't alone.

Directly behind her was a Lashkar hardman, using her as a human shield. The man had his *carok* pressed against Bahn's throat.

CHAPTER FORTY

"Let her go," Bolan commanded.

"I will not hurt her," the other man responded. Though he spoke with a pronounced accent, his English was clearly understandable.

"Let her go," Bolan repeated.

"I am on your side now," the man pleaded. He was in his mid-twenties, wild-haired, and though he sported a beard it was shorter than most of the other Lashkar soldiers and better groomed. He stared intently at Bolan and slowly removed the knife from Bahn's throat. "I can help you."

Bolan shifted his gaze to Bahn. Her face was bruised, and most of the buttons had been torn loose from her shirt. Whatever they had done to her, they hadn't broken her spirit. She gestured at the man behind her, then nodded at Bolan. When he pried the tape from her lips, she winced, then told him, "I walk out on you and you still come to the rescue. That's gallantry for you."

Bolan was in no mood for wisecracks. He held out his hand to the other man, indicating that he wanted the *carok*. As the terrorist handed over the weapon, Bolan asked Bahn, "Is he telling the truth?"

"Yeah," she replied. "I think so."

Bolan eyed the man suspiciously. As he began to interrogate him, he used the knife to cut Bahn's binds. "If you're on our side, why did you keep her in here instead of getting out and helping us?"

"I could not see you," the other man said. "I thought maybe you were UIF. I thought you were retaliating for what happened to Jahf-Al's men."

"What was that about?"

"Pohtoh's arrogance. That's what it was about." There was an edge of bitterness in the man's voice. "He cares nothing about Islam or the cause of our people. He cares only about Moamar Pohtoh."

Bolan helped Bahn out of the vehicle and told the prisoner to follow with his hands over his head. The man complied.

"Did Pohtoh kill Jahf-Al along with the others?" Bolan asked.

The man shook his head. "No, Jahf-Al is still alive, but his days are numbered."

"There's a plan to kill him," Bahn interjected, rubbing her chafed wrists. "I don't know the details, but I heard some of them talking and they want to off him in a way that makes it look like our doing."

"For propaganda?" Bolan wondered.

"Probably," she replied.

Bahn stared at the body of the Hummer driver for a moment, then shuddered. Quickly regaining her composure, she told Bolan, "I'd suggest we find a way out of here, fast, and haul ass to the camp in Dayimatan before they can get their plane off the ground."

"What plane?"

"A fire-fighting plane," the prisoner said. "From search and rescue in Samarinda."

"That plane went down," Bolan said.

The prisoner shook his head. "No. We had men stow away on board in Samarinda. They took it over once it had flown beyond radio range, then they flew it to Dayimatan. At least that was their plan."

"For what reason?" Bolan wanted to know.

"They are going to empty the retardant and replace it with chemicals. The ones the government was trying to get rid of." He pointed past Bolan at the containers set back deep in the cave. "They took three times as much as is stored here, maybe more."

For Bolan, the pieces were starting to fit. "They're going to dump poison into the smoke clouds drifting toward Jakarta," he guessed.

"Some of it, yes," the prisoner said. "They are not sure it will work, so the rest they will fly into Jakarta directly. With all the fires, they think no one will be suspicious of the plane until it is too late."

"Too late for what?"

"They want to do like the World Trade Center," the prisoner explained. "They want to fly the plane into the parliament while it is in session."

CHAPTER FORTY-ONE

Even with the Hummer's four-wheel-drive, it was impossible to get past the crumbled remains of stalactites blanketing the cave floor, but the prisoner knew of an alternative route, and nearly twenty minutes after the Stony Man warriors had completed their inspection, they were back out in open air. Dusk was falling and the setting sun had turned the smoke clouds an appropriately fiery red. Grimaldi was at the wheel with Kissinger riding shotgun, while Bolan and Jayne Bahn sat in the rear. On the bench seat in between, Raki Mochtar sat across from the prisoner, whose hands had been secured behind his back. As an added precaution, both Mochtar and Bolan had their guns out. Much as they wanted to believe they'd finally gotten their hands on a cooperative member of the Lashkar Jihad, the precautions seemed necessary.

Bolan interrogated the prisoner as they made their way through the forest, taking the same, lone dirt road that linked Dayimatan with the lumber camp where Herb Scoville had been beheaded.

The prisoner said his name was Wahid Ma'ruf. He claimed that he, like so many other young men in Indonesia, joined the Lashkar Jihad as a disaffected youth from an underprivileged family. Unlike the others, however, he was fervent in his belief in Islam and had been drawn not so much to the criminal allure of the terrorist group as their purported ideology. He had reluctantly bought into the Lashkar's bloody campaigns against Christians in Sulawesi and the Mollucas, rationalizing them as an unfortunate but necessary means to a greater end. Once the Lashkar had begun to swell its ranks by assimilating other, even more violent groups, Ma'ruf had come to realize that military and political concerns far outweighed any religious considerations. By then, however, he'd felt it was too late for him to bow out of the organization. He'd risen too far in the ranks and knew too much to be allowed to just walk away. Several close friends had made such a choice, only to be tortured and murdered in front of their peers as a warning against desertion.

And so he had served as best he could, trying not to draw attention to himself and, whenever possible, wrangling his way out of any assignment or mission likely to involve bloodshed or other acts contrary to his understanding of the Koran. His mastery of English—self-taught during his teen years as a con artist swindling tourists in Yalim—made him valuable to Moamar Pohtoh, earning him a place, if not in the Lashkar leader's inner circle, at least in the immediate periphery.

The more time he spent around Pohtoh, the more Ma'ruf had come to see the man as self-aggrandizing and power hungry, and the more he'd become disillusioned with the entire Lashkar Jihad. He'd kept his misgivings to himself, however.

Less than a week ago, Ma'ruf had been part of the group that helped smuggle Hamed Jahf-Al into the country after his flight from Islamabad. Jahf-Al, the prisoner explained, had shaved his beard and used makeup to cover the telltale birthmark on his forehead, then disguised himself as part of an air-courier team flying derrick supplies to the oil fields in Muara Badak, just north of Samarinda. From there, the Nile Viper had been transported to his current hideout in Dayimatan. The old quarry site, with its isolated location and network of underground tunnels, had apparently been a primary training site for the Lashkar Jihad since its inception, and at present Ma'ruf estimated that at any given time up to seven hundred men were based there.

Ma'ruf, who'd received pilot's training during his early years with the Lashkar, had flown the plane that brought Jahf-Al to Dayimatan. His first impression of the Nile Viper had not been favorable. He'd found Jahf-Al to be a kindred spirit to Pohtoh, equally brash and conceited, equally quick to preach violence as the only viable means of achieving his objectives. Though he was never present at the so-called "summit meetings" between the two leaders in Dayimatan, Ma'ruf had heard secondhand that the first few days of talks, centered around their mutual goals and ideologies, had gone well. Once they'd gotten down to particulars, however, it had become clear that Jahf-Al and Pohtoh were of two minds, each feeling he should have the final say on any plans for increased Islamic militancy throughout the Indonesian archipelago. The previous day's meeting had been reduced to a shouting match, with the two men nearly coming to blows. Afterward, Pohtoh had conferred with his top aides and then come forth with an apology, acknowledging that in recent weeks the UIF had been instrumental in helping the Lashkar Jihad win its string of victories against governmental forces trying to clamp down on the group's activities. He had extended the olive branch to Jahf-Al, agreeing to let the Egyptian direct strategy in stepped-up attempts to strike decisive blows against both the Indonesian government and its Western allies, particularly the United States.

Ma'ruf claimed he'd been suspicious of Pohtoh's quick turnaround, and this day's events had confirmed his suspicions. Invited to tour the mountain facilities where Iman Agung had assembled the aerosol bomb that would soon go off inside the U.S. consulate in Samarinda, Jahf-Al arrived early that morning with his security entourage, wandering into an ambush that took place inside the mountain caverns just as the first news of the consulate bombing had begun to spread.

Ma'ruf had not been present for the killings. Against his will, Pohtoh had assigned him to accompany a pair of assassins to a lumber mill where they, in turn, planned to ambush a CIA officer who was under the impression he was making follow-up contact with some American soldiers the Lashkar Jihad was attempting to recruit for a top-secret mission. With his English-speaking background, Ma'ruf was to help with the interrogation before the American was executed.

"Herb told me about the meeting when he showed up at the restaurant a few minutes after you'd left," Jayne Bahn told Bolan, picking up the story. By now they'd been on the road for nearly an hour. The sun was down and the Hummer's front beams lit the way before them, illuminating the rain forest around them and drawing a steady stream of flying insects and large moths with wings the size of table tennis paddles. They had already passed the site Lieutenant Wais had pegged as a possible Lashkar stronghold. The camp had been abandoned several weeks ago in favor of the mountain facility, which had been determined to be a better storage area for the diverted pesticides. It would be at least three hours before they reached Dayimatan.

Bahn explained that Scoville told her the mercenaries were the same men who'd thwarted the al-Arqam kidnapping in the Philippines and that they'd fabricated a supposed rift with the U.S. senators to make it easier for them to infiltrate the Lashkar Jihad.

"I talked him into letting me come along for the rendezvous," she went on. "We left at around eleven, because Herb said we'd have to drive through the night to reach the timber mill. I'd thought about leaving a message, but Herb was worried that if you knew we were going he'd suddenly have a small army on his hands."

"He was probably right," Bolan conceded. "Of course, if he'd told us he'd probably be alive right now, too."

Bahn had no answer for that. She continued, "We showed up at the mill right on schedule and went to meet the mercenaries at one of the barracks. Herb said they'd camped out there because it was close to the spot where they'd been meeting up with the jihad recruiters."

"Not very smart," Kissinger called out from the front seat. Like Grimaldi and Mochtar, he'd been silent since they'd set out from the caves, listening to Ma'ruf's interrogation. "Hell, the Lashkar were probably skulking in the brush the first time Scoville met with the guys."

"Do you mind?" Bahn snapped irritably. "The man's dead, for Christ's sake! Show a little respect."

Kissinger traded a look with Grimaldi and once again fell silent.

Bolan guessed what had happened next. "When you reached the barracks, the mercenaries weren't there."

Bahn shook her head. "No, they weren't. We had our guns out, but Pohtoh's goons got the jump on us. I tried to put up a fight but got clobbered over the back of the head and passed out." She hesitated a moment, her fingers reflexively grabbing at her buttonless shirt. Her voice stiffened slightly. "When I came to, Ma'ruf here was pulling one of the goons off me."

"What he was doing was wrong," Ma'ruf interjected. "For me, it was the last straw."

"Good for you," Mochtar piped in for the first time.

"The goon pulled a gun on Ma'ruf and laughed at him," Bahn continued. "I saw an opening and tried to take the guy out with a karate kick, but..." She paused, taking a deep swallow, then added, "Anyway, I couldn't get him off me. That's when I got this shiner. I kept trying to fight him off, but—"

"You don't need to go into that if you don't want to," Bolan interrupted.

Bahn sighed and looked out the window a moment. "Afterward, he dragged me to my feet and put the tape around my mouth, then tied my hands and led me to the mill. Ma'ruf came with us and he kept yelling at this creep, but the guy just laughed back at him."

"Because he was the one with the gun," Ma'ruf said angrily. "They are all like that. They think because they have the gun they can do and say what they like."

"Unfortunately, they're usually right," Bolan said.

"The other goon was just as much of an animal," Bahn said. "He had Herb tied to the chute and was already cutting him. They didn't tie me down next to him because Herb had told them I was just some floozy he'd picked up. I couldn't believe they went for it."

"It's because you're a woman," Ma'ruf said. "It was easier for them to believe him than think you might actually be important enough to have information."

"That, plus the fact they wanted to take me back and peddle me around to the rest of the gang." Bahn glanced at Ma'ruf, then back at Bolan. "That's what saved me. Ma'ruf convinced them I was more useful to them alive than dead."

"I played to their weakness," Ma'ruf said. "It was the only way I thought it would work. But the things I said... I am ashamed."

"It's called acting," Bahn assured him. "I know you didn't mean it."

"What about the interrogation?" Bolan asked.

"They told me what to ask him," Ma'ruf said, "but I knew they didn't understand any English, so I just told him how sorry I was. That I was a coward for not trying to do more to stop what was happening."

"They tell you to interrogate the guy and instead you wind up being the one who's confessing?" Kissinger said.

"I should have done more," Ma'ruf repeated. "But that is what has become of me. Always afraid, always a coward."

The prisoner stared down at his feet and fell into an abject silence.

"Herb played along," Bahn said, getting back to what had happened. "He pretended he was being asked all these incriminating questions, and he gave Ma'ruf hell, but not nearly as much as he did the other two."

"How so?" Bolan wondered.

"Well, like most people, the first words Herb picked up when he got stationed here were all the profanities," she said. "He knew them all, and when he wasn't chewing out Ma'ruf, he was letting the goons have it with both barrels. When he saw it was getting to them, he laid it on even thicker. They cut him some more, thinking it'd shut him up, but he kept going on."

"He was baiting them," Bolan guessed. "So they'd kill him before they could get him to talk."

Bahn nodded. "Finally they'd had enough and one of them just off and whacked him. I didn't see it coming and... God, I tell you, I wish to hell I had, because I'm going to spend the rest of my life seeing his head go down that slide to the river."

CHAPTER FORTY-TWO

As the Hummer continued to make its way through the forest, they had several encounters with animals that had strayed onto the road. Twice it was bearded pigs who blocked their way, another time an orangutan that Grimaldi at first mistook for human. In each case, Grimaldi had only to flash his brights to scare the creatures off. Eventually, he was forced to slow again as he spotted a thick, oblong object lying at an angle across the road, blocking their way.

"Log," Grimaldi said. "Cowboy, you want to hop out and do the honors?"

"Will do."

Kissinger had opened his door and was about to climb out when Ma'ruf told him, "That would not be a good idea."

"Why not?"

"Take a closer look," he said. "It is not a log."

Grimaldi flashed his brights on the obstruction. "Son of a gun," he said. "You're right. It's a crocodile."

The reptile was huge, more than fifteen feet long and weighing half a ton. It was facing away from the truck and showed no signs that it was about to move.

"They come up from the swamp sometimes when they are hungry," Ma'ruf explained. "If that is the case, I would advise against provoking it. It would be likely to attack."

"Enough said," Kissinger said, quietly closing the door. "I think I'll just stay put."

Grimaldi tried flashing his brights, then turned the headlights off and on a few times in quick succession. The crocodile showed no signs of moving.

"Maybe it's asleep," Mochtar said.

"What do we do, then?" Grimaldi wondered. "I don't feel like trying to run him over."

"It probably wouldn't work, anyway," Bahn warned.

"We could shoot it," Kissinger suggested.

"I don't think a handgun would do it," Bolan said. "And I don't want to risk using the assault rifles."

"We have to do something," Grimaldi said. "The clock's ticking. We can't afford to twiddle our thumbs waiting for it to move."

"Maybe he just can't see the headlights." Bolan reached for his backpack, pulling out the last of his flares. "Let's try throwing this ahead of him."

"Might work," Grimaldi said. "Who wants to get out and try it?"

"Use the sunroof," Bolan said, passing the flare to Mochtar, who in turn handed it to Kissinger.

"Much better idea," Grimaldi said. He powered the

window back and Kissinger rose through the opening. Once he'd activated the flare, Kissinger hurled it a good twenty yards past the crocodile, leaving in its wake an arc of sparks that drifted slowly down toward the road.

Whether it was the sparks or the flare itself, the ploy succeeded. The crocodile stirred, then slowly began to crawl away from the road, turning away from the bright glow of the flare. On a hunch, Grimaldi quickly turned off his headlights as well as the Hummer's engine, not wanting to draw the creature's attention.

He wasn't quick enough.

One moment it looked as if the crocodile was going to shuffle its way back to the swamp without incident, the next, it suddenly veered and scrambled toward the Hummer with a speed that took Grimaldi by surprise. Before he had a chance to react, the Hummer shook violently and rolled backward a few feet. Kissinger was nearly knocked off his feet. He quickly dropped back into his seat as the crocodile struck again, once more plowing its broad snout into the vehicle's front end. Again the Hummer trembled and rolled.

"Sucker thinks we're a can of sardines," Kissinger said.

Grimaldi switched on the lights and started the engine, hoping to give the croc second thoughts, but it only seemed to antagonize the creature more. Again it lunged at the Hummer, this time taking out one of the headlights. Steam began to drift up from under the hood.

"He got the radiator," Kissinger said.

It turned out the crocodile had also rammed the quarter panel tightly against the right front tire, because when Grimaldi threw the Hummer into reverse and tried to back up, the vehicle began to fishtail sideways on the loose dirt road. Grimaldi quickly took his foot off the gas.

"We've got a problem," he told the others.

"No shit," Kissinger muttered.

"We need to take him out," Bolan decided, reaching for one of the M-16s.

"How?" Mochtar asked. "We can barely see him now." Indeed, all anyone could see of the crocodile as it launched yet another assault was its tail and hindquarters.

Bolan was going to hand the assault rifle to Kissinger, but he doubted Cowboy could get a good angle on the reptile from the sunroof. And even if he could, the beast was butting the Hummer so relentlessly there'd be little chance of getting off an accurate shot.

Between attacks, Bolan moved past Bahn and threw open the rear door.

"Are you insane?" she called after him. But Bolan was already outside, slamming the door shut behind him.

Bolan carefully circled the Hummer, taking a step back as the vehicle jolted his way under the force of the next charge. As he neared the front of the vehicle, he heard the rear door open again. Bahn got out, car-

rying another of the M-16s, and Mochtar was crawling past Ma'ruf into the rear so that he could do the
same.

"Get back inside!" Bolan shouted.

"Not a chance!" Bahn retorted.

Bolan knew it was pointless to argue. He waited for
her and Mochtar to catch up with him, then they inched
closer toward the front of the Hummer, which, at the
same time, continued to inch backward each time the
croc pounded the front end.

Finally Bolan could see the croc fully in the one remaining headlight. It struck the Hummer, then dropped
to the road only long enough to coil its squat legs for
the next lunge. The beast's snout was bloody, but it
showed no signs of weakening or letting up.

"Aim for the head," Bolan advised, raising his rifle.

"What head?" Bahn said. "All I see are jaws."

"The light's reflecting off its eyes," Bolan said.
"Aim there. On three."

Mochtar joined them in drawing a bead on their
reptilian target.

"One..." Bolan murmured, lining his sights on the
beast. "Two..."

Once the croc had rammed the Hummer again and
dropped back to the ground, Bolan shouted, "Three!"

In unison, the three M-16s rattled. The croc recoiled
slightly as the rounds plowed into it. Then, undaunted,
it turned on its attackers and widened its jaws, giving
Bolan and the others a good look at its razor-sharp teeth.
Without letting up on the trigger, Bolan shifted aim and

fired into the beast's mouth. The beast let out a loud roar and began to charge forward. Enough of the rounds found their mark, however, and as it tried to lunge upward, its legs gave out and the beast lurched to the ground, landing a few yards short of its mark. Bolan and the others had instinctively stepped back, and they continued to fire into the croc until they were sure it was dead. Even then, they continued to give the beast a wide berth.

Bahn looked out into the surrounding rain forest. "Please tell me they don't travel in packs."

CHAPTER FORTY-THREE

It took all of their combined effort, but Bolan, Kissinger and Mochtar managed to drag the dead beast off the road and into the brush. Bahn stood watch a few yards away, rifle braced at the ready. No other crocodiles appeared, however.

Once the men were finished, they paused to catch their breath. Kissinger glanced down at the huge reptile with renewed wonder.

"Hell," he said, "you could make enough boots and wallets out of this guy to open your own store."

"The tribes around here use the leather for shields and roofing for their huts," Mochtar said.

"I understand the shield part," Kissinger said. "That hide's gotta be the toughest thing this side of Kevlar."

Bahn agreed. "I can't believe how many shots it took to bring him down."

Bolan wandered over to Hummer. The hood was up and Grimaldi stood before the mangled front end, a flashlight propped to one side so he could see what he was doing.

"How's the radiator?"

"Got her plugged," Grimaldi said. "Took all our canteens to refill it, though, and without any additives there's still a risk of overheating."

"That's a chance we'll have to take," Bolan said. "We need to move on before anybody comes looking to see what all the shooting was about."

"Almost there," Grimaldi said, lowering the hood. Ma'ruf had made himself useful, prying the crumpled quarter panel off the front wheel with a tire jack. He stood back as Grimaldi shone the flashlight on the tire, making sure the treads were still intact. Satisfied, he called out to the others, "Okay, we're out of here."

Once they were all back inside the vehicle, Grimaldi keyed the ignition and listened to the engine. He didn't like what he heard.

"Not running all that smoothly," he said.

"The way it got knocked around, I'm amazed it's running, period," Kissinger said.

"Well, here goes nothing..." Grimaldi put the Hummer and gear and drove forward. The vehicle wobbled and crabbed slightly to the right. "Front end's out of alignment."

"We'll get it looked at once we pass the next Jiffy Lube," Kissinger said. "Meantime, let's just cross our fingers."

They continued on, traveling by the illumination cast by the Hummer's one working headlight. No one spoke, allowing Grimaldi to keep an ear on the engine. The forest had quieted some as well. The windows were down and Bolan listened intently, dreading that at any second he was going to hear the drone of the Hercules C-130 flying overhead, bound for Jakarta with its toxic cargo.

Several minutes passed. The engine and radiator were both holding up, and Grimaldi had gotten used to compensating for the misaligned front end. When they passed a small stack of boulders arranged in a tell-tale formation alongside the road, Ma'ruf spoke up.

"We're coming to a spot where the river crosses the road," he told Grimaldi. "You'll have to stop a moment so we can lay the bridge across."

"Bridge?"

"You will see."

They rounded a bend, then Grimaldi slowed the Hummer to a stop. Lying on the road before him was a row of ten tree trunks, each the width of a telephone pole. The trunks, each twenty feet long, were lashed together with vines and thick wire cables, giving the appearance of a raft. Beyond the trees, the road gave way to the slow-moving river before continuing on the other side.

"Okay, I'll bite," Grimaldi said. "What good's the bridge if it's just lying on the road instead of reaching across the river?"

"We have to move it into place," Ma'ruf explained. "There are times we use the stream for hovercrafts, and there's not enough clearance if the bridge is left in place."

"Move it?" Grimaldi said, eyeing the tethered logs. "It's got to weigh a few tons at least."

"There is a swivel mechanism run by a generator," Ma'ruf said. "It will only take a few minutes."

"Wonderful." Grimaldi shut off the engine but left the headlight on.

"I will need a hand," Ma'ruf said as he and the others got out of the Hummer. "Someone will need to shine a flashlight on the generator while I get it started."

The others hung back as Bolan grabbed a light followed Ma'ruf to the river.

"Does this link up with the lake where we left the chopper?" he asked, gesturing at the sluggish waters.

"Yes," Ma'ruf explained. "It runs all the way to Dayimatan as well. It is a longer distance than by road, but in the hovercraft you can make better time."

Bolan quickly saw that the bridge was not as crudely put together as he'd first thought. The logs rested on a three-inch-thick steel plate that, in turn, was bolted to a large swivel joint. The driveshaft was buried under the ground, reaching all the way to a large gas generator hidden in the foliage by the side of the road.

As Bolan shone his light on the generator, Ma'ruf primed the engine with one hand while using the other to unlatch the driveshaft's locking mechanism. He then yanked hard on a pull cord. With a high-pitched whine, the generator came to life. Ma'ruf stepped back, reaching past Bolan for a lever rising up from a housing buried in the dirt. Once he'd pulled the lever, the bridge groaned and began to slowly pivot on the swivel mount, swinging out over the river.

"Pretty ingenious," Bolan said.

Ma'ruf nodded. "And if you look, you will see there is another bridge set up the same way across the river, for when we are coming from the other side."

As they waited for the bridge to align itself with the road, Bolan's thoughts turned once again to the plane the Lashkar had hijacked. He asked Ma'ruf how they'd been able to land the Hercules out here in the middle of nowhere.

"They used the old road leading to the quarry," Ma'ruf explained. "It runs straight as it comes into Dayimatan and was wide enough to use for a runway."

"What about this plan to dump toxins into the smoke clouds?" Bolan asked. "The people I've spoken to said it wouldn't work because the chemicals would just drop through the smoke."

"Not if they're converted properly," Ma'ruf told him. "I did not ask about specifics, but we have scientists and I heard them talking about something called a nebulizer. However it works, it apparently turns the poisons into vapor or some kind of aerosol, where the particles are small enough that they will suspend themselves in clouds. They did some tests with smaller aircraft, and it seemed to work."

"And if they were to crash into parliament," Bolan wondered, "how can they be sure the toxins will be released and not just incinerated?"

"Again, I am not a scientist," Ma'ruf said. "I think

it has something to do with where they place everything in the plane. Apparently there is some temperature at which you will get vapor without the poisons being burned off."

Bolan listened with a growing sense of foreboding. It sounded to him as if there were a wide margin for error in what the Lashkar hoped to achieved, but even if the Hercules failed to unleash any so-called death cloud, the mere act of crashing into Jakarta's parliament could be a devastating enough blow to undermine the government and give Pohtoh his chance to seize control of the whole country. The plane had to be stopped, at any cost.

Finally the bridge was in place. Ma'ruf locked down the driveshaft and shut off the generator. "Now we will reach Dayimatan within the hour," he assured Bolan.

"Let's just hope we're not too late," Bolan said as they headed back toward the Hummer.

Ma'ruf suddenly stopped and looked downriver, hearing something.

"What is it?" Bolan asked.

Ma'ruf listened intently, then whispered, "Hovercraft. Coming from the mountains. I wonder if it's..."

A blinding shaft of light suddenly sliced through the forest, illuminating the bridge. Bolan squinted and held his hand before his face to block the harsh glare. Fifty yards downstream, he saw that the searchlight was mounted on the front hull of a large hovercraft headed their way. On board the vessel were at least a dozen armed men.

CHAPTER FORTY-FOUR

Bolan collared Ma'ruf and pulled him to the ground as a burst of rounds whizzed passed them into the foliage. It was a twenty-yard scramble to the Hummer, where the others had already taken cover. Bolan figured it was safer to retreat, so he crawled back to the generator. Ma'ruf was right behind him.

Bolan yanked out his Desert Eagle and fired at the advancing hovercraft, then shouted to the others, "Toss me another gun, then spread out before they take out the Hummer!"

Kissinger quickly stuffed his Colt into one of the backpacks and tossed it Bolan's way, then grabbed an M-16 and sprinted with Mochtar into the brush alongside the road. Grimaldi wasn't about to write off the Hummer. He slid behind the wheel and cranked the engine, ducking low to avoid the gunshots raking the side panel. Bahn got in with him and rose through the sunroof, returning fire with her carbine.

"I'm taking a leap of faith here," Bolan said once

he'd fished the Colt from the backpack. Holding out both the Colt and his .44 to Ma'ruf, he asked the prisoner, "Which of these can you handle?"

Without hesitation, Ma'ruf took the Colt. "You don't have to worry," he assured Bolan. As if to prove himself, the prisoner waited out a volley of shots chipping away at the bridge, then rose from cover long enough to draw bead on the hovercraft and fire. A second later, the spotlight shattered and the jungle fell dark.

"Keep up the good work," Bolan told Ma'ruf. He then broke from cover. The Hummer had reached the bridge, screening him from the gunmen aboard the hovercraft, who continued to fire blindly in the sudden darkness. He waited for the vehicle to bound up onto the logs, then leaped onto the rear fender and grabbed hold of the roof rack with one hand, leaving the other free to fire at the hovercraft.

The boat had cut its engines and was drifting toward the south bank. Kissinger and Mochtar had already taken up positions behind rocks along the road, and when those aboard the craft tried to come ashore, they drove them back with twin bursts from the M-16s. One of the terrorists cried out in pain while the other splashed into the river.

On the other side of the hovercraft, a Lashkar hardman propped a bazooka onto his shoulder and took aim at the Hummer as it cleared the bridge. His aim was low, and the bridge took the initial impact. There was enough concussive force behind the fired round, however, to drive shrapnel up through the underside of the

Hummer and tip the vehicle up onto its two left wheels. Bolan was thrown clear, and Bahn inadvertently kicked Grimaldi squarely in the head as she tumbled halfway out of the sunroof. Grimaldi lost consciousness for a fleeting second, and when his foot slipped off the clutch, the engine died. By the time he came to, the Hummer lay on its side and he was lying on top of the door, his face out the window, pressed into the dirt.

Bolan quickly bounded to his feet and leveled his Desert Eagle at the hovercraft. There was little to see but shadows. He finally picked out the one most likely to be the man with the bazooka and fired. His shots were echoed by those of Ma'ruf, and between the two of them, they managed to take the shooter out before he could finish the Hummer off.

Bahn was trying to crawl out through the sunroof when Bolan reached her. He gave her a hand and helped her to the ground.

"I think that's what the crocodile had in mind," she told him, staring at the upended Hummer.

Bolan peered in through the sunroof and saw Grimaldi still pinned behind the wheel.

"You all right, Jack?"

"I will be once I stop seeing stars," Grimaldi groaned. "Go on, take care of business."

Bolan joined Bahn near the front of the Hummer. Their eyes had readjusted to the dark, and they could make out the hovercraft clearly now. It had come to a stop on the other side of the bank, just short of the bridge. Two men were scrambling from the front deck to the embankment when they were caught in Mochtar and Kissinger's cross fire.

"I'll go along the banks and see if I can get another angle on them," Bolan whispered to Bahn. "Don't shoot unless they fire first. They've got their hands full elsewhere and hopefully they'll lay off us."

Bahn nodded.

Bolan reloaded his .44, then dodged clear of the Hummer and made for the river. On either side of the bridge more tree trunks had been driven into the riverbed flush with the embankment to help keep the current from washing out the bridge. The upper ends of the tree posts rose three feet above the banks, providing Bolan all the cover he needed. Soon he was crouched directly across the river from the moored craft. It was larger than the hydrofoil they'd encountered in Samarinda, a good thirty yards long, rising above the river on a series of skids supported by squat uprights. He was at eye level with the deck, and there was activity aboard the craft, though not the kind he'd expected. A fight had broken out among three, possibly four men, who were shouting at one another vehemently, ignoring the shots that continued to pelt the craft's exterior.

Bolan thought at first that maybe Kissinger and Mochtar had already managed to storm their way aboard, but he couldn't recognize any of the voices. Finally, there were shots aboard the vessel and Bolan saw one of the men topple overboard into the river. Moments later, there was a loud curse, followed by another shot.

Bolan still didn't recognize the voice, but whoever had fired the shot was clearly American.

"Hold your fire!" the man called out. He tossed his gun to one side and held his hands aloft. "There's nobody left here but friendlies!"

Bolan was about to respond when he heard movement behind him. He whirled but held his fire. It was Jayne Bahn, scrambling toward him with her carbine. Behind her, Bolan could see Grimaldi pulling himself up out of the Hummer's passenger-side window.

"Did I just hear what I think I heard?" she whispered.

Bolan nodded. "I think we've found the mercenaries Herb Scoville was dealing with."

CHAPTER FORTY-FIVE

Bolan was right.

There had been five mercenaries aboard the hover-craft. Two had been killed in the skirmish. The Lashkar gunners had fared far worse, losing eleven men in all. Three surviving terrorists had managed to leap ashore and bolt into the rain forest while Bolan and Bahn were crossing the bridge. Kissinger and Mochtar had given chase, and far off in the trees there were periodic exchanges of gunfire between the two parties. Now, while Ma'ruf helped Grimaldi evaluate the seaworthiness of the bullet-riddled craft, Bahn stood guard over the bridge, leaving Bolan free to interrogate the soldiers of fortune. The mercs, however, had some questions of their own.

"Who are you guys, anyway?" one of the men asked. He was short and balding, with a goatee, and a scar along his right cheek. "We figured you guys for Berets or Rangers."

"Close enough," Bolan said. "Let's just say we're in the same loop as Herb Scoville and leave it at that."

"Where is he?" the bald man asked.

"We'll get to that," Bolan said. "Right now, it's your turn to talk. And lay it out straight."

The mercs hesitated, trading looks with one another.

"We don't have a lot of time," Bolan told them.

Finally the men began to spell out their background and explain how they'd come to be involved with Herb Scoville as well as the Lashkar Jihad.

The bald man, Dick Otis, was the group's leader. He said he'd served with the Air Force Rangers in Operation Desert Storm, as had another of the surviving mercenaries, A. C. Rojas. The third—and youngest—survivor, Paul Hager, claimed to have combed the caves of Afghanistan with a contingent of fellow Marines after the fall of the Taliban in late 2001. The two fatalities, JoJo Johnson and Darrell Coles, had been Navy SEALs. All five men hailed from the Northwest, and became acquainted with one another on a Seattle-based VFW Web site chat room. They'd all shared a common interest in becoming soldiers of fortune, and it was Otis who'd first proposed forming a small, self-run mercenary unit that, instead of enlisting with foreign governments, would instead hire itself out on an assignment-by-assignment basis. In time, they moved together to a remote farm near Spokane, where they spent six months training themselves to fight as a team.

A mutual friend introduced Otis to William Ruppert two months before Ruppert's daughter was kidnapped in the Philippines. When Otis received a frantic call from the real-estate baron telling him of the kidnapping, he convinced Ruppert that he'd have a better chance of seeing his daughter alive if he worked around official channels and took matters into his own hands.

As he listened, Bolan could hardly fault Otis's reasoning. After all, Stony Man Farm itself had come into being as a clandestine special-ops force because of concerns that official protocols and restrictions were hampering the effectiveness of sanctioned outfits like the CIA and the military's various elite commandos. In many ways, Otis's mercenaries were kindred spirits with the Stony Man warriors, the main difference being that the mercs were motivated by financial gain.

Bolan interrupted Otis for a moment, telling the mercenary that he already knew about his group's connection with Herb Scoville. He also told Otis that his men had fallen under surveillance by Indonesian Military Intelligence once they turned up in Jakarta.

"Yeah, we knew that," Otis said. "And so did Scoville, so he helped us drop out of sight, then got us over here and maneuvered a rendezvous with the Lashkar."

"How'd he pull that off?" Bahn asked. She'd wandered over from the bridge and been eavesdropping on the interrogation.

"Informants," Otis said. "He used them as intermediaries so he'd stay out of the loop. Or so he hoped. Kinda looks like he wound up being double-crossed."

"Maybe so," Bolan said. "But let's stay on track. You met with the Lashkar Jihad. Where?"

"They've got a safehouse in Samarinda. Near the

marketplace. It was mostly dog-sniffing. You know, checking each other out. It was pretty clear their biggest concern was that we could be trusted, so we really had to play up this falling out with those senators."

"Man, did we talk some trash," Hager interjected. "Badmouthed everybody from the President on down, and they lapped it up."

"They figured you'd come to work for them out of spite," Bolan said.

"Exactly," Otis said.

A. C. Rojas, spoke up, saying, "The thing is, we never really figured to be in the loop long enough to carry out whatever mission they were talking about. Scoville just wanted to use us to find out where Pohtoh and Jahf-Al were hiding out."

"He said we could have first crack at 'em and the reward money," Otis said, "but once he knew for sure where they were, he was going to come after them with the big guns."

"Same thing he told me," Jayne Bahn murmured, more to herself than the others.

"What's that?" Otis asked.

"Never mind," she told him.

Bolan asked the mercenaries about the rendezvous they were supposed to make with Scoville back at the old lumber mill.

"We'd just found out the Lashkar wanted to take us to one of their training camps," Otis explained. "We set up a pickup time with them, then arranged to have Scoville meet us first. He was going to rig us with homing devices so he'd be able to track us, hopefully to Pohtoh and Jahf-Al."

"But something happened," Bolan guessed. "You missed the rendezvous."

Otis nodded. "We were on our way to meet him when the Lashkar intercepted us. They said there'd been a change of plans and the schedule had been moved up."

"We figured they must've had us under surveillance," Rojas said.

"No kidding," Bahn interjected caustically.

"What's *your* problem?" Rojas snapped back.

"The Lashkar pushed up the schedule and got you out of the way so they could nab Scoville when he showed up for the rendezvous," Bahn said, her anger rising. "They tortured him, then lopped his head off because he wouldn't say whether you guys were working for him."

"Jesus," Otis muttered.

Hager shot a glance at his two comrades. "I told you they were on to us!"

"Hey, you think it didn't cross my mind, too?" Otis retorted.

"Look," he said, speaking to Hager as well as Bolan, "once they got us on the hovercraft, they blindfolded us and tied our hands behind our backs, then stuck us down below the deck. They said it was just a precaution and that they wanted to keep the location of their camp secret, but I didn't buy it."

"We've been on the river all day," Rojas stated. "A few hours ago we stopped somewhere and picked up some more men, then just kept going. A while ago we heard some shooting, and the Lashkar got all bent out of shape. We heard rifles being passed around, and a few minutes later the bullets stared flying. Otis here told them to untie us so we could help."

The bald man turned to Bolan. "Anyway, when nobody answered me I figured they were too busy fighting you guys and wrestled off my blindfold. Once I got my hands on a knife, I cut us free and we came up on deck. That's when we lost Coles and JoJo. I don't know if you got 'em or the Lashkar, but they got drilled right off. We didn't know who was shooting at us, either, but I figured with the Lashkar we were dead meat, so we grabbed whatever we could get our hands on and laid into 'em. Somewhere in all the ruckus I heard one of you guys shouting from shore and figured the cavalry'd come to the rescue."

"That's not exactly why we were here," Bolan said.

"What now?" Rojas asked Bolan.

Bolan said. "They were probably taking you to Dayimatan," he said. "It's an old quarry they've been using as a base of operations and we think Pohtoh's there along with Jahf-Al. We were on our way there to…"

Bolan's voice trailed off. He glanced out at the road, as did Bahn. They both raised their rifles, then lowered them when they saw Kissinger and Mochtar approaching. Marching ahead of them, hands over his head, was one of the Lashkar soldiers they'd chased into the forest.

"Look what the quicksand spit up," Kissinger called out.

Bolan took a closer look at the new prisoner and was taken aback.

"Sergeant Latek!"

CHAPTER FORTY-SIX

"You know this guy?" Dick Otis asked Bolan as Latek was brought over.

"Yeah," Bolan said, eyeing Latek with contempt. He quickly told the mercenaries how Latek was part of a KOPASSUS force that had been ambushed outside Samarinda and about the subsequent battle with the Lashkar at a riverside campsite in the nearby rain forest. "A couple of us nearly got ourselves killed trying to pull him and a colleague from a quagmire."

"Only it turns out the bastard never went in," Kissinger said, shoving Latek so hard the sergeant lost his balance and fell into the tall grass near the embankment. "He tossed his helmet in, then screamed for help and hid in the brush while we risked our necks going in after him. Right, Sergeant?"

"I can explain," Latek groaned. He started to get up, but Kissinger stepped forward and prodded him hard with the tip of his assault rifle until he dropped back into the grass.

"What's to explain?" Kissinger said. "You were in on the ambush. When you radioed the surveillance team, they were already dead. You were just signaling the men who killed them so they could make sure that truck would catch us on the straightaway. And I don't know how you tricked up your HAZMAT suit so they could tell you apart from the rest of us, but that's why you pulled through without a scratch after all the shooting."

"No, it wasn't—" Latek cried out.

"And afterward you kept up the charade," Kissinger went on, talking over Latek's protests. "When you pointed out the smoke from that campfire, you knew damn well there'd be men down there in the jungle waiting for another go at us."

"It's not true!" Latek insisted. "I am still loyal to KOPASSUS!"

Otis turned to Bolan. "He was our contact for the Lashkar at the safehouse we told you about in Samarinda," he said. "He never mentioned being part of the military."

"It was part of my cover!" Latek insisted. "I am a spy for KOPASSUS!"

"He's lying!"

Latek glanced over his shoulder toward the hydrofoil. His face registered shock when he saw Ma'ruf leap down from the deck and stride over.

"He's lying!" Ma'ruf repeated, pointing a finger at Latek. "He is a spy, all right, but not for KOPASSUS. His loyalty is with Moamar Pohtoh and the Lashkar Jihad!"

"No!" Latek shouted.

"I have seen you with Pohtoh!" Ma'ruf shouted back. "Several times! Laughing together like brothers!"

Latek glanced at Bolan pleadingly. "He is confusing me with someone else."

Bolan didn't answer. He stared past the sergeant, almost as if he were looking through him. His focus seemed to be on the river, barely visible in the faint moonlight. Suddenly, without warning, he strode forward and grabbed Latek by the collar, then jerked him to his feet. Taken by surprise, Latek let out a choked cry. When he tried to lash out at his attacker, Bolan grabbed his right arm and twisted it behind his back, then spun Latek so that he was standing before the row of trunk pylons separating him from a five-foot drop into the river. Bolan forced Latek to kneel atop the posts, then used his free hand to grab the sergeant by the hair and force him to look down into the water.

There, a pair of crocodiles, every bit as large as the one that had attacked the Hummer earlier, were drifting silently toward the body of one of the slain Lashkar soldiers who'd fallen from the hydrofoil during the battle. As Latek watched in horror, the two beasts converged on the body and began tearing at it with their powerful jaws, picking the man apart as if he were made of straw.

"They'll still be hungry when they're through with him," Bolan growled in Latek's ear. "And the way I hear it, they prefer live meals."

To underscore his point, Bolan let go of Latek's hair and shoved him forward just enough so that it seemed that if Bolan were to release his arm, the sergeant would tumble into the river. As it was, the extra pressure on his twisted arm popped Latek's shoulder out of place with a sound like cracking knuckles. He let out a pained howl.

"Now, then," Bolan suggested, "when I ask you something, you answer, and you answer fast. If I get the sense you're lying, I'm going to rip this arm of yours all the way off and feed it to the crocs as an appetizer. Do you understand me?

"First question," Bolan went on. "How long have you been playing both sides of the fence?"

"A few months," Latek confessed. "They made threats against my family—"

"Save the excuses," Bolan interrupted. "Just answer."

"I understand," Latek said.

"The Lashkar have someone else on the inside back in Samarinda, yes?" Bolan said. "Either with KOPASSUS or Military Intelligence."

"No," Latek said.

Bolan tugged on the sergeant's arm. "The truth!"

"There is no one else!" Latek insisted. "We hoped to place more people eventually, but right now it's only me!"

"What about Colonel Tohm?"

Latek shook his head. "No! For all his faults, he is loyal to the government. We never even approached him."

Bolan weighed the implications. If Latek was indeed telling the truth, it meant that nothing had come of Lieutenant Wais's ploy to corral the KOPASSUS troops and feed them the story about a move on one of Pohtoh's strongholds. It also meant that it was unlikely Bolan or the others could expect any backup force to help them carry out their mission. He twisted Latek's arm again and resumed the interrogation.

"What about the fire-fighting plane you hijacked?" Bolan demanded. "Is it still in Dayimatan?"

"I don't know," Latek confessed. "There was a problem with the landing gear when it landed. They couldn't take off until it was fixed."

"How long did they think it would take?"

"I don't know," Latek said.

"And they still plan to fly it to Jakarta?" Bolan asked. "To crash it into the parliament while they're in session?"

Latek stole a glance back at Ma'ruf, then nodded.

"Yes, that is still the plan," the sergeant said.

"Then we have time," Bolan stated. "If parliament doesn't open until sometime in the morning, they probably won't take off until dawn, right?"

Latek shook his head. "No. The plan was to fly to Pontianak under cover of night so they could refuel before crossing the sea. If the plane has been fixed, it will have already taken off."

Bolan turned toward the hydrofoil and shouted out to Grimaldi, who had just come up from the lower deck. "How's the boat?"

"Lotta cosmetic damage," Grimaldi called back, "but I think she'll run."

Bolan turned his attention back to Latek. "You were headed back to Dayimatan, correct? They'll be expecting you."

Latek nodded.

Bolan loosened his grip on the prisoner, then pulled him away from the river's edge and shoved him back into the grass. There was some rope lying in the dirt near the pylons. Bolan grabbed it and tossed it to Rojas.

"Go ahead and tie him up."

Rojas nodded and motioned for Latek to put his arms behind his back. The sergeant meekly complied, grimacing from the pain in his shoulder.

Bolan looked around, formulating a plan, then told the others, "Strip the robes off the dead, then everybody get on board. We'll try to play Trojan horse."

While the others began to disrobe the slain terrorists, Bolan turned to Ma'ruf. "You're going to have to tell me how the camp's laid out. I'll need as much detail as you can give me."

"I'll do my best," Ma'ruf promised.

Once Dick Otis had helped himself to one of the Lashkar robes, he wrapped it around his right hand, then strode over to where Rojas was helping Latek to his feet.

"My turn," Otis said. He lashed out with his wrapped fist, striking Latek squarely on the chin. The sergeant reeled backward, yet somehow managed to remain on his feet. Bolan was about to intervene but checked himself.

"What were your plans for us!" Otis shouted at Latek. "What was this big mission?"

"What does it matter?" Latek responded weakly. "It's not going to happen."

"Wrong answer." Otis stepped forward and swung again. This time Latek went down. Otis towered over him.

"You said it was important that we be white," he said. "That we look all-American. Why?"

Blood trickled from the corner of Latek's mouth where he'd been struck. He stared up at Otis and told him, "We were going to have you kill Jahf-Al."

"I gathered that much," Otis said.

"We have some stolen uniforms we were going to give to you," Latek said. "U.S. Marines. We were going to have you dress as Marines when you killed him. One of you was going to have a bayonet, so that after Jahf-Al was dead you could behead him. We would have it all on camera."

CHAPTER FORTY-SEVEN

"That's why they sent out that fax making it look like the consulate bombing was Jahf-Al's doing," Bolan said, speculating. "First they make him an even bigger hero to the militants than he already is, then they cut him down, which turns him into an even greater martyr."

"And if the blame falls on the U.S., it rallies even more converts to the cause," Kissinger said, following through on the logic behind the Lashkar's plot to kill the Nile Viper. "Pohtoh comes forward with a little show of grief and 'humbly' says the UIF torch has been passed to him, and who's going to argue?"

"Especially once he kills us and claims he's avenged Jahf-Al's assassination," Dick Otis concluded. "Nice plan, if it had worked."

The three men were standing on the foredeck of the hydrofoil as it made its way upriver toward Dayimatan. Bahn, assault rifle in hand, had taken up a position in the rear of the craft. She'd tucked her hair up under a headpiece and had donned one of the slain Lashkar gunner's robes, as had Mochtar, who stood up on the observation platform with Wahid Ma'ruf. Directly below them, Grimaldi was at the controls, pushing the boat as hard as he dared. Down below, A. C. Rojas and Phil Hager were standing guard over Latek. Against his better judgment, Bolan had decided to spare the traitor's life, at least for the moment, in exchange for Latek's promise of cooperation once they reached the Lashkar stronghold.

There was a radio aboard the hydrofoil, and though its signal couldn't reach Samarinda, they were able to call ahead to Dayimatan and plant their cover story. Ma'ruf had made the call, reporting that both the hydrofoil and mountain base had been attacked by Dayak tribesmen, a credible story insofar as there had been ongoing skirmishes between the Lashkar and the tribe, which objected to the terrorists' ongoing use of roads and riverways that passed through their territory. Ma'ruf claimed that most of the troops who'd been aboard the boat had remained behind to restore order, while he was continuing on to Dayimatan with the mercenaries. He'd assured the person he was talking to that the mercs were unaware that the Lashkar knew of their link to the CIA. As he'd put it, "They are too busy dreaming about the money they think will be coming to them." That had been good for a laugh back in Dayimatan.

There remained one hurdle to overcome before they reached the quarry site, and after another five minutes on the river, Ma'ruf spotted it from the observation platform.

"We're coming to the checkpoint!" he called down.

"Okay, let's get down below," Bolan told Kissinger and Otis.

Bahn caught up with the men as they reached the cabin entryway.

"Make sure to keep your back turned to them," Bolan advised her.

"Duh," Bahn said with a grin.

Once they climbed down into the cabin, Jayne motioned for Latek to stand, allowing the three men to take his place sitting on a bench seat alongside Rojas and Hager. Bolan called out a warning to the prisoner.

"Remember, you're just window-dressing. You stay put at the controls with your mouth shut and let Ma'ruf do the talking, is that clear?"

Latek nodded and glumly shuffled toward the stairwell, his gait limited to the twenty inches of slack on the rope linking his bound ankles. Grimaldi appeared at the top of the steps. He'd just finished pulling a robe over his head.

"Move it!" he told Latek.

"I'm moving as fast as I can!" the lieutenant snapped back.

As Grimaldi helped Latek up the steps and then led him off to the wheelhouse, the other men grabbed strips of cloth torn from one of the other robes and tied them around their heads. The material was thin enough to see through it, but it would give the appearance that they were sufficiently blindfolded. Similarly, the lengths of rope they wrapped loosely around their ankles would make it look as if their feet were bound together. Once they'd completed the tasks, the men placed their hands behind their backs, concealing the pistols they would bring into play if they failed to pass the cursory inspection Ma'ruf had told them they could expect from the checkpoint guards. Bahn, meanwhile, took a seat in the shadows directly across from them and cradled her carbine across her lap, making sure the cuffs of her robe covered her hands.

Grimaldi soon rejoined them and remained standing. He most closely matched the stature of the average Lashkar soldier and had therefore been given the task of pretending to help Bahn guard the mercenaries as they were brought into Dayimatan.

"All set," Grimaldi said. "Checkpoint's coming up."

Ma'ruf had taken over the controls from Grimaldi, and as he slowed the engines, the men fell silent. A few seconds later, there was a light knocking on the ceiling directly above them. It was followed in quick succession by three more quick thumps, then another after an interval of two seconds. The men waited tensely, but the sounds stopped.

Bolan sighed faintly with relief. Ma'ruf had been tapping the wheelhouse floorboards as he counted the number of soldiers stationed at the checkpoint. He'd forewarned the others that as many as three dozen men could be standing guard, as the checkpoint marked a boundary shared by the Dayak and another tribe, the

Gylwrin, with similar reservations about the Lashkar's forays into their territory. This night, fortunately, it appeared there were only four guards on duty.

"Piece of cake," Otis murmured.

"We'll see," Grimaldi said, pacing before Bolan and the mercenaries.

"Quiet," Bolan said.

Soon Ma'ruf had the engine idling and Bolan could hear him calling out to somebody on shore. There was a slapping sound as a mooring line landed on the deck of the hydrofoil. The plan was for Ma'ruf to handle the mooring and any conversation with the guards while Latek remained in the wheelhouse and Mochtar stayed up on the observation deck in his Lashkar disguise. If all went well, the guards would buy the same story Ma'ruf had already relayed to Dayimatan and content themselves with a quick, cursory glimpse at the would-be captive mercenaries before waving the boat on.

As the hydrofoil was being secured to the docks, Bolan saw the drifting beam of a searchlight fall across the upper deck. Ma'ruf started to tell the guards his tale of how the boat had come to be so bullet-riddled. Suddenly his voice was drowned out by a persistent tapping. It was coming from the wheelhouse again, but Bolan was sure that Ma'ruf had already moved out onto the deck, which meant it had to be Latek giving the signal. Bolan stopped counting after a dozen taps. Latek was either trying to throw them off or else he was trying to warn them that there were more soldiers at the checkpoint. Which was it?

After someone shouted angrily from the docks in Javanese, the tapping abruptly ceased. The shouting, however, continued.

"Oh, shit," Bahn muttered under her breath. She glanced over at Bolan and whispered, "They want to know what the tapping's all about and they're asking about the guy on the observation deck."

Overhead, Bolan next heard the scuffling of feet in the wheelhouse, followed by a frantic cry from Latek. He was calling out something in Javanese. Bolan didn't need Bahn to translate.

"Bastard just blew our cover!" Bolan growled, jerking off his blindfold, even as the first exchange of gunfire began to rattle through the night air.

CHAPTER FORTY-EIGHT

Sergeant Latek had been exaggerating about the number of soldiers manning the checkpoint, but not by much. As Bolan led the charge up to the deck of the hydrofoil, he saw a Jeep with six Lashkar gunmen speeding toward the docks, more than doubling the enemy they now had to contend with.

"Stay low!" Bolan called out to the others as they spread out along the deck.

Latek lay facedown on the deck after toppling down from the wheelhouse. He'd been shot, and blood seeped through an exit wound in his back. Bolan exchanged a quick look with Ma'ruf, who'd taken cover on the foredeck, brandishing a 9 mm Ruger semiautomatic. Ma'ruf nodded.

"We should've done it back at the bridge," he said matter-of-factly before turning his attention back to the enemy.

Bolan planted himself and raised his Desert Eagle into firing position, tracking the Jeep's driver with the gun's sights. The moment the Jeep finally came to a complete stop, he pulled the trigger, sending a 3-round burst through the front windshield, shattering the glass. The driver pitched forward and the Jeep's horn began to blare.

The other men in the vehicle were already clambering to the ground, taking cover alongside the four guards who had first come out to greet the hydrofoil. One of them had been shot in the chest by Ma'ruf and lay dead on the planks, his blood spilling through the cracks into the water.

Bolan and the others had a slight advantage as long as they remained on the boat, as the deck railing lay more than two feet below the level of the docks, allowing them to fire upward at their more-exposed targets, while the men on shore found most of their volleys burrowing into the dock planks.

Mochtar was the lone exception. Even after he'd dropped to the floor of the observation platform, he was still an easy target, and as bullets began to clang off the platform railing, missing him by inches, he returned a quick round of gunfire, then scrambled backward and began to lower himself quickly down the ladder leading to the far side of the wheelhouse.

He almost made it.

As he was lowering himself down the last two rungs, a round fired from the shore skimmed across the roof of the wheelhouse and plowed into his shoulder, just below the collarbone. The impact threw him off balance and he missed the last rung of the ladder. First he knocked his head against the wheelhouse roofline, leaving him dazed, then his right foot struck the deck at an angle and he lost his grip on the ladder altogether. Arms flailing, he teetered over the railing and into the river.

On the other side of the boat, Bolan knew at once what had happened. He downed another of the soldiers on the docks, then bolted from cover, bounding over Latek's body so that he could pass through the wheelhouse. Standing by the ladder, he peered over the railing and saw Mochtar floating facedown in the river.

Without hesitation, Bolan holstered his .44, climbed up onto the railing and dived into the river. The water was cold and murky. Bolan surfaced as quickly as he could. He saw that the current was pulling Mochtar along; soon he'd be drifting beyond the cover provided by the boat. Bolan drew in a quick breath, then swam with the current, gaining on Mochtar while conserving his energy for the real challenge, which began the moment he reached the younger man and propped his head above the waterline. Mochtar sputtered, coming to, but he was still too groggy to help his own cause. It was up to Bolan to keep him afloat and at the same time swim against the current to get back behind the boat before somebody on shore saw them and started firing.

Seconds seemed like minutes as Bolan struggled toward the boat, slowed by not only Mochtar's deadweight, but also by their wet clothes. He felt as if he were moving in slow motion. All the while the gun bat-

tle raged around them. Bolan could faintly hear the
shots above the sounds of his labored breathing, but he
had no idea how the others were faring. For all he
knew, he might wind up hauling Mochtar back to the
boat only to find it overrun by the Lashkar gunners.

Bolan was still a good twenty yards from the hydrofoil's nearest front wing when he glanced downriver
and saw the one thing he'd dreaded most when he first
plunged into the dark waters.

CHAPTER FORTY-NINE

Watching the beast drift closer, Bolan shifted his grip on Mochtar, freeing one hand and reaching for his holster, doing his best not to stir the water around him. Mochtar groaned and stirred.

"Keep still," Bolan told him.

Bolan drew his .44, but he knew it was pointless. The crocodile was too low in the water to present much of a target, and there was no way he'd be able to get off an accurate shot while treading water and holding on to Mochtar. Their only hope was that the creature would pass them by, and that hope faded as Bolan saw the beast began to veer toward them. It was less than fifteen yards away.

Bolan slowly raised his gun.

Before he could fire, there was a sudden splash a few yards in front of him. It looked as if someone had just jumped into the river. Before he could see who it was, the crocodile attacked, widening its massive jaws and tearing into its victim. The water came alive as the beast thrashed fiercely about, slapping its tail against the surface.

Bolan tightened his grip on Mochtar and kicked with his legs, distancing them from the crocodile's feeding frenzy. Preoccupied, the creature paid no attention as they made their way to the hydrofoil. Mochtar, now fully conscious but still somewhat disoriented, gasped in Bolan's ear.

"What's happening?"

"Just getting out of a little jam," Bolan told him. "Hang on."

When they reached the nearest wing, Bolan grabbed hold, then pulled Mochtar over and told him to do the same. As he paused to catch his breath, Bolan strained his ears, trying to hear over the loud splashing made by the crocodile as it finished off its prey. He heard a few gunshots, then a voice, calling out to him.

"Up here!"

Bolan glanced up and saw Kissinger leaning over the foredeck, extending a pole down toward the wing. Grimaldi stood behind him, holding Kissinger by the waist so that he could lean farther out.

Bolan grabbed the strut supporting the wing and pulled himself up out of the water, then helped Mochtar up as well.

"Can you take the pole?" he asked.

Mochtar nodded feebly, transferring his grip to the pole. Bolan steadied him as Kissinger began to pull. Slowly Mochtar rose toward the deck. Dick Otis appeared beside Kissinger and Grimaldi and reached over the side. Once he was able to grab hold of Mochtar's wrist, he told him, "I've got you."

Mochtar let go of the pole. Otis pulled him upward and Grimaldi moved over to help the wounded man onto the deck. Mochtar collapsed onto the deck, clutching his shoulder. Blood seeped through his fingers.

Bolan, meanwhile, stood on the strut and reached up. Kissinger set the pole aside and gave Bolan a hand, pulling him up to the deck.

"Who do you think you are, Mark Spitz?" Cowboy asked.

Bolan shook his head. "I was thinking more along the lines of Johnny Weissmuller."

He bent over, took in a few deep breaths, then moved to the railing and stared into the dark waters. The crocodile was still working on what was left of the man who'd taken Bolan and Mochtar's place on the menu.

"Latek," Kissinger explained. "Turns out he was worth taking along after all."

Bolan moved over to Mochtar's side. Grimaldi was leaning over the younger man, inspecting his gunshot wound. He already had the bleeding in check.

"How bad is it?" Bolan asked.

"Looks nasty," Grimaldi said, "but hopefully it missed any vitals."

"It stings a little when I breathe," Mochtar wheezed.

"Have you coughed up any blood?" Bolan asked.

Mochtar shook his head.

"I'll track down a med-kit," Kissinger said.

Bolan told Mochtar to stay put, then made his way

to the side deck. Glancing ashore, he saw bodies strewed across the docks and around the Jeep, but there was no sign of activity. Near the doorway to the passenger cabin, Rojas and Bahn were crouched over Hager, trying the staunch the flow of blood from a gunshot wound to his neck. It wasn't working.

"He's gone," Rojas finally said, pulling his reddened hands away.

"Where's Ma'ruf?" Bolan asked.

Bahn gestured with her head as she wiped her hands on her pants. "He went to check things out."

Desert Eagle in hand, Bolan climbed up to the docks and cautiously made his way toward the Jeep, side-stepping the bodies of the fallen Lashkar gunners. In the back of the Jeep he noticed a footlocker strapped down securely inside a slightly larger box, cushioned by a layer of foam pellets. Curious, Bolan unfastened the straps and raised the lid of the footlocker. Inside, beneath a layer of folded HAZMAT suits, were more than two dozen small slabs of C-5 plastique stacked in neat rows, each stick separated from the others by a sheet of bubble wrap. There was also a smaller third container, the size of a cigar box, filled with a bound roll of wire, several detonators and an equal number of digital LCD timers.

Bolan was still pondering his discovery when Ma'ruf stepped out of a small clapboard shack set near the road leading to the docks.

"We got them all," he announced as he strode over to the Jeep.

"At least for now," Bolan said. "Any chance they could hear us back at the camp?"

"Not likely. Dayimatan is still five miles away." Ma'ruf glanced at the open footlocker and told Bolan, "They use explosives for tunneling through the quarry."

"And for bombs," Bolan ventured.

"Yes," Ma'ruf said. "For bombs, too."

Bolan glanced over his shoulder at the road. "Does that lead to the camp?" Bolan asked.

Ma'ruf nodded. "It leads to the old access road where they have the plane."

Bolan circled to the front of the Jeep. The driver had fallen away from the steering wheel but was still sprawled across the front seat. The soldier dragged the body from the car, then got behind the wheel and stared out through the fractured windshield as he started the engine. It seemed to be running smoothly.

Bolan turned off the ignition, then glanced back at the explosives.

"What are you thinking?" Ma'ruf asked.

"Let's have another look at that diagram you drew for me earlier," Bolan said, getting out of the Jeep. "I think there might be a better way to pull this off."

CHAPTER FIFTY

An hour later, the hydrofoil emerged from the rain forest and rounded a bend that led to Dayimatan's old quarry. Ma'ruf was at the controls in the wheelhouse. Peering through the windshield, he saw a broad clearing off to his right. He breathed a sigh of relief when he saw the Hercules C-130 resting in the middle of the old access road. The landing gear had apparently been repaired, because men were unloading containers from two flatbed trucks parked near the cargo hatch and carrying them up a ramp into the plane's hold. It looked as if it would be awhile before the plane took off. Beyond the plane, up atop a knoll dotted with acacia trees, Ma'ruf saw a pair of helicopters, both Sultan EG-23s like the one that had been abandoned back in the mountains. Unlike that chopper, however, these were combat-equipped gunships. Ma'ruf had been concerned that both choppers might be in use. To find both of them where he'd last seen them was a good omen.

He checked his watch.

Their plan could still work.

Guards soon appeared along the riverbanks. Ma'ruf greeted them somberly, explaining that the boat had been attacked a second time by Dayak warriors.

"We lost everyone," he told them. "There's just me and three of the mercenaries."

The guards bought Ma'ruf's story, recounting the other recent attacks on Lashkar troops in the region.

"Pohtoh has had enough," the guard said. "He's decided it is time to move camp."

"To where?" Ma'ruf asked.

"East," the guard replied. "To Ertonon. We will be leaving in the morning."

Ma'ruf understood Pohtoh's reasoning. Ertonon was located higher up in the mountains, sixty miles northeast of Dayimatan. It was an area less contested by other tribes, and the mountains were as honeycombed with caves as the range where they'd originally stockpiled the stolen pesticides. It would be an easier locale to defend and, if need be, to flee from.

"Pohtoh is waiting for the mercenaries," the guard told Ma'ruf. "He wants to finish things with Jahf-Al before we leave."

"I understand," Ma'ruf said.

The guards stepped back and traded salutes with Ma'ruf, who proceeded to guide the hovercraft another quarter mile. There, he veered the craft from the river into a lagoon leading to a dock not unlike the one at the checkpoint. The quarry lay just beyond view on the other side of a long plateau. The plateau was busy with activity. As many as three dozen Lashkar soldiers were stacking provisions they'd hauled up from the quarry. Nearby, a driver was carefully backing up a semitrailer to the base of the plateau.

Ma'ruf cut back on the engines as he drew near the docks. A handful of soldiers were on hand. Ma'ruf moved from the wheelhouse and helped moor the hovercraft alongside the docks, then grabbed an assault rifle and told the soldiers, "Let me get the Americans."

Ma'ruf went to the passenger cabin and climbed down the steps. Bolan, Kissinger and Otis sat on the bench seat much as they had back at the checkpoint. This time, however, both their blindfolds and binds were secured tightly. Grimaldi, Bahn, Rojas and Mochtar were nowhere to be seen.

"The plane hasn't taken off yet," Ma'ruf whispered to them as he directed the men to stand. "I'll proceed as planned once I turn you over."

"Are you sure you can do this?" Bolan whispered back. "Remember, we have backup plans."

"The other plans are not as good," Ma'ruf replied. "Let me do this."

Keeping his rifle trained on the men, Ma'ruf helped guide them up the steps to the deck. As he made his way behind Bolan, Kissinger whispered to him, "We've backed some long shots in our day, Striker, but this one takes the cake."

HALF A MILE from Dayimatan, Jack Grimaldi pulled off the road and drove the Jeep to a stop behind a tall cluster of vine-infested brambles. He shut off the engine and looked over at Raki Mochtar, who was grimacing in pain.

"Sorry about all the bumps," he told the wounded man.

"They hurt less than those crocodile's teeth would have," Mochtar said. His shoulder was bandaged and his left arm was in a makeshift sling to cut down on the chances of reopening the wound.

Jayne Bahn was in the back of the Jeep. Like the men, she was still wearing a robe taken from one of the slain Lashkar terrorists. She and Grimaldi had also smeared their faces and hands with river mud. The ruse wasn't likely to fool anyone for more than a fleeting second, but given the odds they were up against, they were determined to seize any possible advantage. Tucking a loose strand of hair under the headpiece rounding out her disguise, she climbed out of the Jeep, telling the men, "Let's get a move on."

There was a faint smell of smoke in the breeze as they abandoned the Jeep and crossed over the road to a ditch. Glancing up, Grimaldi said, "Looks like we've got a fire cloud drifting in."

"That could help us," Mochtar said, wincing with each step as they walked along the bottom of the ditch.

"I don't know about that," Bahn said. "I know it'd give us more cover, but I'd just as soon see where we're going."

They'd gone nearly fifty yards when the ground beneath their feet turned a shade darker, blackened by a recent fire.

"Up the rise here," Grimaldi said, recalling the directions Ma'ruf had given them. They turned and started up the slope, soon coming upon a quarter-mile stretch of charred terrain. Ma'ruf had explained that the land had been cleared more than six months ago to provide lumber for barracks and other facilities at the quarry. There was some new growth pushing up through the scorched earth, but for the most part all Grimaldi and the others could see were tree stumps poking up from the ground at irregular intervals. There were hundreds of them.

"They almost look like gravestones," Bahn murmured as they made their way through the obstacle course.

"I guess they are, in a way," Grimaldi said. "One for each dead tree."

The terrain was hilly, rising in spots and then dipping into shallow valleys. Ma'ruf had told them to keep an eye open for a pronounced indentation along the highest ridgeline, and once they spotted it they veered course toward it and proceeded with even more caution, crouching low and using the exposed trunks for cover.

"I don't see any sentries," Bahn said, keeping an eye on the landmark as she moved forward alongside Grimaldi. "He said if there were any, they'd be up along the crest."

"Let's play it safe," Grimaldi said. They paused behind another of the trunks and waited for Mochtar to catch up with them.

"How are you holding up?" Bahn asked.

"I'll manage," Mochtar said.

"Are you sure?" Grimaldi pressed. "If you have to, you can switch over and come with me."

Mochtar shook his head. "It's important that I go with her. You can handle your end alone."

Grimaldi grinned. "Thanks for the vote of confidence, Rock, but the truth is I could use at least a couple more guys. And you two could use a small army."

"Well, unless Able Team and Phoenix Force beam down from the U.S.S. *Enterprise,* that's not going to happen," Mochtar managed to joke. "So let's stick to the plan. I can gut it out."

"Good man," Grimaldi said.

By now they were on their way up the final rise leading to the upper ridgeline. Grimaldi told Mochtar to stay put and keep them covered as he and Bahn crawled the last dozen yards on their stomachs. Mochtar propped his carbine on the trunk before him, then watched the other two slowly inch their way up the slope. Once they reached the crest, Grimaldi turned and waved Mochtar forward.

When he reached the indentation, Mochtar saw the gaping mouth to a tunnel large enough for a small truck to pass through. Ma'ruf had told them that most of the lumber was transported to the quarry through the tunnel, as it was quicker than overland. There was still no sign of any sentries guarding the opening.

"Our lucky day," Bahn said.

"Still, you better watch yourselves once you head down," Grimaldi cautioned.

She nodded and turned to Mochtar. "How's your sense of direction? Better than mine, I hope."

"I have a good sense," Mochtar said. "And I remember all the turns Ma'ruf described."

"Then you're definitely coming with me," she told him. "One wrong turn down there and who knows where the hell we'd end up."

"Good luck," Grimaldi told them.

"You, too," Mochtar responded. "We hope to see you soon."

Grimaldi nodded, then watched as Bahn and Mochtar headed into the tunnel. Once they'd vanished into the shadows, he turned his attention from the cave and inched closer to the far side of the scallop in the ridgeline. When he reached the rim, he peered out into the night. Fifty yards away was the knoll leading to the helicopters. Grimaldi could see more than a dozen men milling around both gunships. It didn't seem to matter which one he should try to gain access to. From the looks of it, it was going to take more than a robe and a smeared face for him to get close to either one. Still, he had to make a decision and go for it. He shifted his gaze back and forth, trying to calculate which was his best bet. He finally opted on a less scientific approach.

"Eenie, meanie, miney, moe."

SURROUNDED BY total darkness, A. C. Rojas shifted uncomfortably and wiped the sweat from his brow. His legs were starting to cramp up on him and the air inside the enclosed space was getting stale, reeking of perspiration and the faintly cloying smell of motor fuel. All he could hear was the labored sound of his

own breathing and, now and then, the lapping of the
lagoon waters against the hydrofoil's struts.

Good thing I'm not claustrophobic, he told himself, shifting his legs slightly in hopes of increasing
the circulation.

Another few minutes passed. Rojas raised his left
hand close to his face and pressed a recessed button on
his watch. The time flashed with a dull, luminescent
glow. 11:36.

Twenty-four minutes to go.

Rojas doubted he could stay cooped up that long.

He waited a few minutes longer, then reached up and
gently pushed at the plywood above him. The board
tilted and Rojas slowly sat up. He was concealed in a
storage space beneath the bench seat in the passenger
cabin of the hydrofoil. Through the open doorway he
could catch a glimpse of the docks. He listened intently.
When he failed to hear any signs of activity, he swung
the seat all the way up, then cautiously climbed out. He
was wearing one of the HAZMAT suits taken from the
back of the Jeep at the checkpoint. He stretched his legs
briefly and drew in a few deep breaths, then moved to
the stairwell and peered out. He'd heard Ma'ruf tell the
dock hands that there were problems with the hydrofoil's engine and that they would need to have me-
chanics look at it in the morning before they considered
using it for transport. The hands had apparently bought
the story, because the dock was deserted.

Rojas deliberated whether he should leave the craft.
If he could clear the docks without being seen, Ma'ruf

had explained there was a lower walkway that would allow him to reach the periphery of the quarry without being seen from the plateau. If he went for it now, however, he would still have to wait out the clock, and it seemed more likely someone would spot him near the quarry than if he stayed put. Better, he thought, to wait until the last minute.

Rojas stepped back from the stairwell. He'd left the bench seat up so that, if need be, he could quickly return to cover. Pacing the cabin, he fidgeted with his pistol, making sure it was loaded and that the sound suppressor was securely in place. He patted his fanny pack, making sure the grenades were still there.

Finally he stole another glance at his watch.

11:42.

Eighteen minutes to go.

BOLAN STOOD impatiently on what he assumed was some sort of platform. He was still blindfolded, and his hands were still tied behind his back. The Lashkar hardmen had cut the binds around his ankles after frisking him on the docks, and he'd led the procession as he, Kissinger and Otis had been guided along a path leading to the plateau where troops continued to stockpile supplies. From the plateau, they had been marched across a short wooden bridge to the platform. In the distance he could hear the hissing of the semitrailer's tailgate as it was lowered, as well as the grunts and mutterings of men as they brought still more supplies to the loading area. The way the sounds carried and seemed to echo faintly, Bolan guessed he was somewhere near the edge of the quarry pit. Kissinger and Otis were standing close by, and Bolan had counted the voices of three other men speaking to one another in Indonesian. Ma'ruf wasn't among them. He'd excused himself after leading the would-be mercenaries ashore, saying he wanted to check on the plane.

Several minutes passed. The delay was beginning to concern Bolan.

"What's taking so long?" he called out, hoping one of his guards could understand English.

"You wait," a guard told him.

"I'm tired of waiting," Bolan said. "We want to do what we came here for."

Bolan was answered by a blow to the ribs with the butt of an assault rifle. He staggered slightly, brushing up against what felt like a wall of chicken wire.

"You wait!" the guard repeated.

Another of the guards chuckled faintly. Bolan fell silent, anger and frustration building inside him as he listened to his captors murmur to one another.

Finally, someone whistled far below and Bolan heard the groan of an engine. Moments later, the platform shook slightly, then began to descend into the quarry.

An elevator, Bolan thought.

The platform vibrated noisily as it continued to carry the men downward. Taking advantage of the sound, Otis leaned close to Bolan and whispered, "They're complaining about having to work while most of the others get to sleep."

"You speak Indonesian?" Kissinger spoke up softly.

"Not very well," Otis told them. "Just enough to get by."

"No talking!" one of the guards shouted over the creaking of the elevator. A second later, Bolan felt the barrel of a gun press against his cheek.

"You shut up," the man holding the gun warned him.

Bolan and the others fell silent. The elevator groaned to a stop. Bolan heard the creak of a gate opening, then he felt a tugging on his sleeve. He followed Kissinger and Otis out of the elevator. They were led single file along a dirt path. The scuffling of their footsteps resonated loudly in the night air. Bolan assumed they were at the base of the pit. Ma'ruf told them the execution would take place there, but soon he found himself being led into a tunnel.

Not good, he thought to himself. This would throw the entire plan off. He couldn't say anything without drawing suspicion.

They hadn't gone far along the shaft when Bolan and the others were steered through a narrow opening, then told to stand still. The guards removed the blindfolds. Bolan blinked, then looked around him. They were in a small chamber, the size of a prison cell, carved out of the bedrock. The only light came from the flickering of an oil lamp ensconced in the wall. The only furnishings were a pair of army cots, upon which were piled a half-dozen rumpled uniforms of the U.S. Marines.

As one of the guards untied Bolan's hands, he told him, "You change clothes now."

Bolan rubbed his chafed wrists and stole a glance at his watch. A sinking feeling roiled in his stomach.

11:48.

They had only twelve minutes.

Once all three men were untied, the guards stood back, blocking the entrance to the tunnel, holding their assault rifles at the ready.

"Change clothes," one of them commanded again. "No talking."

Bolan fished through the uniforms for one that looked as if it might fit him, then turned his back to the guards and began to strip. As he did so, he exchanged looks with Otis and Kissinger. They, too, seemed aware of the time and had a look of grim resignation on their faces.

The men dressed wearily. Bolan's uniform was a close fit, as was Kissinger's. Otis had trouble getting into his shirt and switched it for another. They were tying their boots when there was a disruption at the doorway. Bolan glanced up and found himself staring into the face of Moamar Pohtoh.

CHAPTER FIFTY-ONE

Pohtoh was in his mid-thirties but looked much older, with gray streaks in his beard and shoulder-length hair. His dark eyes stood out in his face, gleaming with far more vitality than his haggard features. He stood just under six feet tall and was wearing a simple white robe not unlike those of the guards on either side of him.

"So, here are our CIA coconspirators," he said with a faint smile. His English was not as clear as Ma'ruf's, but Bolan and the others had no problem understanding him.

"You're mistaken," Bolan told him. "We work on our own."

"That is not the information I was given," Pohtoh countered.

"Your information was wrong," Bolan said. "Yes, the CIA tried to recruit us, but we didn't make any deals with them."

"Why should I believe you?" Pohtoh replied calmly.

"Does it really matter?" Bolan said. "All you're concerned about is having us kill Jahf-Al for you. Whose side we're on doesn't make any difference. Either way, he'll be dead and you'll have what you want."

"True enough," Pohtoh said. "But aren't you concerned about your payment?"

"There won't be any payment," Otis interjected as he finished buttoning his shirt. "We all know that. Once we've done our job, there's nothing to stop you from killing us, too."

"But that was not the agreement." Again Pohtoh was smiling. "We discussed money."

"And we played along," Otis said. "Face it, you can't send out a videotape of us killing Jahf-Al and have anybody buy it if we're alive to say it was a setup."

Pohtoh's smile faded. He frowned, eyeing Otis and the others with suspicion. "Now I'm confused," he said. "If you felt this 'assignment' would cost you your lives, why go through with it?"

It was Kissinger's turn to speak up.

"I lost family on that cruise liner Jahf-Al bombed," he said, laying out the story he and Bolan had worked out on their way to Dayimatan. "I want the satisfaction of having my revenge."

"At any cost?" Pohtoh asked.

"At any cost," Kissinger countered evenly. "Do you think you're the only people who believe in suicide missions if the cause is worth it?"

Pohtoh regarded the men thoughtfully for a moment, then said, "I am impressed. A little skeptical perhaps, but impressed nonetheless."

Bolan stole another glance at his watch.

11:52.

"Let's get it over with," Bolan told Pohtoh. "Where is he?"

"Jahf-Al is being readied," Pohtoh said. "You'll have your chance soon enough."

"Now or never," Bolan bartered.

Pohtoh laughed. "You're dictating terms?"

"You heard me," Bolan responded. "Get your cameras and let's get rolling."

"Or else?"

"Or else you've got no show," Bolan said. "Unless you want to dress some of your men up to do the job in our place."

"That would hardly be credible," Pohtoh said.

Bolan stared hard at Pohtoh and reached for the top button of his uniform. "You've got thirty seconds, then the uniform comes off."

"We can force you to cooperate," Pohtoh warned.

"That would hardly be credible," Bolan said, parroting the leader. "Twenty-five seconds..."

Pohtoh stared at Bolan and said nothing.

"Twenty seconds..."

"Fine, fine," Pohtoh said, waving his hands dismissively. "You want to feel in control. I can appreciate that. Very well. We will, as you say in Hollywood, let the show begin."

THE HERCULES C-130's engines were already warming up when Wahid Ma'ruf approached the fire-fighting plane.

Good, he thought to himself. That would help.

However, when he glanced up at the nearby knoll, Ma'ruf saw a handful of soldiers still standing around the two Sultan helicopters. Clearly Grimaldi had not yet been able to make his move to board one of the choppers.

Ma'ruf glanced at his watch.

11:50.

He had to do something.

The plane's spray tanks had already been filled with chemicals and one of the flatbed trucks had been emptied, but the second truck was still half-filled with containers. Instead of the impregnable casks the herbicides had been stored in when they'd left the agri-compound in Samarinda, the fluids had been transferred to five-gallon clear plastic drums, the same type used for holding drinking water. The plastic containers would easily burst open when the plane crashed into the parliament, insuring a broader dissemination of toxins. By the same token, their fragility required careful handling as they were transferred from the truck to the cargo hold of the Hercules. At the rate they were moving, Ma'ruf figured it would take at least another five minutes to finish loading. That would be cutting things too close.

He moved away from the plane and shouted up to the men standing around the helicopter, telling them to come down and help with the loading.

"Immediately," he stressed. "We need to take off before the smoke obscures the runway."

After a moment's hesitation, the soldiers began to

jog down to the plane. Two of them, however, remained atop the hill. Ma'ruf was about to call out to them, but checked himself. He was worried about raising suspicions. Grimaldi would have to manage to get past the last two men on his own.

Ma'ruf pitched in and helped load the last of the chemicals. Inside the cargo hold, two men with clipboards carefully orchestrated the placement of the containers. Ma'ruf recognized them as the same scientists who'd help develop the bomb that had gone off at the consulate in Samarinda. As with that bomb, they were seeing to it that the chemicals were stacked in such a way as to maximize their deadly effect when the plane exploded into parliament.

"Are we ready?" Ma'ruf asked once the last of the containers had been brought aboard.

One of the scientists looked over the stored chemicals, more than ninety containers in all, each strapped securely in place on a bed of foam padding.

"Yes, everything is ready."

"Then pray to God for success with the mission," Ma'ruf said, ushering the men to the cargo ramp.

The first scientist paused at the head of the ramp and stared at Ma'ruf. "You're not staying aboard, are you?"

Ma'ruf nodded. "To copilot," he said.

"But the plan was to use just one pilot," the scientist protested. "You are too valuable."

"We must be prepared for all contingencies," Ma'ruf reasoned. "And what could be more valuable than to see this mission through?"

"You've cleared this with Pohtoh?"

"It was his suggestion," Ma'ruf lied. "And it will be my honor. Now, go."

The two scientists headed down the ramp, shaking their heads as they whispered to each other. Ma'ruf helped close the cargo ramp, then strode carefully past the stacked containers, making his way to the front of the plane.

Inside the cockpit, the pilot, a middle-aged Lashkar terrorist, whirled in his seat when Ma'ruf came through the door.

"Ma'ruf!" he exclaimed. "What are you doing here?"

"I could not let you have all the glory, Elghir," Ma'ruf said with a grin. He dropped into the copilot's seat and quickly gave the same explanation he'd given to the scientists.

"I'm capable of flying this mission alone," Elghir protested. "But if it is Pohtoh's wish, so be it."

Reaching beneath the folds of his robes, Ma'ruf asked Elghir, "Have you gone through the checklist?"

The pilot nodded. "We are ready for takeoff."

"That is what I hoped."

Ma'ruf slowly withdrew a knife from his robe. Before Elghir could react, he leaned across the console and plunged the six-inch blade into the pilot's chest. He twisted the blade sharply, then left it in place and watched the life drain from Elghir's eyes.

"Forgive me," he told the pilot.

He quickly dragged the man from his seat and took

his place at the controls, then drew in a quick breath and stared at his watch.

11:55.

Ma'ruf whispered to himself, "It is time for atonement."

GRIMALDI MADE his move the moment some of the men began to walk downhill away from the helicopters. Using the charred tree trunks for cover, he slowly made his way toward the knoll, cutting the distance by half before coming to a sudden halt, realizing he'd run out of trunks to hide behind. That there were still two armed men posted near the Sultans gave him pause as well. He remained crouched behind the last trunk, hoping they'd move and join the others. The men stayed put, however, talking to one another as they lit up cigarettes.

Grimaldi checked the time.

11:56.

Shit, he muttered under his breath. He couldn't afford to wait much longer.

From where he was hiding, the knoll blocked Grimaldi's view of the Hercules C-130. He was wondering how Ma'ruf had fared with his end of the mission when he suddenly heard the plane's engines get louder. Seconds later, the Hercules came into view, gaining speed as it rolled down the access road.

Grimaldi glanced back at the men on the hill. They, too, were watching the plane, backs turned to him. Grimaldi saw his opportunity and went for it.

Even as he was moving clear of the trunk and breaking into a run, Grimaldi was tearing off his robe, wary that it would flap too loudly and tip off his approach. Underneath he was wearing one of the HAZMAT suits taken from the Jeep. As he reached the base of the hill and started up, he drew his gun, finger close to the trigger. He was within twenty yards of the men when one of them spotted him. Without hesitation, Grimaldi fired a silenced round into the man's head, then quickly shifted aim and took out the second man with another two shots.

When he reached the top of the knoll, Grimaldi dropped onto his stomach, wriggling past the bodies and glancing down the other side. The other Lashkar terrorists were still down by the flatbed trucks, watching the Hercules take off. Grimaldi glanced to his left and saw the plane rising up into the smoky haze. Soon it disappeared from view.

Grimaldi crawled over to the nearest Sultan and climbed into the cockpit. He quickly checked over the controls, assuring himself the chopper was ready for takeoff at a moment's notice. When his eyes fell on the console clock, he felt a stab of panic. The clock read midnight. He quickly checked his watch and let out a breath. The console clock was off.

It was 11:58.

"WHICH WAY?" Jayne Bahn asked, standing at a junction where the tunnel split off in four separate directions.

"All the way to the left," Raki Mochtar told her.

Bahn was about to move on when she saw Mochtar close his eyes and clench his teeth.

"You're bleeding again," she said, noticing the growing patch of crimson soaking through his robe.

"Let's keep going," he told her.

"Are you?"

"Go!" Mochtar whispered harshly, gesturing with his good arm. "Let's go!"

"All right!" she said, starting down the other branch of the tunnel. "Excuse me for being concerned!"

Mochtar forced a grin. "I was wondering when you'd start giving me a hard time like everyone else."

Bahn grinned back. "Welcome to the club."

So far their journey through the quarry tunnels had been devoid of complications. They'd taken a wrong turn early on but had quickly corrected themselves, and though they'd passed two different chambers teeming with Lashkar soldiers—one a barracks where nearly five dozen men had been sleeping, the other a storage area where troops were preoccupied with loading supplies for the transfer to Ertoron—they had yet to contend with a face-to-face confrontation.

That changed as they rounded the next bend.

Up ahead, two men brandishing Uzis were striding directly toward them, talking to each other excitedly.

Mochtar quickly stepped in front of Bahn, motioning for her to walk directly behind him. He was betting that with nearly seven hundred men at the camp it was unlikely that anyone could remember everyone's face, much less their names. Without breaking stride, he looked directly at the men and nodded perfunctorily, doing his best not to interrupt their conversation.

Mochtar was betrayed, however, by his bleeding gun-shot wound and the fact that his left arm was concealed beneath his robe in its sling. One of the soldiers noticed and stopped abruptly while gesturing for the other to do the same.

Bahn was ready for them. When she stepped out from behind Mochtar, she had her pistol out. Without hesitation, she drilled the man closest to her through the heart. The other man was drawing his Uzi into play when Mochtar beat him to the draw and took him out.

Both shots had been fired through sound suppressors, but Bahn and Mochtar nonetheless froze in place momentarily, eyeing the tunnel in both directions on the chance someone might have heard the shooting.

"What now?" Mochtar whispered.

"Let's leave them and keep going," Bahn said. "We should almost be there."

Mochtar paused long enough to grab the dead men's Uzis.

"Just in case," he told Bahn, handing her one of the weapons.

After another forty yards, they came to a chiseled corridor lined with passageways leading into separate small chambers. The one Ma'ruf had told them about was the last one on the left, less than ten yards from the opening that lead out to the quarry pit itself. There was an eight-inch-thick steel pocket door built into the chamber entrance, but, as Ma'ruf had predicted, it had been left open.

Mochtar went in first. Bahn followed. They found

themselves in a fortified bomb shelter, complete with provisions, communications equipment and a stockpile of weapons. Stacked in a neat pile just inside the door were a dozen full-body HAZMAT suits. Mochtar stared covetously at the communications setup.

"If only we had a little more time," he said.

"Well, scratch that," Bahn replied.

Ma'ruf told them where to locate the panel switch operating the door. Bahn quickly tried it. With a pneumatic hiss, the door slid shut in a matter of seconds. When she pushed the switch again, it reopened, just as quickly.

"Okay, all set," she said. "Ready?"

Mochtar checked his watch and replied, "We better be."

It was 11:59.

MA'RUF HAD been right.

Hamed Jahf-Al's execution was to take place in the quarry pit after all. There was a trio of mercury vapor lamps. Only one was situated at the bottom of the pit, while the other two rested on posts up at the periphery, one near the elevator, another on the far side of the quarry. Though the lamps were high-powered, they had a lot of area to cover—the pit alone was almost half the size of a baseball stadium—and the illumination they provided was diffused to a pale, otherworldly shade of yellow.

An open area was stripped bare of all adornment save for a few large boulders and the bodies of three UIF bodyguards whose lives had been spared back at the mountain enclave so that they could now serve as background props for their leader's final appearance as ruling head of the United Islamic Front. The men had been brought out to the pit only a few moments before, then summarily gunned down by some of the two dozen armed Lashkar Jihad soldiers on hand to insure that Pohtoh was adequately protected as he watched his handpicked crew of American mercenaries kill and then decapitate his long-time rival. As for the rest of Pohtoh's men, a dozen or more were still up near the plateau while the rest were in the surrounding caves, either asleep or gathering more supplies for the next day's relocation march to Ertonon.

Pohtoh's had ordered the use of three handheld video cameras. Each one would tape Jahf-Al's killing from a slightly different angle so that Pohtoh could later choose which footage best depicted the savagery of the beheading.

Now, as midnight fast approached, the moment of truth was at hand.

Crouched beside the largest of the boulders, Bolan, Kissinger and Otis—all dressed in their secondhand Marine uniforms—clutched M-16s filled with blanks and stared out at the slain UIF bodyguards strewed on the ground twenty yards ahead of them, supposedly just felled by their carbines. The cameramen stood a few yards behind them, and another twenty yards back stood Pohtoh, perched on a four-foot-high platform, holding a Mannlicher sniper rifle with a high-powered scope. His own bodyguards stood in formation around the platform.

Satisfied that everything was ready, Pohtoh called out loudly, "Bring us the great Nile Viper!"

As Bolan and the others silently watched, three figures began to slowly materialize out of the darkness of the cave directly across from them. Two were Pohtoh's men. Between them, half-limping, half-staggering, was Hamed Jahf-Al. Pohtoh had secured a makeup specialist, and Jahf-Al was outfitted with a wig and beard that accurately recreated the visage that had been plastered across newspapers and the nightly news for the past five months. The snakelike birthmark on his forehead was clearly visible in the pale overhead light, as was the dulled-over, vacant gaze in his eyes.

Once they reached the slain bodyguards, the two soldiers moved off to either side, leaving Jahf-Al to stand alone among the corpses, dazed and trembling, barely able to stand on his own two feet.

"They've got him drugged," Otis murmured under his breath. "Hardly seems fair."

"I'm all choked up," Kissinger whispered back.

Bolan didn't respond. Crouched between the other two men, he drew his M-16 tighter to his body and reached out with his right hand, slowly loosening the bayonet with which he was supposed to behead Jahf-Al. As he did so, he glanced over his shoulder. Moamar Pohtoh had raised his rifle and was taking aim at his rival's chest.

Had he been looking at his watch, Bolan would have seen that it had just struck midnight.

CHAPTER FIFTY-TWO

When they had been laying out their plan back at the checkpoint on the river, Rojas had told Bolan and the others that years ago, while playing center field for a minor league baseball team in Palm Springs, a scout told him he had one of the best throwing arms he'd ever seen.

Now was his chance to prove it.

Two minutes earlier, he had successfully made his way from the moored hovercraft to edge of the quarry, giving him a clear view of the preparations for Hamed Jahf-Al's execution. As he watched Moamar Pohtoh raise his rifle and take aim, Rojas pulled the pins on the two smoke grenades he'd just removed from his fanny pack. In quick succession, he threw the two projectiles into the pit.

Even as the second grenade was leaving his hand, a hundred yards behind him the timed plastique charges inside the hydrofoil detonated. With a resounding explosion, the craft turned into a fireball, showering debris along the docks and across the river.

STARTLED BY THE explosion, Moamar Pohtoh released his finger from the trigger of his Mannlicher and glanced over his shoulder. The guards surrounding him did the same. They saw a burst of light where the hydrofoil had gone up in flames and heard screams as several of the men on the plateau were knocked off balance by the force of the explosion, tumbled down the slope and fell over the edge of the quarry, plummeting to their deaths.

Seconds later, there were two smaller explosions on the ground. Clouds of smoke began to rise where the grenades had landed. Before the guards could respond, a hail of 9 mm gunfire from one of the cave entrances slammed into them. Four men went down immediately; another five cried out in agony.

As Kissinger and Otis dived to their right, then scrambled back to their feet and rushed toward the cave, Bolan whirled, holding the bayonet by its gleaming blade. Pohtoh was barely visible above the rising bank of smoke. Bolan took quick aim and let the bayonet fly. End over end the blade hurtled through the smoke, finally sheathing itself in Pohtoh's chest. Dumbfounded, the leader of the Lashkar Jihad stared down at the hilt, then slowly dropped his rifle and pitched forward over the railing to the ground. He was dead before he landed.

Bolan broke into a run, quickly catching up with Kissinger and Otis. As they neared the cave, they saw Bahn and Mochtar standing in the opening, firing their

Uzis through the smoke screen at Pohtoh's remaining bodyguards.

Several of the guards had regained their wits and managed to find cover behind some of the nearest boulders. As the smoke drifted past them, they spotted Bolan and the others and raised their rifles, hoping to nail the men before they escaped into the cave. Before they could take aim, however, they suddenly became aware of a loud droning sound overhead. Glancing upward, their eyes widened with horror.

Streaking toward them out of the heavens at a speed of more than four hundred miles an hour was the Hercules C-130 fire-fighting plane with its lethal cargo of pesticides.

"HURRY!" BAHN SHOUTED over her shoulder as she approached the bomb shelter.

The others were close behind. One by one, they followed her into the shelter. Bolan was the last one in. Bahn had her hand on the wall switch, and the moment the Executioner passed through the opening, she triggered the door. A second after it hissed closed there was a deafening roar. The shelter walls shook violently and the ground trembled, knocking everyone off their feet. Bolan rolled to one side as a storage locker came crashing down to the floor.

There were a quick series of secondary explosions, all weaker than the first, and the shelter continued to reverberate. Then, slowly, the loud din began to fade.

Soon, save for a ringing in their ears, those in the

shelter could hear nothing. There was a strange, unsettling silence.

Bolan slowly rose to his feet and looked at the others.

"Everyone all right?" he asked.

They all nodded.

The stack of HAZMAT suits had collapsed in the explosion. Silently, Bolan and the others reached into the pile and began to pull the suits on over their clothes. Once he'd finished, Bolan tipped the storage locker onto its side and opened the door, then started handing out gas masks. Kissinger finally broke the silence.

"If I never have to wear one of these clown suits again, it'll be too soon."

THE FORCE of the explosion had propelled clouds of toxic vapor deep into the caves, and as they made their way through the haze-filled tunnels, Bolan and the others had to move carefully to avoid tripping over the bodies of Lashkar troops who'd been overcome while trying to flee. Passing one of the caves being used as a barracks, they saw dozens of men sprawled dead on the floor and on the rows of cots. The chamber where supplies had been stored was filled with corpses as well.

After a few hundred yards of twists and turns, signs of the vapor began to fade. The group encountered a handful of surviving Lashkar troops, but the terrorists were in a state of shock and went down without much of a fight.

Finally, eleven minutes after they'd left the shelter, Bahn and Mochtar led the group out through the same opening where they'd entered the tunnel complex. Grimaldi was waiting for them in the Sultan. He'd already picked up Rojas, and the mercenary helped the others aboard.

"That scout was right," Kissinger told Rojas. "You were right on the money."

Rojas grinned. "Too bad I couldn't hit a curve ball."

"Where's Ma'ruf?" Bolan asked as he clambered aboard.

"He never ejected," Grimaldi called out from the cockpit. "I guess he wanted to make sure the plane hit dead center."

Bolan stared out the cabin window and saw a bright glow shining through the thick clouds still rising up from the quarry.

Mochtar was the last one in. "All aboard," he called out weakly as he pulled the cabin door closed. His robe was drenched with blood, and he was close to passing out.

"Hang in there," Bolan told him as the Sultan rose up into the night.

"I've been thinking," Mochtar said, smiling faintly. "Maybe picking fruit back at the Farm's not such a bad gig after all."

EPILOGUE

Major Abdul Salim hung up the phone and turned to Bolan.

"That was General Suseno," he said. "We've pinpointed a small force of Lashkar troops on the move in the mountains near Ertonon. We'll be sending in KOPASSUS units to engage them once we've softened them up with air strikes."

Bolan nodded. "I hope it goes well."

"We have them where we want them," Salim said. "On the run and without a leader. Hopefully we can wipe them out before they have a chance to regroup."

"Even if they do, they won't be the threat they were just a few days ago."

It was Salim's turn to nod. "We have you to thank for that."

"It wasn't just me," Bolan said.

"Of course," the major said. "But without your help, I shudder to think how different the situation would be."

They were in Salim's room at the hospital. The major was still hooked up to IVs, but his condition was improving. He'd eaten his first solid food since being brought to the facility, and the color had come back to his face. The doctors had yet to set a timetable for his rehabilitation and release, but he was anxious to get back into uniform and resume his duties.

"I still can't believe Sergeant Latek was our turncoat," he murmured, staring out the window. Outside, the morning sky was leaden, still filled with smoke from the fires raging in the mountains. At least for now, however, the smoke seemed less foreboding.

"At least he was the only one," Bolan said.

There was a knock on the door frame. Bolan glanced over his shoulder. Jayne Bahn stood in the doorway, carrying an overnight bag and a carry-on.

"My taxi's here," she said.

Bolan introduced Salim to Bahn, then took the woman's luggage and told her, "I'll walk you out."

Out in the hall, a work crew was repairing the damage from the earlier shootout. They'd already cleaned the blood off the floors and were nearly done replacing the sections of the walls that had been hammered with gunfire.

"I just saw your friend Rocky," Bahn told Bolan as they waited for the elevator. "He says now that he's got some of your blood in his veins he might have to stick with commando work."

Bolan grinned. Over the objections of the hospital staff, he'd donated two units of blood to help Mochtar out as he went into surgery for the gunshot wound to his shoulder. The procedure had been successful and Mochtar was expected to join Bolan, Kissinger and Grimaldi when they left Indonesia at the end of the week.

"So, what's next for you?" Bolan asked the bounty hunter as they rode the elevator to the ground floor.

"Cayman Islands," she replied. "Chasing down some embezzlers. Sounds pretty boring, eh?"

Bolan shrugged. "I hear the weather's nice."

The elevator stopped. They got out and crossed the lobby. "I've been there a couple times before," she told Bolan. "I know this nice romantic bungalow over-looking the ocean. Be a great place to recharge your batteries. Interested?"

Bolan smiled as he opened the door for her. "Don't think I'm not tempted."

She sighed. "Still playing hard to get, are we?"

"Maybe when the time's right," Bolan told her.

The cabdriver already had his trunk open. As Bolan set down the luggage, Bahn leaned over and kissed his forehead.

"That bump's nearly gone," she said.

"I'm as hardheaded as they come," Bolan told her.

"Tell me about it." She pulled a business card from her purse and slipped it into the pocket of Bolan's shirt. "When the time's right, you know where to find me."

With a wink, she got into the cab. The driver closed the door, then circled the vehicle and got behind the wheel. Bolan waited at the curb, then waved as Bahn rode off into the busy traffic. He was about to return to the hospital when he suddenly changed his mind and headed north along the sidewalk.

A few minutes later, he was standing outside the American consulate. The building was still cordoned off, and HAZMAT crews were inside trying to rid the ducts of any last traces of the lethal chemicals unleashed by the Lashkar's bomb attack. A makeshift memorial had been set up near one of the barriers surrounding the consulate perimeter. An enterprising vendor had set up a cart nearby, selling flowers and candles. Bolan bought two candles and took them over to the memorial. He set one candle before a large, framed photograph of Ambassador Stansfield, the other next to a smaller, wallet-sized photo of the Marine he'd spoken to the day he'd come out of the computer room where the bomb had been placed. Once he lit the candles, he stood back, taking in the memorial. Then he glanced up at the U.S. flag flying at half-mast in front of the consulate.

Standing tall, Bolan saluted.

THE DESTROYER

POLITICAL PRESSURE

The juggernaut that is the Morals and Ethics Behavior Establishment—MAEBE—is on a roll. Will its ultra-secret enforcement arm, the White Hand, kill enough scumbags to make their guy the uber-boy of the Presidential race? MAEBE! Will Orville Flicker succeed in his murderous, manipulative campaign to win the Oval Office? MAEBE! Can Remo and Chiun stop the bad guys from getting whacked—at least until CURE officially pays them to do it? MAEBE!

Available April 2004 at your favorite retail outlet.

THE Destroyer®

BLOODY TOURISTS

With the tiny Caribbean tourist trap of Union Island looking to declare its independence from the U.S., president-elect Greg Grom launches a "Free Union Island" movement, touring Dixieland to rally support. And amongst all the honky-tonks and hee-haws, some weird stuff is happening. Ordinary beer-swilling, foot-stomping yahoos are running amok, brawling like beasts on a rampage. Remo Williams is pretty sure Greg is slipping something into the local brew, but the why is another matter for him to solve.

Available in January 2004 at your favorite retail outlet.

James Axler
Outlanders®

MAD GOD'S WRATH

The survivors of the oldest moon colony have been revived from cryostasis and brought to Cerberus Redoubt, leaving behind an enemy in deep, frozen sleep. But betrayal and treachery bring the rebel stronghold under seige by the resurrected demon king of a lost world. With a prize hostage in tow to lure Kane and his fellow warriors, he retreats to the uncharted planet of mystery and impossibility for a final act of madness.

Available February 2004 at your favorite retail outlet.

GOLD EAGLE®

GOUT28